Warning: This book contains triggers. If you have
triggers of any kind, do not read.
There are no animals or children harmed in this story.
Reader discretion advised.

This book is dedicated to all the beta readers who helped me make this novel the best it can be. You rarely get credit in the author world, and I feel like you deserve the spotlight, too. So, with this story, we all sign it together.

♥

Melissa

Chapter One
The Beginning

It's the last day of high school. I should be excited to finally finish this chapter of my life, but I find myself conflicted. The thought of leaving the familiar and starting something new in a different city with new people sends my mind reeling. Taking a year off before starting college never crossed my mind. It has always been my plan to graduate, enjoy my summer and dive right into my new adventure.

My boyfriend Jayce hooks his arm around me and tugs me closer, a massive smile plastering his face. His lips press into the top of my head as we stroll down the main hall of Southside High for the last time. We didn't get into the same college, but he's only an hour away, and we plan to see each other every weekend.

Maureen, my best friend since kindergarten, races toward us, slinging her backpack across the ground like a bowling ball, trying to wipe out our legs. Jayce and I separate, letting the bag slide between us. Maureen has always been overly affectionate. I love her, but I could do without her hands constantly touching me. She wedges herself between Jayce and I, hooks her arms around ours and says, "Who's ready to party?"

Every year, the graduating class has a bonfire behind the school. Railroad tracks separate the school zone from a long-abandoned industrial area that is likely contaminated with hazardous materials. Woods surround the former factory, providing cover from the outside world, and a small pond and park are located just beyond the tree line. No one goes inside the vacant building, ever. It's not only boarded up, but word is, it's haunted by the people who died in a fire there a decade ago.

I peer over my shoulder as we continue walking, Maureen leaving her bag where it landed in the hall without a care in the world. She will start college in the fall with Jayce. I'm bummed we didn't all end up together, but at least I can hang out with them both on the weekends. You know, two birds, one stone.

We approach the exit, and instead of unhooking arms with us so we can go through the door one at a time, Maureen turns us sideways, and we shuffle in a line through the opening. She giggles and looks up at me, then turns to do the same to Jayce before releasing our arms and skipping across the parking lot. Maureen is not only blessed with a petite frame and perfectly silky long blonde hair, but she's rich. Well, at least her family is. Her father owns a chain of porn shops around the state. They live in a big fancy house on the west side of town, where the line between the city and the town is clear. Duplexes, apartment houses and raggedy homes suddenly cease after the sign "Now entering the Westside Neighborhood." It's like someone purchased the plot of land on either side of the road, leaving an acre-sized gap between the city and town, so as not to contaminate their precious space.

She's not stuck up or anything. In fact, she's more like us than she is the other Richies from the west side. Jayce and I think it's because of who her father is. I imagine being a porn shop owner doesn't sit well with the doctors, lawyers and investors in the area.

We shake our heads as Maureen leaps into her mom's Porsche Boxster convertible and plops into the passenger seat. She waves at us like Princess Diana as her mom cruises out of the parking lot and disappears.

I turn to Jayce, stretch my neck and peck his soft lips. He wraps his arms around me, pulling me tight against his body and presses his tongue into my mouth. His deep, penetrating kiss sends prickles through my body and a tingle between my legs. We have yet to have sex.

Although we've done other things to bring each other pleasure, waiting to have sex until the school year ended was something I made clear to Jayce when we started dating.

The end-of-year party is a perfect opportunity in his mind. We'll all be drinking, our inhibitions will be lower, and my mind won't be so focused on the future. The only problem is, I'm afraid. What if he gets me pregnant? What if someone sees us? What if…?

Jayce removes his tongue from my mouth and says, "See you at the bonfire."

I smile broadly, the heat in my face rising as my cheeks redden. "I'll be there."

He has this charisma about him that I find irresistible. His ability to turn me into putty excites and annoys me at the same time. I can't get mad at him, no matter how hard I try. All he has to do is flash me his crooked smile and bat his long lashes over his brown eyes, and I melt. He has me, mind, body, and soul; he has it all. As he climbs into the back of his friend's pickup truck along with four other guys, I find myself wanting to throw myself in the back and ride home with them.

A car horn beeps as I cross the street, and I flip them the finger. I'm on the crosswalk for God's sake.

I kick rocks down the sidewalk as I close in on my house. Both my parents are at work for another couple of hours. I insert my house key in the lock, turn and push the door open.

Boozer, our black lab, leaps on me, his paws slapping my chest, nearly knocking me back out the door. I push forward, grabbing his paws and placing them on the floor. "Down, Boozer."

He wags his tail hard, slapping the entryway table, jarring it. The lamp on top wobbles, and I grab it before it falls and roll my eyes. "Come on, dip shit, let's go potty."

His feet scrape against the floor as he races ahead of me. When he reaches the kitchen, he skids on the throw carpet and slams into the door, rattling it. I shake my head and wonder if this is why he was at the shelter for a year before we adopted him. He's dumber than a box of rocks.

I open the back door, and he jogs into the yard. After circling the same spot three times, he hunches over. A line of shit cruises out of his ass at breakneck speed, landing on the ground in a pile like chocolate soft serve.

That's one thing I'll give him; he can hold his bowels and bladder for hours without an accident. He flicks his back legs at his poop, completely missing it, and walks toward the only tree in our backyard. One day, I'm going to time how long it takes for him to pee. I stand there, waiting impatiently for the urine stream to stop flowing so I can go inside and get ready.

My phone pings, and I gaze down at the screen.

It's Jayce.

Can't wait to see you later.

I hover my finger over the keyboard, ready to respond, when my phone pings again.

It's Maureen.

Tonight's going to be epic.

Three dots appear and disappear, and seconds later, a photo of her manicured nails holding a bottle of Vodka appears.

I send Maureen a thumbs-up emoji and Jayce a heart. Boozer rubs his face on my leg, wraps his paws around it, and thrusts his pink lipstick into my shin. "Ewwww, Boozer. Get your dick off my leg," I yell, pushing him back. He smiles up at me, his tongue dangling, oblivious of my wishes, and tries again. "Get, you freak." I yank my leg from his grasp and storm inside, swinging the door around behind me.

A note from my mom sits on the kitchen table.

Don't forget, your father and I are going to dinner tonight.

Oh, I didn't forget, I think to myself as I climb the flight of stairs to my bedroom. My closet is full of clothes, yet I'm struggling to find something to wear. Perhaps it's because I know tonight Jayce is supposed to take my virginity, and I want it to be perfect. The problem is, the more I think about it, the more scared I become. I've seen the size of his cock and the way just his fingers inside me hurts, I worry about the pain he will cause me. He's told me many times before he'll be gentle, but it's not just that. Having sex changes things.

If there's one thing my mother instilled in me since I got my first period at the age of twelve, it's that sex can be scary. She told me stories about people who only had sex once and got pregnant or contracted diseases. Instilling fear was partly her intention, and the other part was to make me think it through beforehand. Now, I find myself second-guessing my promise to Jayce.

My fingers hover over Jayce's number. Calling him to tell him I've changed my mind about tonight seems rude. I need to tell him in person.

I haul out a graphic T-shirt, leggings, sneakers, and a matching hat. It's the most unsexy thing I can think of wearing tonight.

After taking a hot shower, I pull on my pants, put on my shirt, and tie my sneakers.

Maureen has already texted me twice, wondering when I'll be ready. I'm her ride, so she's growing impatient. I tie my hair in a ponytail and pull my hat down low on my forehead before jogging downstairs. Muddy footprints scatter around the kitchen when I enter, and Boozer stands at the open door, wagging his tail.

Flies buzz around my head, and I swat at them as I yell at Boozer. "Bad dog. Get inside." He bobs his head at me and crosses the threshold. I take paw wipes, clean his feet, and pat his backside. "Go lie down." After doing a quick sweep across the floor with the wet jet mop, I lock up the house and make my way to Maureen's.

When I pull into the driveway, her mom stands in the doorway, arms crossed, arguing with her.

It's her outfit. It has to be. Her mini skirt barely covers her ass, and her cleavage is seconds away from busting out of the top. Her mom stuffs a white sweater into her hands and grits her teeth as she says, "Take it."

Maureen rolls her eyes, tucks the sweater under her arm and storms away. Her emerald green skirt complements her green eyes but does little to hide her body as she sits beside me, flashing a partially bare cheek. "Gosh, she's annoying," Maureen says, slamming the car door before glancing at me. "How do I look?"

"Like a slut," I say with a broad smile.

We burst into a bout of maniacal laughter as I back out of the driveway and speed down the street.

She scans my outfit and shakes her head. "What happened to wearing something sexy?"

I grip the steering wheel tighter, whitening my knuckles. "I changed my mind."

Her eyes widen as she places her hand on my forearm, gripping it tight. "You changed your mind about banging Jayce tonight."

My head snaps in her direction. "I didn't say that."

She nods. "You don't have to. Your outfit says it all."

I slap the turn signal down and pull into the parking lot across from the park. "Don't make a huge deal of it."

I exit the car and round the front as she climbs out and says, "Oh, I'm not. Did you tell Jayce yet?"

"No," I murmur as I press the door lock button on my car, and we cross the street.

Maureen shimmies her skirt down as we enter the grass and walk along the pond, heading for the man-made path that leads to the party spot. She pulls the bottle of vodka from her oversized bag and passes it to me. "Here, some liquid courage."

I twist off the top and take a big swig. The liquid burns its way down to my empty stomach, and I cough at once. "That shit is strong." I pass it back to her, and she takes a swig.

She shakes her head and wrinkles her nose before swallowing hard. "It's 80 proof."

We press through a row of bushes and weave around a thick blanket of brush before coming into a clean flat space, a small fire burning in the center.

Jayce drops a pile of sticks into the flames and approaches us. He glances briefly at Maureen with raised eyebrows before wrapping his arms around me and whispering, "What are you wearing? Did you get your period or something?"

My face flushes, and I feel it drain of color. He's disappointed, I can hear it in his tone. "Can we talk?" I gaze up at him as he runs his fingers through his hair.

He directs me away from the growing crowd and behind a wide tree. "You changed your mind, didn't you?"

I put my head down and nod. "I'm sorry."

He places a finger beneath my chin and tilts my head to face him. "It's fine." He sighs heavily. "If you're not ready, you're not ready."

"Will you wait for me?" I ask, a tear developing in the corner of my eye.

He cups my face in his hands. "Of course. You know I love you."

I slip my hands around his waist and hold him tight. "I love you too."

Maureen's voice carries through the woods. "Let's get this party started," she shouts, and it's followed by hooting and hollering from multiple people.

"Come on." I nod toward the sound of the party. "Let's have some fun."

Within an hour of our arrival, the size of the party grew exponentially. This happens every year. Seniors invite friends from other schools and the neighborhood, and they drink up all the alcohol they didn't help pay for. When the crowd gets too large, a fight or two always breaks out. Not only that, as night falls and the flames grow higher, neighbors who work in the morning will start calling the police to break up the party.

Two girls face off in front of the flames, screaming at each other. Maureen wanders over, carrying her bottle of vodka, and staggers between them. I don't know what she says to calm them down, but next thing you know, they're taking swigs from the bottle and talking as if they're friends. Maureen is such a social butterfly.

Jayce strolls around the fire, grabs a beer from the red igloo cooler on the ground and pops the top open, tossing the cap into the flames. He's been a little off since I told him, but I'm not upset. I broke our promise, not him. He sucks down a big swig of beer as Maureen struts toward him and hands him her liquor bottle. She continues walking by him and disappears into the woods. Even through the flames, I can see the look in his glossy eyes as she wanders away, his focus on her barely covered ass.

How could he not? I'm having a hard time not looking, along with many other girls and guys, at the party. If Maureen's skirt shifts, even just a little, boom—you can clearly see the black lace bikini underwear she's wearing.

I stagger to the side as someone crashes into me, and two guys get into a pushing contest beside me. They exchange words briefly before the one closest to me swings at the other, and a brawl ensues. I roll my eyes and storm around the fire pit, searching for Jayce.

He's no longer standing where he was before the fight broke out. I scan the crowd twice before peering into the woods in the direction Maureen went. He probably went to check on her. I press through the dense landscaping, fumbling along the dark path until I breach the tree line in front of the closed factory.

I rub the goosebumps from my arm as I approach the eerie building. Glass along the perimeter crunches beneath my sneakers as I round the corner and spot a piece of plywood resting beside an entrance to the building. A small opening, big enough to climb through, catches my eye. I creep close to the hole and stop breathing to listen. Low voices come from inside; one of them is Maureen.

What the hell is she doing? This place is both dangerous and haunted; everyone knows this. I step through the opening and move cautiously through the space. A small amount of moonlight shines through the broken upper windows as low voices turn to moans. I stand behind a tall pile of pallets and gaze around the stack. My eyes widen at the sight of Maureen on a metal table, her legs wide open, Jayce slamming his cock into her. I cup my hand over my mouth to stifle my scream, not wanting them to hear me.

"I missed you so much," he murmurs in her ear before licking her neck and ramming his dick into her again.

She grips his hair and kisses him hard. "Fuck me from behind like before."

Like before?

Have they been fucking behind my back this whole time? Tears cascade over my hand as he grabs her violently, throws her over the table, and reenters her from behind, his hand holding her throat. She cries out with every thrust, a sinister smile on her face. Heat rises in my cheeks as my heart pounds, and my blood boils. I saved myself for him, and this whole time, he's been fucking my best friend behind my back.

He lied to me. They both did. They've been running around together having this secret relationship for who knows how long. I'm a fool.

I'm a fucking fool.

Chapter Two
A Heart on Fire

I back away from the pallets, tears streaming down my face, my heart shattering and joining the shards of glass crunching beneath my feet as I jog back in the direction of the bonfire. Branches and prickly bushes slice my face and arms, tearing at my flesh as I work my way toward the flames in the distance. When I stumble into the open, I drop to my hands and knees, sobbing.

The two girls who were previously fighting spot me from the other side of the flames and make their approach, no doubt coming to console me and find out why I'm distraught. They make it within a few feet of me when someone yells, "Cops."

Everyone scatters in different directions, some knowing where they are going, while others do not. Luckily for me, I paid attention to the curved tree I passed on my way here. I hustle to the opening and jog behind several others until we reach the far side of the pond. We fork off, some heading around the right side of the pond, while others head around the left. I went left.

In the distance, I see someone leaning against my car. Once I get a little closer, I realize it's Maureen. She's holding one hand on her chest, panting heavily, and her nearly empty bottle of booze in the other.

I want to hurt her—punch her right in the face for what she's done, but now's not the time. Flashing lights turn down the street along the pond, going in the direction of the old factory. I reach my car, unlock the doors and climb in without saying a word to her.

She flops into the seat beside me and adjusts her skirt. I stare through the windshield, unsure of what my next move may be. Do I kick her out of the car and let the cops pick her up? Do I pounce on her like a cat and gouge out her eyes?

"Let's go, sister," Maureen says, staring at me expectantly.

I turn the key, put the car in reverse and slam my foot on the gas, kicking up rocks. "Where's Jayce?" I ask.

Her eyes drift to the side mirror and then to the rearview mirror. "I don't know."

Lie one.

"He went into the woods looking for you, I think. You didn't see him?" I glance at her before focusing back on the road.

"No."

Lie two.

"How long have you been fucking my boyfriend?" I ask as I enter the highway.

Her head snaps in my direction. "What the hell are you talking about? I'm not fucking your boyfriend."

Lie three.

Three strikes.

"I was there," I say, my foot pressing the gas to the floor. "I saw you in the warehouse."

Her face goes blank, and she gawks at me with stunned silence before saying, "Fuck, Tessa. I'm so sorry. We didn't mean for it to happen. We didn't mean to hurt you." She reaches for me, and I pull my arm away.

"How long?" I ask.

She doesn't reply right away, as if she's debating whether to lie or tell me the truth. Her phone pings in her cleavage, and she glances over at me as she removes it, her eyes welling with tears. "It's Jayce."

He sent her a text, not me. My phone is silent. He doesn't care as much if I get caught, that's clear to me now.

"Do you love each other?" I ask, my hands gripping the wheel tighter, my head starting to pound as my blood pressure rises.

The tension in the air grows even further. If I had a knife, I could slice it right down the middle, creating a larger divide than she and Jayce have already created.

"Yes," she murmurs as she frantically types on her phone.

I snatch it from her hand and read the screen.

She knows.

She didn't hit send yet. I delete the message, roll down the window and chuck her phone onto the highway.

"Hey," she yells, glancing over her shoulder. "Do you know how much that cost?"

"How could you do this to me, Maureen?" I press the gas harder, the gauge surpassing eighty.

"Tessa, slow down." Her hand grips the dashboard. "Please. I'm sorry. We're sorry. We were going to tell you. I swear."

I grit my teeth, forcing words through them. "I'm only going to ask you this one more time. How long?"

"Almost a year," she blurts.

A single tear rolls down my cheek as my mind goes blank and emptiness fills the void where my heart should be.

I hate her. I hate them both, but I hate myself even more for being so blind to what was happening right under my nose. The bridge ahead has a fast-moving creek below, and I think about driving off it, killing us both.

"Tessa, I'm sorry. You know I love you like a sister."

The car jerks to the right as I turn and scream in her face, making her tightly clutch the handle above her. "A sister wouldn't have fucked my boyfriend, whom I love. A sister wouldn't have betrayed me. A sister wouldn't have lied. I hate you. I hate you. I hate you!"

Snot drains from her nose as she sobs. "Tessa, please slow down and watch the road."

"Watch the road? Watch the fucking road? Fuck you, Maureen!" Her eyes widen as I swerve the car in the direction of the guardrail. The sudden impact crumples the front end of the vehicle, and the sound, like that of cracking thunder, pierces my eardrums, making them ring as my head flies forward and then back. The air bag strikes me in the face, breaking my nose with an audible crunch.

For a few confusing moments, there is no audible sound other than the throbbing and ringing in my ears. As the ringing grows quiet, the sound of metal popping and a strange hissing noise takes its place.

A stabbing pain sears through my thigh, and something warm and wet drips down my face. Spots float before my eyes as I twist my neck and cry out. Maureen's head is embedded partially in the windshield, her face unrecognizable, her arms twitching. Moisture seeps into my pants, and I gaze down at a piece of metal lodged in my leg, blood squirting around it.

Smoke rises from beneath the hood, and my legs heat up as a small fire ignites. I cover the hole in my leg with my fingers the best I can to slow the bleeding, but it's coming so fast. I glance left and realize I'm staring partly at the sky.

What the heck?

I turn my head right and look around Maureen's dangling body. The creek rages below, the water white and foamy as it speeds under the bridge. We're dangling sideways over the edge, a part of the car hung up on something, keeping us from falling.

Metal crunches and grinds, and we shift down slightly. I grab the roof with trembling hands, tears streaming down my face as the fire under the hood grows. Sweat beads on every inch of my body as the car becomes an oven. Maureen's arm twitches again, followed by her hand, then nothing. She stops moving—stops twitching.

My throat clenches, and a violent cough escapes me. The smoke thickens around us, and I can't stop coughing, the air growing thin and unbreathable.

A flame rises beside Maureen's open doorway. It moves in rhythm, and I wonder if I'm hallucinating as I sit trapped between the airbag and the steering wheel, suffocating and bleeding.

Dying.

Without warning, the flame forms into a human-like entity that dives into Maureen's body. Her head shifts side to side, fracturing the rest of the windshield before sitting back in her seat, My bottom lip quivers as I reach for her and touch her hand. "Maureen?"

Her mangled face rotates toward me, and I flinch away as flames rise in her eyes and her bloody mouth opens wide.

"Siiiiiinnnner," a voice roars from deep within.

I thrash in my seat, trying frantically to get away from her as her face melts slowly before her entire body falls in slow motion from the car, plunging into the fast-moving water below.

The flaming entity curls into the seat and manifests into a half-man, half-creature. His upper body is fit with rippled abs and a devious smile on playful lips. The wavy black hair on his head is as smooth as silk, and his sharp features make him handsome in a cruel sort of way.

Black irises pierce into my soul beneath long lashes. The lower part of him is completely naked and on fire. His cock is long, thick, and swollen beneath the inferno, and his legs are hairy, too hairy, as if they belong to a goat. Instead of feet, he has charred hooves.

Flames lick at my toes, burning them. I stomp my feet, trying to put the fire out as I cry out. "Please," I shout out of the window beside me, my voice hoarse and dry. "Help me!"

"Still a virgin, my Little Sinner," the creature beside me says with a sadistic cackle.

How could he know that? How could he know something I've only told Jayce and Maureen?

"I can read your thoughts," it says as I turn to face it.

He looks different now, more man than creature. His clawed hand reaches for me and touches my cheek with a sharp nail that drags gently down to my chin, before tearing the airbag away from the steering wheel, making me gasp.

"Little Sinner, do you want me to save you?"

Fire swoops into the car's cabin, filtering through every nook and cranny. I shriek and nod my head, saying anything to stop the burning. "Yes!" I shout, coughing hard as smoke chokes its way into my lungs, burning them. "Save me." A burnt-hair smell fills my nostrils as the hair on my arm singes. I glance at the man now sitting beside me and wheeze. "Please. I'll do anything."

His hand wraps around my throat, and his long tongue glides over my face before traveling down between my legs, stopping just inside my upper thigh before returning to his mouth.

"Anything?" he asks as his tail lashes back the flames crowding my legs, sending them back under the hood.

The car stops moving, and the smoke vacates the cabin, suddenly swirling on the hood like a tornado, waiting for the creature's command to reenter.

A smoldering piece of paper, blackened around its edges, floats into the car. He snatches it and places it in front of my fluttering eyes, weakness overwhelming me. "Sign it in blood."

"What does it say?" I whisper, staring at the unfamiliar language, my mind growing foggy.

"Does it matter if it saves your life?" he asks.

My head bobbles as my blood continues oozing out of me.

"You're running out of time, Little Sinner. Make your choice. Die here, and I'll take your soul to hell, or sign here," he points to the bottom of the page. "And stay among the living and be mine."

I push my fingertip into my bloody wound and smear a crimson signature across the page.

The man-creature chuckles, sending a chill down my spine. He slides the paper away from me with two fingers, rolls it, and throws it into the fire before turning to me. "Now, you belong to me, my Little Sinner."

My eyes roll back in my head. The strength in me is gone. The fight in me is gone.

I'm dying.

The sound of twisting metal grinds through my ears before a burning grip wraps around my body, and I fade into the darkness.

Sensing someone hovering over me, I force my eyes open. I'm no longer in the car, but beside it, and the man-creature is staring down at me. I gaze up at him as I cough and moan, the pain reminding me I'm still alive. His tongue extends from between his lips and snakes its way to my waistband. I stifle a cry as it slips beneath my leggings and into my underwear, where it flickers against my clit like a serpent, tasting me.

"Mmm," the creature moans.

The roar of a motorcycle draws the creature's attention away from me. His tongue slithers out of my pants and retreats back into his mouth. As the sound of the motorcycle grows near, he leans over me, his face in mine, and tightens his hand around my pussy. "Mine." Flames rise in his eyes, and I scream as he backs away from me and vanishes into the fire. I toss my head back and cry out—screaming for my friend, screaming for Jayce's betrayal, screaming for my life.

My head falls to the side, and the heat from the flames stings my face. It's blurry now, the mangled car, the smoke and fire billowing around it.

Hands suddenly grab me, and the distance between me and the inferno that once was my car grows.

My back scrapes against the highway as someone leans over me, shuffling backward. I can't see their face; it's blurry along with everything else. My eyes are reduced to slits, barely able to stay open.

"Stay awake," a man's voice says as I close my eyes. "I've called 911. Help is coming."

My leg shifts as the stranger tears the hole in my pants wide open. "I have to stop this bleeding."

I sense his hesitation right before he says, "I'm sorry."

A heavy pressure presses down on my leg, and I shriek, trying to reach for him to make him stop, but my arms won't raise high enough; I'm too weak.

I writhe back and forth, barely moving, but it's enough to ease some of the pain.

"Please, stop moving. I have to do this, or you'll bleed to death." The pressure returns, greater this time as he repeats, "I'm sorry."

Blue and red lights flash around us and seconds later, two silhouettes appear above me. "I'll take over," one of them says. The pressure on my leg releases only to return with force. I cry out into the darkness that's slowly taking over my vision. A hand brushes my hair off my cheek before cupping my head. "You're going to be okay." A face appears above me, shifting in and out of focus. I catch a quick glimpse of him and realize he's young like me. My eyes drift past him to the sky, the moon a bright, beautiful circle drawing me to its light.

Everything turns black, and I feel myself letting go of this life. Voices shout, but they fade farther and farther away as I drift into the quiet darkness of death.

*   *   *

Beeping draws me from the dark into a blurry light. Every inch of me is on fire, not just from the flames that scorched my skin but from the pain penetrating every muscle and bone beneath it. A vice-like pressure squeezes my temples, crushing my head. My eyes widen as I try to breathe, but a tube blocks my airway. A figure appears over me, and a woman with a soft voice says, "Cough hard."

I force out a cough, and the tube scrapes out of my mouth.

She turns away from me, and a man, wearing a white lab coat with a stethoscope around his neck, says, "There you go." He leans over me with a flashlight, his brows furrowing as he raises each of my eyelids and shines it into my eyes. "You were lucky someone came by the accident when they did, or you wouldn't be here."

Someone? What about the something that was there before that person arrived? Was that just a dream?

"Did I die?" I rasp out in a scratchy voice, my throat burning and raw.

The doctor sighs heavily before saying, "Yes, but we got you back pretty fast, so there should be no lasting effects." He shifts his focus to my leg wrapped in bandages. "I pulled out a three-inch piece of metal from your thigh, which did some damage, but I repaired it. There will be a scar, and the site will likely be tender for the rest of your life."

I shake my head, trying to rid it of the fogginess. "How long have I been here?"

His hand grips my wrist and raises it. "Two days." He turns my arm slightly, showing me the bandages. "You have some first and second-degree burns, which we've treated and will send cream home with your parents to apply in the places you can't reach."

My parents. The mention of their names sends a wave of panic and fear over me. I wrecked my new car. Not only that, I killed my best friend.

"The police want to speak with you as well," the doctor says, drawing my eyes to his.

My heart pounds as the memory of what I did floods back in. The monitor beeps above me, alerting everyone that my vitals are going haywire. The doctor pats my hand and says, "Relax. They just have a few questions to clear some things up."

I'm not ready to talk. What do I say? What do they know? Do they know I did it on purpose?

A man in khaki pants and a blue button-up shirt and red tie enters the room and stands at the foot of my bed, clipped to his waist, a gun, cuffs, and a shiny gold badge. He nods to the doctor who does the same before exiting the room, leaving us to talk. The light above him reflects off his shiny, bald scalp as he leans over and says, "Hello, Miss Salavatori. My name is Detective Peterson. I have a couple of questions about the accident."

I rub the blanket covering me between my fingers, the friction heating them. "I don't remember much," I lie.

He nods and says, "Well, tell me what you do remember." He seizes a chair from by the door and drags it to the side of the bed, scraping the floor the entire way, unnerving me.

I rub the chills from my arms and say, "We were at a party—"

"By the abandoned factory?" he interrupts.

I nod and continue. "The police came, and we ran. Maureen and I…"

My eyes flit to his. "Did you find her? She fell into the creek."

He shakes his head. "We're still looking."

"She never wears her seatbelt. No matter how many times…" I choke on my words, a wave of fresh sorrow flooding through me.

"How did the accident happen?" His pen hovers over his notepad. "Did you swerve to miss an animal? Were you speeding and lost control? Because there are no skid marks at the scene indicating you tried to stop?"

I don't reply. I keep my head down, focusing on my fingers. My breath catches in my throat, and the monitors start beeping again as my heart pounds. Under the nail of my right pointer finger is caked blood. "No," I whisper to myself.

"No, what?" The detective asks, leaning closer and examining my fingertip. "Is that your blood embedded under there or…?"

This can't be real. I didn't make a deal with the creature sealed with my own blood, did I? If I did, where is he? Why hasn't he appeared? What exactly did that piece of paper I signed say? I glance at the detective. Could he be it, using the detective's body to torment me with questions?

"Look, I know you just woke up, but I need answers."

"Maureen did it," I lie again. "She was really drunk and grabbed the wheel while I was driving, making us swerve."

The pen scratches across his notepad as he writes down what I'm saying. "And why did she do that?"

"She was trying to make the car bob and weave to the music that was playing, and she…"

A loud thump rattles the window, drawing our attention. The detective stands and peers outside. "Must have been a bird." He turns back to me. "Your toxicology readings indicated your blood alcohol barely registered. Not much of a drinker, huh?"

"No."

He stands at the foot of my bed, grips the rail, and says, "Who cut off your seatbelt?"

"What?" I ask, confused by the question.

The detective takes his phone from his pocket, turns the screen toward me, and shows me a photo of the melted seatbelt, clearly cut. "Who else was there? Because the paramedics and the Good Samaritan who stopped said you were already out of the car when they got there."

"I don't know. I told you, I don't remember." Another lie. What am I supposed to say? A man-creature must have cut me free with his talons and pulled me from the vehicle while I was blacked out?

My mother appears at the door, her eyes bloodshot and wet with tears. "My baby. Oh, my sweet innocent girl." She wraps her arms around me, her embrace stinging my burned skin. Her eyes pierce through the detective's, giving him a death stare. "Really? You couldn't wait a day?"

The detective tucks the notepad in his pocket and shoots my mother a soft smile, "I think I have what I need." He pulls a business card out of his back pocket and holds it out to my mother. "In case she remembers anything else."

She refuses to take it, her mama bear instincts kicking in, not allowing her baby cub to experience any more trauma. "Leave it there." She nods to my bedside table.

The detective sets the card on the surface and slides it toward me with two fingers. "Call me."

I look away from him. I'll never call. Not a chance.

"So, now that he's gone, who was the third person at the scene?" My mother asks, raising her eyebrows.

I don't like lying to her, never have. She can sniff out a lie better than a hound can sniff blood. I close my eyes and decide to tell her the truth about what I saw inside that car—what it did to Maureen, to me. I open my mouth to speak, and an alarm sounds overhead. The lights dim, then flicker, and a static voice crackles over the PA system in the hallway. "Code Red. Lobby. This is not a drill."

A nurse speeds into our room, "Stay here. We're sheltering in place. There's a small fire in the lobby." She exits the room, closing the door behind her. Another door slams outside my room, and another as the staff goes room to room and door to door, securing patients.

As the alarm overhead continues to screech, the fear inside me builds, and I don't know why. I want to go home and crawl under the covers where it's safe.

My mother places a reassuring palm on my forehead. "It's going to be okay."

I force a nervous smile, and after several agonizing minutes, the alarm falls silent. The door swings open, and a nurse peeks in. "All set. Someone turned on the lobby fireplace, and a magazine left on the hearth caught fire. They think a draft may have blown it toward the flames or something."

My mother thanks the nurse and stands. "Well, it's getting late. Your father will be by tomorrow to see you." She kisses my head and combs my hair with her fingers. "Love you, Tessa bear."

"Love you too."

She strolls through the doorway and vanishes around the corner.

I stare at the blank television screen, my eyes stuck and watering. My chest tightens, and I clutch it as I sob uncontrollably. My friend's dead, my boyfriend's a cheater, my car's totaled, I'm in the hospital, and all I can think about is the man-creature that saved me. His words filter into my head, and goosebumps raise the hair on my arms. He said I belong to him now. What does that even mean? And him tasting me, what was that all about?

A shift in light draws my attention to the open door. The hallway grows darker and darker until there's nothing but a black opening where the door should be.

I grip the sheets beneath me, my nails folding over as a soft orange glow lights up the blackened space. My heart races, and the monitors above me bleep their warnings to whomever will listen as a single burning piece of paper floats into the room, landing on the floor beside my bed. Etched on its surface in black jagged letters is one word.

Mine.

Chapter Four
Jayce

The hallway lights suddenly brighten. I grab my call button and press it repeatedly as the burning paper slowly turns to dust. A nurse swoops into the room, dispersing the remnants of the page and huffs. "Yes?"

"There was…" I point to the floor where she's standing. "I…" I'm at a loss for words. Now that she's here, I'm suddenly unable to form whole sentences.

She rolls her eyes, picks up my water carafe and shakes it. "I'll get you some more ice water." The second she exits the room, another figure appears.

Jayce swipes his bloodshot eyes, clearing them of tears. Judging by his unruly hair and disheveled clothes, he hasn't slept.

"Hi," his voice cracks as he enters the room fully.

I turn my head and stare out the window. "Get the fuck out."

"Tessa, please. I'm so sorry."

He touches my arm, and I face him, pulling my arm away. "This is all your fault. You did this to me—to Maureen." A wayward tear drips from my lids, soaking into the blanket on my lap. "If you hadn't cheated on me, this would never have happened," I say, raising my voice.

Tears cascade over his cheeks as he collapses beside me, his hands cupped over the edge of the bed. "Please,

Tessa. I need you to forgive me. This is all just too much. I can't go through this without you."

"Go through what? Grieving?" I push his hands away from the bed, and he sits back on his heels as I say, "You grieve for her, not for me—not for what you've done to us." I point to the door. "Go feel sorry for yourself somewhere else. I'm all out of forgiveness here."

"Please, Tessa." He shakes his head. "Don't do this. I need you."

"No!" I shout. "You needed her, and she's gone now, so go cry to someone else about your sorrow. You won't get any sympathy out of me. Now, get out!"

He slowly rises, wiping his face with his sleeve. "Tessa, you're angry, and I get it." He rests his palm on my leg gently. "But I can help take care of you while you're healing and your parents are at work."

If I could spin my head around like the exorcist right now, I would. "Take care of me? I needed you to wait for me. I needed you to love me and be there for me, no matter what. And how did you take care of me? By sleeping with my best friend and betraying me and my trust for almost a year. You are dead to me. I don't want to see you or hear your voice." I sniffle.

"Tessa, I…"

"No, don't call me Tessa. It's Contessa. You've lost the right to call me by my nickname like we are friends, family, or lovers. You are nothing to me, and if you don't leave this room right now, I'm going to scream."

He grabs my head, pressing his forehead against mine. "Please, baby. I'll die without you."

"Good!" I shriek, pushing him back hard with two hands, knocking him down onto the hard tile. "You can join Maureen in hell and fuck her there. Enjoy." I cross my arms and glare down at him as he stares at me, dumbstruck.

"You don't mean that," he staggers to a stand, brushing off the back side of his jeans.

For fuck's sake. What does it take to get him the fuck out of my room?

I grip my call button tightly and slam my finger down on it.

The same nurse as before speeds into my room seconds later, carrying my ice water. She sets it on my table and says, "Did you remember what you called me for before?"

I grip her scrubs and say through clenched teeth, "Get him out of my room. I don't want him to visit again."

The nurse gazes down at my fingers wrapped around the material of her top and nods slowly. "No problem."

I release the fabric, and she turns to Jayce. "You heard her—time to go." She stands between us and points at the door. "Move."

Jayce doesn't move. He stands there like concrete is holding him in place. His face turns pale and gaunt. "No," he whimpers, his voice like that of a whiny child whose favorite toy was just taken away. "She needs me." His eyes lock on mine as a tear drips off his chin.

The nurse laughs outwardly. "Don't test my patience today, kid. It's been a long eight hours, and I still have eight more to go." She positions herself closer to him, her body nearly touching his. "Do I need to have you removed by security?"

He puts his head down and shakes it. "No, ma'am."

"Good." The nurse keeps walking forward as Jayce walks backward out of the room. Once he's completely out of sight, the nurse turns to me. Her mouth opens to say something, but immediately closes as the PA system crackles overhead. "Code Blue, Emergency Room. Code Blue, Emergency Room." It crackles again and falls silent. The nurse vibrates her lips and turns away from me without another word.

I stroke the discolored, burned skin spots on my arms and wonder if they will scar. Tattoo cover-ups are always an option, and I may need to consider them in the future.

I'm so tired, but falling asleep scares me. I flick on the television. A newscaster is standing in front of a burnt-up vehicle sitting on the flat bed of a tow truck. My lips move as I read the tagline.

"One person is dead, and another is hospitalized after a fatal accident on Friday evening."

They found Maureen.

A coroner's vehicle flashes across the screen before the television goes from reporting tragedy to reporting about a local festival happening this weekend. How quickly they move on.

I force my eyes open wider with my fingers, trying desperately to stay awake. What if that's where the demon lingers? He can send a message through a fiery piece of paper, but is that all? Is that what the contract states? There has to be more to this. Nothing in this life is free, and making a deal with the devil, a demon entity, or man-creature is no different. In fact, I'm sure the price of signing my life away in blood will be much greater.

Priceless even.

My head aches as I try to pull the memory of the moment he slapped the fiery page before me, asking me to sign it in blood. The blurry words, all foreign to me, were more like symbols. God, I wish I could remember and see the page clearly.

The PA system crackles overhead. "Code Red. Lobby. This is not a drill."

Once again, my nurse flies into the room. She swings my door around, not quite closing it before racing down the hall, followed by two other nurses.

Seconds later, I hear it, faint at first but growing in intensity.

Screaming.

It's not just any screaming, though; this is blood-curdling, someone lost an arm, screaming. As the gut-wrenching noise closes in, I realize that in between the screams, Jayce is hollering words that drain the color from my face. "It came from the fire. Something was in the flames."

My mom practically falls into the room, her face as white as the sheets beneath me. Her hands shake as she approaches my bed, her mouth open and soundless.

"Mom, what happened?" I ask as she sits awkwardly beside me, the chair rocking to the side, nearly tipping over.

"I…I was talking to Jayce in the lobby." Her hand leaves her lap and gestures toward the open doorway. "And something…I mean, somehow, the fireplace ignited on its own…and…" Her voice trails off.

I reach for her, taking her trembling hand and squeezing it. "What do you mean it ignited on its own?"

She glances at me, her eyes widening. "I mean, one minute it was off and cold as this room, and the next…" She removes her hand from under mine and throws both hands in the air. "…poof, it fires up and shoots out flames that burn your Jayce's arm."

"He's not my Jayce."

The wrinkle in her forehead deepens as she frowns. "What do you mean he's not your Jayce? How about asking me if he's okay? How bad is it? Can I see him?" She shakes her head.

"We broke up. I don't want to see him." I roll over, wincing as the sheet tightens around my injured leg. My mind wanders to the fire that burned Jayce. Was it him? Is the man-creature sending a warning?

I frown as my mom appears in front of me, blocking my view of the window and the outside world. "You two broke up?"

"Yes," I say without further explanation.

She runs her fingers through my hair and cups my head in her palm. "Oh, honey, what happened? I thought you two were happy."

Fuck it. If he didn't tell her, I'm going to. Maybe then he'll stay away.

"Jayce was having sex with Maureen for almost a year. I found out at the bonfire. And by found out, I mean I saw them with my own eyes."

Her hand stops moving on my head, and the air from her nostrils shifts the hair on my head like a huff from a bull. "That son of a bitch." She turns her back on me and covers her mouth with her hand as she murmurs, "I'm glad he got burned."

"Mom!"

She whips around to face me. "Lord, forgive me, but he hurt my sweet girl, so he deserves everything that comes after. It's probably the devil himself who lit that fire in the lobby and burnt him for his sins."

My windpipe narrows, and the air turns heavy and thick. Too thick to breathe. It's him. Even my own mother believes it's possible the man-creature, or should I say, devil came from the flames to punish Jayce.

The devil. That must be what the creature is. My chest aches, and my heart pounds in my chest. I made a deal with the devil. What the fuck have I done?

Pain pierces through my temples. I press my fingers into my head, trying to stop the building pressure.

"Tessa, what's the matter?"

The screaming starts quietly and grows rapidly, becoming unbearable. I cover my ears, trying to muffle the sound, but it doesn't help.

The screaming is coming from me.

I can't stop it. Everything that's happening is too much. My body shakes violently as my mom yells for help in the background. I can't open my eyes; I'm stuck in my own nightmare. I've suffered from anxiety attacks for years, but this feels different. This feels chaotic.

Heat spreads through my body, and I open my eyes as multiple people flood into my room. They all reach for me at once, and I slap at their hands. My feet fly from beneath the covers, and I quickly throw my legs over the opposite side of the bed. I stand, but I fall in slow motion, my leg giving out. Blood sprays out of my hand, dotting the floor with crimson as my IV rips out of my vein.

My mom grabs me by the arms, and we slide to the floor, where she holds me tight and says, "What can I do, Tessa bear?" She sobs, her lips pecking my head. "Tell me how I can help you."

I bawl uncontrollably, gripping her arm with shaking hands as I roll on my side and take on the fetal position. A nurse kneels beside us, presses a piece of gauze on my bloody hand, and says, "I'm going to give you something to calm you down." She turns to the other nurses in the room. "Everyone out. This isn't a circus." A cap pops off the end of a syringe and rolls to the floor by my feet. A cold square of alcohol touches the side of my outer thigh. "Usually we do this intravenously, but since you pulled out the IV, I'm doing it in your muscle." The needle penetrates my skin, and the medication stings as it filters into my leg muscle and surrounding tissue. "Look at me," the nurse says calmly. "I need you to breathe with me. In and out, like this. Nice and slow."

My heart is bordering on explosion. I follow her lead and take a deep breath, releasing it slowly.

"That's my girl," my mom whispers as she curls a wayward hair around my ear. My body trembles, and I close my eyes, wishing the medicine would kick in faster. I focus on my breathing, taking slow, rhythmic, and steady breaths for several minutes. A shoe squeaks on the floor on the other side of my bed. "What happened in here?" A woman's voice says.

An older woman with salt and pepper hair rounds the foot of the bed, wearing brown dress pants and a cream short-sleeve turtleneck. She stares down at us, her hands on her thin waist. Her eyes lock on the needle on the bed and the blood on the floor. "What did you give her, Bernice?"

The nurse beside us stands. "Valium. She was screaming, in a full-on panic, and ripped her IV out when she tried to get away from us."

The older woman nods, pursing her tight lips before dropping her arms with a huff. "Well, you can't leave her on the floor. When that medicine kicks in, she'll probably fall asleep. Come on." She unlocks the wheels of the hospital bed and shoves it over with her hip before locking it again and squatting on my right side. "I'm going to need you to use your good leg and help us help you get back to bed. I don't want to have to lift your dead weight when that injection kicks in. Understand?"

I nod through tear-filled eyes as I blow out a staggering breath.

She gestures to my mom to move, and the other nurse steps to my left. "Count of three," the older woman says to the nurse. "One, two, three, heave."

I'm stuck. My body wants desperately to stay in the fetal position. The older nurse grunts. "Put your good leg down, young lady."

I take another deep breath and relax my leg to the floor, balancing it as they pivot and turn my back to the bed. The older woman's foot slams down on the pedal beneath the bedframe, and it groans lower before clanking to a stop when it reaches the lowest setting. "Sit down."

The mattress sinks beneath me, and they swing my legs onto the bed and cover me up with a sheet. With a quick yank from the older woman, the guardrail bangs into place beside me, securing me in bed. "Why weren't these both up?"

The other nurse looks at her, a perplexed expression on her pale face. "I don't know, I just got here, and it was a total shit show." She glances at me and Mom and says, "Sorry for my language."

"Outside, right now," the older woman says, not taking her eyes off the other nurse."

For being petite, the older woman is a force I wouldn't want to reckon with. She gives off a fiery energy that screams "administrator," and I have a feeling someone's about to lose their job.

"Everything's going to be okay," my mom says, leaning over me.

I want to believe her, but how could I? I've made a deal with the devil, and the terms are unknown to me. My eyes cross, and the room blurs. I try to raise my hand to scratch an itch on my nose, but a sluggish feeling consumes me. My eyelids flutter, struggling to stay open.

"Don't fight it, Tessa bear. You need to rest." A soft hand strokes the side of my face, and the smell of roses floats into my nostrils. I love my mom's Bath & Body Works hand cream. It reminds me of blooming flowers in springtime.

I nuzzle her palm and force my head off the pillow to look at her through the barely open slits of my eyes. "Mom, I don't want to sleep. I'm scared."

"It's okay. I'll be right here when you wake up. There's nothing to be afraid of."

My head falls back to the pillow. The energy drains from me, and I can no longer lift my arms. "What if he comes for me in my sleep?" I whisper.

Her fingers interlace mine, but I can barely feel them. "Who, sweetheart?"

"The devil," I murmur.

Darkness surrounds me, and all sound is muted in the void I've entered. There's nothing here. It's just a smoke-filled room with a single door, a soft glow of orange light creeping beneath it. Strangely, I feel calm and at ease, almost at home in this place. There's no one here to judge me or ask questions about what happened that night. It's just me, well, me and whatever's beyond that door.

I take a step closer, the floor feeling uneven and jagged beneath my feet. Something screeches on the other side of the door, the sound like nails on a chalkboard. I cover my ears as the claws of the unknown drag from the top to the bottom and disappear as fast as they came. Beneath the door, there's a break in the orange light as if something stands on the other side of it, waiting for something.

Waiting for me.

When I take a step back, my heel squishes in something warm and slippery. I freeze, fighting and losing the urge to look down. Beneath my heel is a melted face, the melted face of Maureen. My mouth opens, but the room keeps my screams soundless. I scan her mangled body, lifeless, burned, and lying on the slippery algae-covered rocks.

Twisted metal and crackling fire draw my eyes to the ceiling that was never there. Above me is the bridge, my car hanging by a branch. Water rushes around my ankles, and suddenly I'm in waist-deep water. I dig my feet between the rocks, trying to maintain my balance as the water rages downstream.

I glance at the door, mocking me in the corner. I'm not going to bother running for it; it's locked, it's always fucking locked.

Why? Why is the devil tormenting me with this repetitive nightmare?

The branch holding my car moans and cracks. I dive underwater and try swimming away, but the water dries up. I crawl to the door and fumble with its knob. Locked as always. The walls glide closer and closer until I'm trapped in the center of the room, where they stop. The branch holding my car snaps, and it plunges toward me. I close my eyes and shriek right before it crushes me flat.

* * *

I wake up in a cold sweat, my t-shirt stuck to my sopping chest. The sun peeks between my drapes, brightening the space around me. The mirror across from me vibrates my reflection as my mom's heavy footsteps slap down the hall. A soft knock rattles my door. "Tessa?"

"Yes?"

She tries to open my door, but it's locked. Locking my bedroom door won't keep the devil from getting to me, but it does give me a sense of security, no matter how false it may be.

"I made breakfast. Are you coming down?"

I gaze down at my soaking wet clothes and sheets. "Yeah, let me take a quick shower," I yell.

Her footsteps grow quiet as she walks away and descends the stairs. I've been home for just over two weeks, and my leg still hurts like a bitch when I step down. The doctor said it's because part of the muscle was damaged, and it will take time to fully heal. Until then, I saunter from one room to the next like a decrepit old woman.

I peel off my soaked clothes and toss them in the hamper before dropping onto the toilet seat. My ability to maintain my independence despite my injury surprises my parents, but the last thing I wanted when I came home was my mom helping me in the shower.

My dad installed a grab bar just outside the shower for me to hold on to when I climb in and out. He wanted to put one on the shower wall, too, but I found it unnecessary. I wipe quickly, flush the toilet, wash my hands, and close the toilet lid, resting my towel on top.

The shower water shrieks on with a quick turn of my wrist, and steam fills the bathroom quickly. One of the things I love about my parents' house is that it's enormous, so I get my own private bath. Well, at least, now I do, now that my brother Jessie has moved out. This was his room before it was mine. Before that, I used the bathroom down the hall.

I step under the pounding stream and let the warmth coat my aching neck. Ever since I've been home, I've been plagued by aches and pains. The doctors wanted to give me pain medication, but I refused. I've seen too many family members become addicted to that shit and worse. Besides, I deserve to feel this for however long it takes, even if it's an eternity.

After my shower, I dry off, put on gym shorts and a half-tank, then hobble downstairs. My dad sits at the table beside my mom, giving me a disapproving glare. I peer down at my outfit. "What? I'm not going anywhere."

His eyes drift down to this month's edition of *Guns and Ammo*.

The first time Jayce came to our house, my dad made a point of cleaning his Glock in plain view. He never liked Jayce, and now he blames him for everything that has happened to me up until this point, but I think Jayce has received sufficient punishment. The burn on his arm left deep, permanent scars. He'll never play football or any other sport requiring the use of his right arm again.

A plate of bacon, scrambled eggs, and toast with jelly drops on the table in front of me as I sit down. "Want orange juice?" Mom asks, turning toward the fridge.

"Yes. Please."

Dad glances at his plate and frowns—egg whites piled on a slice of wheat toast. His doctor says his cholesterol is bad and he needs to change his diet. Mom's all gung-ho about it, and he plays along, but I know he secretly swings by the local diner and grabs a special on his way to work a few mornings a week.

The doorbell echoes through the house, and we all stare at each other, no one wanting to leave the table and let their food get cold. Dad clears his throat and gestures with his head for me to get it. I roll my eyes and limp through the living room and swing the front door open.

I gasp at the sight of Jayce standing on my porch, his arm still wrapped in bandages. "What the fuck are you doing here?"

He drops his head and stares at his black Vans sneakers. "Wow, still mad, I guess."

"Are you kidding me? Jayce, I thought I made it clear that I wanted nothing more to do with you." I go to shut the door in his face, but he slaps his palm on it, pushing it back open. "Come on, Tessa, I really need to talk to you."

I roll my eyes, push his arm off the door, step onto the porch and cross my arms. "About what?" My foot taps impatiently on the floor.

His eyes drift from my lips, down to my bare midsection, and stop at the gnarly, still-healing wound on my thigh. "Does it still hurt?"

"Are you dumb?" I uncross my arms and grab his bandaged arm. "Does this fucking hurt?"

He yelps and pulls away from me. "Ouch, Tessa. Yeah, that fucking hurts."

"Good. Now stop asking dumb questions and get to the reason you're ruining my Saturday."

His foot scrapes against the porch as he averts his eyes from mine. "I want to talk about us."

I rub the tension building in my forehead. "For fuck's sake, Jayce, there is no us. We are done. Over. Kaput. Finished. Do I need to say it in another language or put it in writing?"

His eyes search mine for a glimmer of hope he'll never find. "Tessa, we made a mistake. I said I was sorry." He grabs my arm and strokes it softly with his thumb, a crooked smile curving on his lips. "You know we were always meant to be together."

He thinks I'm stupid. This is what he does. He pisses me off and tries to Rico Suave his way back into my good graces with smooth moves and even smoother words. Not this time. This time is different. He not only cheated, but I have a demon who's made it clear to me that I am his. The thought of what it could do to me—to Jayce, raises the hair on the back of my neck. I may not want to be with Jayce, but I don't want him dragged to hell either. A tremor builds inside me, and I cover my stomach with my palm, holding it steady.

I peel his fingers off me and turn away from him. "Goodbye, Jayce."

His hand drops heavily on my shoulder as he spins me around and plants a forceful kiss on my lips. I shove him back hard against the porch railing, harder than I knew I had the strength to do. A sharp pain tears through my leg, objecting to my sudden movement.

The railing cracks, then snaps, and Jayce goes over the side of the porch, landing in the thorny rose bushes lining the front of our house.

"What the hell is going on out here?" My dad steps through the doorway. He places his hands firmly on his hips as Jayce staggers to his feet, his face bleeding from minuscule cuts.

"He was just leaving." I step inside the house and return to the kitchen.

My mom glances across the table at me as I take my seat. "Everything, okay?"

Before I have a chance to respond, my dad enters the kitchen, his face red. "That idiot boyfriend of yours needs to pay for the railing."

"He's not my boyfriend." I stab my cold eggs and fork them into my mouth. "And technically, I broke the railing."

"You broke it?" He sits down and leans back in his seat, gawking at me. "I beg to differ; he's the one who was on the ground covered in scratches from your mother's rose bushes."

My mom puts her hand on her chest. "My rose bushes." She tosses her napkin on the table and stands. "He better not have damaged any of them, or I'm going to make him pay for them too." She leaves the room, presumably to check on her prized flowers.

My dad swipes his face with his palm. "So, how'd you break it?"

"Jayce kissed me after I told him we were over, so I shoved him."

A low throaty laugh comes from across the table before it turns into a full-on cackle. "That's my girl." He takes a bite from his toast, chews it for a few seconds and spits it on his plate. "Fuck this. Want to run to the hardware store with me?" He stands, scrapes his food into the garbage, and rests his plate in the sink. "And by run to the store, I mean, get a real breakfast."

I smile up at him. "Let me get changed, and we can go."

He nods. "Don't tell your mother."

We exchange glances and broad smiles as my mom returns to the kitchen. "What are you two smiling about?"

"Nothing," we say in unison.

I'm more like my dad than my mom in many ways. I firmly believe that cursing is an inherited trait my father passed down to me, along with my ability to defend myself when need be.

Mom glances at us both, lets out a heavy sigh, and says, "Fine, keep your secrets."

Secrets.

I have so many now, and something tells me there will be many more once the demon rears his head again.

Chapter Seven
Awakening

What a long fucking day. Going to breakfast turned into a trip to the hardware store for wood and caution tape, a stop at the pharmacy where my dad and a long-time friend had a thirty-minute conversation about tonight's Buck Moon, and then on to meet my mom at the grocery store to figure out dinner together. My leg is killing me, and all I want to do is lie down and sleep for twenty-four hours.

I fall back on my bed and cover my eyes with my arm. Mom and Dad walked to the neighbor's a block down the street. Apparently, they are having a Moon Party—freaking weirdos. I could have gone, but gazing through a telescope for hours to check out the surface of the moon close up didn't sound exciting to me. It could be the pain or this infernal itching. I scratch either side of my wound with my fingernails, careful not to scratch it open.

A great weight lands on my chest, knocking the wind out of me. "Damn it, Boozer." I shove him off me. "Get down." He licks the side of my leg, then grabs it with both paws, humping the air. I yank my leg away from him. "Get out, you freak." I point to the door, and he smiles up at me, his tongue dangling, utterly oblivious of boundaries. I grab his collar, pull him off my bed, stick him in the hallway, and slam the door in his face, locking it behind me. I collapse back on my bed, stomach first and close my eyes.

* * *

I wake up with a start, feeling the mattress sink at the foot of my bed. Did I forget to shut and lock my bedroom door? I thought for sure I did. My room's pitch black except for a small amount of moonlight peeking through the drapes. "Boozer?" I say to the darkness.

A searing heat squeezes my ankle. I cry out, but something snakes around my throat, silencing me as I yank my leg back, sitting up quickly. Fiery eyes open slowly in the dark as the man-creature moans. "My Little Sinner, did you think I forgot about our deal?"

"Deal?" I say in a strained voice.

The full weight of him suddenly presses down on my chest, and I can hardly breathe. "You belong to me, that was the deal." He releases his hold on my throat and growls in my face. "I saved your life, and now your body is mine."

My breath quickens as he sits back and his tongue rolls from between his lips, disappears inside my shorts, the heat stinging my bare skin like the sun. I squeeze my eyes closed as it curls around my underwear and slithers over my clit, stinging it sharply like a sudden burn from a hot stove. "You can make this easy, or you can make this hard. Either way, there will be pain."

I kick at him with my good leg, and his tail wraps around it and presses it firmly into the mattress. His face slowly morphs into the same one he used from the night of the accident, handsome yet terrifying. "Now, be good for Mastyx, and maybe you'll enjoy this too."

Mastyx, that's his name—not Satan, Lucifer, or whatever.

His hand circles my throat and squeezes it delicately. "I'm going to take what no one else has had before. And every full moon going forward, I'm going to come for you, and you will open your legs for me…" His knee pushes between my legs, forcing them open. "…You will not fight me. You will not try to stop me. Your body is mine to do with as I wish."

Sweat rolls down my spine, soaking into my comforter. "And if I say no?"

He lifts his head to the ceiling, a sinister chuckle escapes his lips, sending chills through my body, hardening my nipples. "Don't."

I can't let this happen. My mind races with ideas of what to do and how to prevent him from taking me. Do I fight? Pray? I mean, would that even work? Prickling courses through me, adrenaline flooding my veins, giving me a sudden surge of bravery. I raise my knee and slam it hard into his heated cock.

He roars, his body separating from mine. I unwedge myself from the front of him and race to my window. I get my hands on the pane when something hot lashes across my calf, dropping me to the floor. The window grows further away as he pulls me back toward him using his long tail. I kick and scream as he hoists me upside down and holds me there, dangling like a piece of meat in a freezer waiting to be butchered.

"Hard way, it is." His tongue lashes out at my shirt, cutting it off me in one quick movement before moving on to my shorts and underwear. I thrash naked in front of him as a devious smile spreads across his face. He scans my bare skin before pulling me close and dragging his nose across my clit. I thrash my body, thrusting my midsection back, trying to tear away from him. Tears spill over my forehead and drip onto my bedroom floor as he holds me at arm's length with a grin of anticipation. "Ahhh, the sweet smell of virginity," he says in a low, throaty growl.

I fly across the room with a quick flick of his tail, my teeth sinking deep into my tongue as I bounce onto my mattress. Metallic liquid spreads into my palate and dribbles out onto my chin. He moves toward me in quiet footsteps, like an animal stalking its prey. My eyes widen, and I use my feet to slide backward across my mattress until my spine strikes the headboard, stopping my retreat.

He crawls across the foot of my bed, and I kick out my leg. He catches it mid-air and holds it tight, pulling me toward him. I open my mouth to scream, but his other hand slaps against my mouth, knocking my lips into my teeth. I wretch at his hand, trying to pull it off my face, but he's too strong. The hand holding my leg heats to an unbearable temperature, burning my flesh. He releases my leg, and it drops to the mattress, no longer having the strength to fight. His tongue slithers from his mouth, gliding down my inner thigh. I swing my other leg at his head, and he catches that one, too. Flames shoot from his eyes and glare down at my scar. "Someone needs a reminder of who's in charge."

Before I can react, his claws dig into my wound, pulling it wide open. Blood oozes onto my comforter as

I grip his hand that's covering my mouth with both of mine, and pull it away frantically. "Please stop!" I cry out.

"I warned you not to fight me, Little Sinner." His fingers press further into my wound.

"I'll stop fighting! Please, stop." I shout, my face wet with tears.

His fingers exit my wound, and he rests his palm on the bleeding hole. "Good girl." He presses down hard, heating the opening like a hot poker in a flame. I scream at the ceiling, my body soaking with sweat and shaking violently. The pain is just as intense as the day it happened. My eyes widen as he removes his hand, and the wound is closed—healed. It's as if he had never ripped it open. My head drops back on the pillow, my body exhausted and heavy with fatigue. Although he's stopped hurting me, the pain lingers like aching bones do with an approaching storm.

My breathing shallows, and most of my body relaxes, feeling defeated, but fear keeps my knees tight together. His clawed hands slide over my knees and yank them apart. He presses my thighs against the mattress and gazes down at his prize. His tongue exits his mouth once more. It slithers along my inner thigh and grazes over my pussy lips, taunting me.

I gasp as it presses inside me slowly at first, stroking and caressing my tight entrance. Without warning, he harshly plunges deeper inside. I jerk away, the tearing sensation causing me to recoil. He grips my hips and pushes further in, moving in and out, burning my delicate walls. I stifle a scream as it singes its way through my organs. Cramps fill my lower abdomen, and a torturous pain bursts inside me like my ovaries are exploding simultaneously. His tongue retreats slowly into his mouth, and he smacks his smooth black lips. "No one, not even new life, will ever be inside you again—no one except me. You are mine, Contessa—my Little Sinner."

Blood pools beneath me, soaking my sheets. I weep openly as I realize what he's done. I'll never carry a child, ever. He's destroyed all the internal parts required to make and carry a baby. The blood keeps coming, and I wonder if he's going to sit between my legs and watch me bleed to death.

He wedges his body between my thighs, positioning his cock in front of my opening. "Now, to take what's mine."

My head launches forward as he grabs it and forces me to look down. "Watch." I pinch my eyes closed, not wanting to see and feel what's about to happen. My head shakes side to side violently, and his hot words filter into my ear. "Open your eyes and watch me take you."

I force my eyes open and grit my teeth at the sight of his cock. The girth alone is the size of my wrist, and the length is nearly as long as my forearm. He's going to tear me into two pieces.

He sits back a little, holding my head with one hand and guiding his cock before my pussy with the other. A playful smile spreads across his face before a dark determination overcasts it. Fire pierces my pussy, and I dig my heels into the mattress, trying to push away from him as he grinds into me. I close my eyes, and he shakes my head, reminding me to keep my eyes on him. He tilts his head back and moans at the ceiling, the veins in his firm, veiny neck popping out, black blood coursing through them. His smooth, muscular chest drops onto mine, and his claws feed through my hair, gripping my scalp. "Oh, Little Sinner, how tight you are for me."

I scream as he rams into me, his hot, fiery cock scorching everything it touches. Bile rises in my throat, my insides popping and snapping with every violent thrust. My nails sink into his spine, raking down his muscular back, and something wet coats my nails.

"Silly, Little Sinner, you can't hurt me," he laughs as he pulls almost entirely out of me and slams his massive cock back into me. I shift higher on the bed, my head thumping into the headboard over and over and over. Spots form before my eyes. I force my hands between my chest and his and push, trying to ease the unrelenting pounding he's giving me. In a matter of seconds, his cock yanks out of me, and I'm airborne, dropping face-first onto the mattress. The weight of his body drops onto my spine and heats up as his cock circles my ass, dotting around the hole like it's testing its tenderness.

"No, please. Not that. Anything but that," I whimper.

His tail wraps around my throat, holding it loosely, just enough to control my movements. A wave of heat flows into my ear canal as he whispers, "You must learn the rules and be taught a lesson. Just like your little boyfriend Jayce." His cock pushes slightly into my ass. "Every inch of you belongs to me, remember that next time you try and fight me, my Little Sinner." I tighten my ass cheeks, trying to stop his hot poker cock from entering. He grips my ass cheeks and spreads them wide. A spitting noise comes from above me, and something hot and wet lands on my asshole. An unrelenting, painful pressure forces me further into my mattress, and I cry out. His cock pushes fully inside my ass, and he moves it rhythmically in and out gently at first as his hot spit lubricates the opening.

I bite down on my pillow as he thrusts into me further and faster. He's killing me slowly, at least that's how it feels.

"I'm not killing you, my Little Sinner."

What the fuck. He just read my mind.

"I did. I own you, mind…" He pulls his cock out of my ass and thrusts it into my pussy. "Body…" His hands wrap around the front of me, and he hoists me up and against his chest, his tail untangling from my throat and whipping around to the front of me, slapping against my clit. "And soul." His massive calloused hands cup my breasts tightly as he thrusts into me over and over. He lets me go without warning, and I fall face-first onto the mattress. He grips my hips, his claws digging into my delicate flesh as he yanks me violently upward to meet his body before pounding into me, harder and faster. His moaning grows louder before it changes to a roar as I scream into my pillow. He blows a breath like a heatwave across my spine, and his hot lava flows into me, burning everything it touches.

I sob into my pillow, snot flowing from my nose like a string, and crimson coats the surface of my pillowcase from my bloody mouth.

"Oh, Little Sinner, you make me feel euphoric." He moans deeply and drops his head against my back.

"You could have found pleasure in this moment, too, if you hadn't fought me."

His cock slides out of me, and I curl into a ball, sobbing uncontrollably.

He swipes the hair away from my face. "There, there, Little Sinner, the worst is over. Each time I see you, it will get a little easier."

A little. That's all I get after what he just put me through. The knowledge that it will be only a little less painful every time after today makes my stomach churn. I lean over the side of the bed, hovering over my waste basket as my mouth waters excessively.

I clench my stomach as vomit launches from my lips and splatters inside the garbage can.

His hot fingers graze my spine. "Little Sinner, tonight was about me, but it won't always be that way. Sometimes it can be about you, your pleasure, if you let it."

My insides quiver, fear coursing through me. But there's something else too, lingering behind it, threatening to take over my trembling frame.

Rage.

I gaze down at my shaking hands and curl them open and closed as flames race through my veins, a surge of adrenaline giving me not only energy but courage. "Pleasure? You call that fucking pleasure. Nothing about it was pleasurable."

"Not for you," he smiles playfully as he stands and backs away from me.

I push off the mattress, but my arm gives way, and I collapse back down. My leg dangles over the edge, and I let my body melt off the bed, too weak and in pain to stand on its own. I take a few deep breaths, trying to calm myself. "So that's what you want, to bring me pain?" My voice comes out hoarse from crying, panting, and screaming.

He kneels before me, his body curving unnaturally as his manly features slowly disintegrate. "I can't help what I am, Little Sinner. If I were all man, there would still be pain. But changing into something more humanlike…" His body transforms completely, and I crawl away from him. His face is nothing but bones engulfed in flames, and his chest, now covered in coarse, sharp hair, moves rhythmically with his breathing. "…will make our encounters easier, don't you think?"

His hooves clunk against the hardwood floors as he closes in on me. I watch in horror as horns slowly rise from his scalp, curling under like a ram. His long hair-covered tail swoops around to the front of him and slides between my legs. I pushed it away, covering my decimated pussy.

"Remember the rules," he hisses, his fiery face growing brighter.

I remove my hands, and his fluffy tail floats over my clit, back and forth, back and forth. It moves over and around it with a pleasurable softness I can't ignore. A tingling sensation spread through my inner thighs. I close my eyes, wondering what sensual feeling this is.

"That is your body's way of telling you it likes what it feels." He's reading my mind again.

He presses harder, rubbing my clit faster and deeper, the tip of his tail tickling my lips like a flickering tongue. The tingling in my thighs grows stronger, and I toss my head back, closing my eyes and panting heavily at the ceiling. I call out, "Oh, my God," as I climax and juices coat the tip of his tail. I breathe heavily, a slight smile creeping in the corner of my mouth. Then I open my eyes and remember who just brought me such pleasure.

"You see, Little Sinner, it's not all bad. You just need to obey." He plunges his tail between his hairy lips and sucks it loudly. "Mmm. Next time, I will use my tongue and catch your juices in my mouth."

A fresh wave of tears spills over my lids. He's a complete creature now, all manly features have vanished.

I can't get away from him, I can't fight him, and my thoughts are no longer my own. He will do as he pleases, and there is nothing I can do to stop him.

I'm his toy, his slave—his prey.

My bottom lip quivers as I gaze up at him. "You've got what you've come for, now leave me be." I wipe the snot rolling onto my lip with the back of my hand. "Please, just go."

"Oh, I'm going, but not because you told me to. I have another matter to attend to tonight." Fire ignites around him, and right before he disappears, he winks.

I wrap my arms around my knees and rock on my bedroom floor, the room reeking of vomit, burned skin, hair, and sex, but I don't have the strength or energy to stand. My body falls slowly to the side, and I'm racked with shame over my response to his touch.

The touch of a beast.

This is my life now, bound by my own fear of death. I've tethered myself to this demon for the rest of my life, but what about death? Will he torment me there, too?

The thought overwhelms me, and another round of sorrow brings massive tears to my eyes. I weep on the hard floor for what feels like hours before exhaustion overwhelms me and drags me into a deep sleep.

"Contessa!" My mom's voice screams from somewhere far away. My bedroom ceiling slowly comes into view as my eyes flutter open. Paleness and panic cover my mom's face as she gazes down at me, tears dripping from her chin. She shakes me hard as my eyes drift closed and my heart begins to pound. "Open your eyes, baby. Stay awake."

A dark figure towers behind her, and I can barely make out my dad's voice. "Tessa, were you in the house?" he yells over Mom's shoulder.

The house? Whose house, I wonder?

Mom's talking again, this time to him, but their words are garbling together, making them incomprehensible.

I cry out as burning pain spreads through every inch of my naked body. A blanket floats over me, and my father's face hovers inches from mine. "I'm going to pick you up. The ambulance will be here any minute."

Ambulance?

My body leaves the floor, and a tremendous amount of pain pierces my skin. The torment continues as my dad races down the stairs of our house, bouncing me around in a panicked state. My eyes roll back, vaguely registering the red and blue lights flashing outside as we emerge on the front lawn.

A gurney bangs to the pavement, unloaded by a paramedic who rushes toward us and reaches under my dad's arms, helping him place me gently on the gurney. "Did she come from the house?" the paramedic asks.

"I think so," my dad says, combing through my hair with his fingers. "Can I ride with her?"

"Of course."

When we reach the ambulance, they wheel me to the side to load me into the back. That's when I see *the house.*

It's far down the street, just past the corner, but not too far for me to know whose it is.

Jayce's.

Fire rages through the attic, practically licking the full moon in the sky, and black smoke roars in angry tufts around the entire structure as firefighters work frantically to douse the flames.

The paramedic shoves the gurney through the ambulance's back doors, jerking me harshly inside. I wince, and a sob breaks free as a fresh wave of pain overwhelms me, threatening to pull me back under.

I grip my dad's hand and mutter one word through trembling lips. "Jayce?"

He kisses the back of my hand, wet tears streaming over my fingers, and whispers, "I don't know, baby."

* * *

I cringe as the gurney bounces out of the ambulance. My dad takes my hand and runs beside us as the double doors of the ambulance bay groan open. The fluorescent lights above me sting my eyes, and I pinch them closed. I roll into a sterile-looking room and am quickly surrounded by unfamiliar faces, my dad fading into the background. I grip the blanket covering me tight between my fingers, not wanting anyone to see.

"Let it go," a nurse wearing a blue mask says kindly. "We have to see everything to treat you." I peer over her shoulder at my dad, biting his nails in the corner. "Where's mom?"

He drops his thumb away from his lips and says, "She'll be here any minute."

Another nurse gestures for my dad to step behind the white curtain to give me privacy. It's not just his presence that makes me uncomfortable; it's all of them.

I don't want any of them to see.

A bright light flashes into my eyes, and a masked woman wearing a white lab coat curls her fingers around the blanket covering me. "We'll get you a fresh blanket. This one's covered in dog hair and can get in your wounds."

I gaze down at the blanket that was at the end of my bed. It's coated with a layer of Boozer's hair, and now so am I. I release the blanket from my grasp, and they fold it away from my upper body and legs until I'm completely exposed.

Everyone's eyes widen before they take turns exchanging glances of confusion. A cold stethoscope lands on my chest, and the doctor clears her throat before saying, "My name is Dr. Francis. Can you take a deep breath for me?"

I'm not sure how she could hear my breathing over my pounding heart. She continues moving the stethoscope around my chest, listening intently. "Lungs sound clear."

Sweat pools behind my spine, the heat from my skin making it hard to stay cool. I feel like I spent hours at the beach without sunscreen. I shift uncomfortably on the stiff mattress. A nurse gently lifts my leg, and I cry out, my body screaming in pain. She freezes, letting the initial shock of pain wear off before continuing to lift them one at a time, examining the gash across my calf that Mastyx's tail caused. She nudges the doctor with her elbow. "This one's a second-degree burn." She points to my hips, ankles, and other parts of my body. "The others are all first degree."

"Are those handprints?" The doctor's voice muffles through her mask.

Everywhere Mastyx touched me, left a mark, his prints, but the only one that may scar is the one on the back of my calf.

"Okay. Let's bring in the portable X-ray and double check her lungs," the doctor hooks her stethoscope around her neck. "Bring in a SAFE kit as well."

The nurse furrows her brow. "Are you thinking assault?"

Assault. Sexual assault. That's what they are talking about. The kit she's referring to is one they use to collect evidence for detectives. I learned that long ago, watching Law & Order: SVU.

My body suddenly tremors uncontrollably. A steady and soft hand rests gently on my forearm. "You're okay. You're safe now," the doctor murmurs.

Safe? Nowhere is safe.

The doctor's hand leaves my arm, and a cold draft chills me to the bones, sending goosebumps across my skin. The nurse slides a warm blanket over me.

The curtain clanks partly open and then closes, the doctor disappearing behind it. Low voices speak on the other side, and seconds later, my mom moves the curtain aside and approaches me slowly, her hands squeezing the top of her purse, her knuckles whitening. "Hey, Tessa bear."

She sits beside me as a nurse rests empty blood vials on my side table and wraps a rubber strap around my bicep. "First, I'm going to take some blood, then I'll clean your wounds, spread some cream on them, and cover them. I'll give you IV fluids and a little medication to help with pain after that," the nurse says, hanging a fluid-filled bag above me. "The doctor will be back in shortly to do a vaginal exam."

My mom takes my hand, squeezing it gently as the needle penetrates my vein and a vial fills with my blood.

Tears spill over my cheeks on either side, entering my ears and soaking the pillow beneath my head. The nurse finishes taking my blood, inserts the IV and injects something into the port before grabbing a packet from the side table and dispensing a cream into her gloved hands. She grips my calf, and I clench my teeth before belting out a pent-up scream.

Her eyes squint and her shoulders rise as she cringes, moving faster now, trying not to drag on the agonizing treatment process. A wrap tightens firmly around my calf, and I squeal and yank my leg away from her.

The nurse puts her hand up. "I'm sorry. I know it hurts, but I'm almost done. The worst is over."

A strange rushing noise pierces my skull and radiates through my head, making my ears ring. My eyes cross, and my mom's face blurs as I fight to keep my eyes open, exhaustion and pain trying to drag me into the depths of unconsciousness.

"If you need anything, here's your call button." The nurse sets the call button beside my hand and smiles at me with her eyes, the rest of her face hidden behind a mask.

Mom dabs her eyes with a tissue. "Tessa bear, I have to tell you something."

The doctor steps back into the room, holding a small box.

It's the kit. The rape kit.

The doctor sits on a rolling stool at the foot of my bed and opens the box. My heart pounds, the thought of what she may find sending my stomach into a frenzy. I yawn broadly, my mouth stretching wide open as my pain slowly fades, the medication the nurse gave me taking effect. My body suddenly feels heavy and relaxed, and my eyes cross, making it hard to focus on her face.

"I'm going to start the exam now, Miss Salavatori. I'm going to try and make it as comfortable for you as possible, but if it gets to be too much, let me know and I'll stop," the doctor says, sliding the blanket above my knees and resting it on my stomach.

"Tessa, look at me." My mom squeezes my hand tighter. "I have to tell you something."

The doctor's hand touches the inside of my thigh, putting a slight pressure on it, trying to get me to open my legs more. My ass shifts backward inadvertently, and my knees clamp shut. Her hand cups my knee and tugs gently. "This will be over soon, just breathe."

I try. I take a deep breath and focus on my mom's mouth, her words coming out slow and distorted, the medication coursing through me jumbling her words. "Tessa, it's about Jayce."

Something pushes inside me, and I shriek, crushing my mom's hand in my grasp.

"It's just the speculum, Miss Salavatori, breathe. I have to open you up a little to document the extent of damage."

Damage. She sees the damage Mastyx did to me.

"Tessa." My mom takes her other hand and cups it around our joined hands. "There was a fire at Jayce's house and he…" She chokes on her words. "And he didn't make it."

I force my eyes open wider, trying to fight the drugs dragging me into unconsciousness. "What did you say?"

Click. Click. Click.

The speculum pinches me, and I release my mom's hand and grip the sheets, my legs instinctively trying to push my body up and away from the burning pain between them.

Mom stands, her face hovering over mine. I pinch my eyes closed and cry out as something scrapes the fried walls of my vaginal opening.

"Sweetheart, Jayce is dead. He died in the fire. I'm sorry." Her voice carries through the noise, the screams, the shrills of fiery heartache that jolts through every ounce of my body and soul.

"What?" My head bobbles when I lift it, trying to look at her lips, wondering if the words that just spilled through them were my mind betraying me.

Delirium and a violent tremor envelop my body; the weight of what's happened to me, what's still happening to me, is too much—a loss like no other.

My bladder releases, soaking the mattress beneath me. The doctor's last words float through the air before darkness pulls me into the abyss.

"Jesus Christ."

Chapter Nine
Unanswered Questions

After spending a few days in the hospital, the doctors released me a day early to attend Jayce's funeral service. The police, my parents, and even Jayce's parents keep hounding me with questions I can't answer—won't answer. I kept telling them I wasn't there. I don't know how the fire started, and I don't know how all these burns got on my body.

No matter how vehemently I deny knowing anything and insist that the last time I saw him was on my front porch, they don't believe me for obvious reasons.

How could I tell them the truth? No one would believe me anyway, so I deny anything and everything.

Maureen and Jayce's parents huddle together in the pew, their bloodshot and suspicious eyes drifting across the aisle to mine and back to the casket. They blame me. I know it. I'm linked to both of their children's deaths.

My mom pulls me against her side. "Ignore them."

She knows they blame me, too. Both my parents do. They came to our house separately, but for the same reason: they wanted answers.

Why am I still alive, and their child is dead? What am I not saying? She knows something. Why won't she tell us what really happened? Let us talk to her; we'll get her to speak.

It's as though my guilt radiates from my body and sets off their parental intuition radar.

I close my eyes and wipe the tears from my cheeks. Jayce wasn't a bad person, and he certainly didn't deserve to die, no matter how shitty of a boyfriend he was.

Mastyx did this. He knew that Jayce would keep coming back. He's always had a persistent and persuasive way about him. The official cause of the fire was a candle left unattended on a coffee table, but I know better. Mastyx probably used the flame of that candle to gain entry into Jayce's home.

The officiant concludes his prayer and directs everyone's attention to the closed casket. "If anyone would like to come up and say their goodbyes that aren't going to the cemetery, please do so now." He steps away and takes a seat in the front row.

No one moves. It's like everyone was waiting for someone else to go up and say goodbye. It's not like you can touch him for the last time or put any memorabilia in his casket. His body was burned beyond recognition, and they had to use dental records to identify him.

I peer over my shoulder and across the aisle. Everyone stares in my direction, wondering if I'll make the first move. "Fuck this," I murmur and stand, my leg shaking, still weak from the accident and Mastyx.

My mom grabs my wrist. "Tessa, maybe you shouldn't."

I curl my fingers around hers. "It's what they want." I scan the crowd. "They want to see how I react, if I cry, if I am even grieving for him. I'll give them what they want if it will bring them closure." I shimmy past my dad and limp toward the casket, my eyes having a hard time not focusing on the candles burning at the top of tall candlesticks placed at the head and foot of Jayce's navy-blue casket. I kneel on a small, padded stool in front of it and run my fingers over the gold trim. "Hi," I say just above a whisper.

The candle flame rises to my left, lighting up my face. I shift away from it, knowing it's Mastyx reminding me that he can see and hear me through the flames. I swallow hard and clear my mind.

Choose your words wisely, Contessa, I think to myself.

The flame lowers to its original height, and I mutter the only thing I can think to say, "I'm sorry."

"Sorry?" A man's staggering voice comes from behind me. I peer over my shoulder as Jayce's dad rises from the pew and stalks closer. "What are you sorry for, Contessa Salavatori? Did you kill my son?"

I scan the room behind him. Everyone is staring at me.

Everyone.

He steps within a few feet, and my body trembles. In the background, my dad wedges himself between people, trying to make his way to the aisle.

Jayce's dad bends at the waist, his face inches from mine. "Answer me!" he shouts, the faint scent of old beer floating from his lips.

I lean away from him, trying to create distance between us, but he takes a step forward, closing the gap. I'm cornered like an animal against a tree, only my tree is his son's casket.

All that comes out when I open my mouth is a jumble of sounds. I can't form the words, but in my head, I'm screaming for help, hoping my dad will hear it and shove his way to me.

Without warning, the candlestick sitting at the foot of Jayce's casket topples over, lighting the ankle of Jayce's dad's pants on fire, burning him. He cries out and stands erect right as my dad tackles him sideways against the catafalque holding the casket. It launches backward, and the casket falls in slow motion toward my dad and Jayce's. They quickly reach for it, grabbing it frantically with both hands, but with the weight and momentum of it, they don't stand a chance. It tumbles hard to the floor, popping open between us, Jayce's charred remains rolling to a stop at his mom's feet.

A blood-curdling scream echoes around the church, and multiple mourners quickly exit out the back while others run to the front, trying to see what they can do to help.

My eyes lock on the blackened corpse, its face twisted, and its mouth stretched wide open in a permanent scream—a witness to something horrifying.

A glimmer of orange flashes briefly in its eyes and disappears just as fast. It only lasts a second, but I know it was *him*. I begged for help, and Mastyx came. No matter how demented his methods are, he stopped Jayce's dad from tormenting me.

The pastor yanks a silk cloth covering an altar nearby and covers the remains. Jayce's mom screams down at me, "You did this, you fucking whore. You—"

A hand crosses her face, with a loud slap, shutting her mouth at once. My mom straightens her dress as Jayce's mom covers the quickly developing red mark on her cheekbone. "Don't you ever talk to my daughter like that again."

Inside, I'm laughing but also afraid. I know now isn't the time, but I've never seen my mom hit anyone before, and I'm low-key proud to call her mine. My dad hooks his hands, one of which has a bleeding cut, under my arms and lifts me from the floor. "Are you okay, kiddo?"

I nod as the pastor shakes his head at us. My dad excuses himself and kneels to the floor, apologizing for his actions.

It looks like I'm not the only one who will eventually go to hell.

The pastor places a reassuring hand on my dad's shoulder, then rises and guides Jayce's parents to an open doorway off to the side to calm them. I imagine he's speaking to them about forgiveness and offering apologies for what happened.

Multiple people work to return the corpse and casket to their original position, some of them gagging, others trying to maintain their composure.

The wailing sound from mourners returns, combined with the hushed whispers and outright accusatory statements of the town gossiper's blasts through the church like a static radio playing two stations at once. I cover my ears, the chaos searing through my temples like an icepick.

Flakes of charred dust litter the floor where Jayce's body once rested. My eyes lock on the onyx powder, wondering if it will stain.

"Tessa?" My mom places her hand on my shoulder, jarring me slightly. "Are you sure you're okay?"

My head moves on its own, nodding as the pastor follows Jayce's parents out of the side room they were just in.

They walk straight for us, and I step back, bumping into my dad, who places his arm around me and moves me behind him as they stop in front of us.

"I'm sorry." Jayce's dad's voice cracks. His eyes drift down to the blackened outline on the floor and tears spill down his face.

My mom rests her hand on his shoulder and says, "We are sorry for your loss." She turns away from him and applies a slight pressure to my upper back with her palm. "Come on, Tessa, let's get you home."

Okay, maybe her sudden forgiveness of the man who screamed at me will get her a ticket back into heaven, but in my opinion, there's no excuse for treating me like that. Perhaps she did it for appearances' sake, not wanting anyone to have any more ill will toward me than they already do.

They already think I've killed two people after all. I hear the whispers and the rumors. But no matter how much they talk, they'll never know what's really going on because I'll never tell anyone.

The sun burns my eyes as we exit the church. I slide my sunglasses down over my eyes and rub mom's hand that's firmly holding me around my waist, as she helps me down the long flight of stairs leading to the parking lot.

When we reach the car, a flyer for a craft fair coming next month flutters in the breeze under the windshield wiper.

My mom crushes it in her hand. "Seriously? People have no sense of decency."

I reach out to her. "Don't do that." I take it away and smooth it out on the roof of the hot car. "I know it's odd, but I do need to find a hobby since I can't go anywhere this summer anyway. Maybe I can save some money to buy a new car."

"You're not going to be driving again for a while, young lady. Not after lying about going to a party and crashing the car." She pulls open the back passenger door and gestures with her hand. "Not to mention, my heart can't take the worry. Now, get in."

I slide carefully into the back seat, trying not to set off the blistering pain that plagues my singed flesh. My mom pushes the door closed, and I lean my head against the window as she climbs in, turns the car on, and cranks the air conditioning.

Warm, stale air blasts through the back center vent, striking me in the face. I sit up, roll down the window, and close my eyes, letting the sun warm my cheeks. We sit there, idling in the parking lot, waiting for my dad to emerge from the church.

"What a shitshow," Mom says, talking more to herself than to me.

The church doors swing open a few minutes later, and my dad exits, shaking Jayce's dad's hand before giving him a heartfelt hug. Guess he's back in heaven now, too.

What do I have to do?

It's been two weeks since Jayce's funeral, and life around the house has returned to normal. My mom went back to work, confident I can be alone now, and my dad, well, he only takes time off for funerals or emergencies, which there have been a lot of in the last few months. We are falling back into our regular Monday-through-Friday family routine—breakfast, work, dinner, bed, repeat.

During the day, I work on my crafting projects for the upcoming craft fair. Ever since I saw the charred remains of Jayce, all I could think about was, why couldn't they bleach them—at least make them white again? That's what gave me the idea to do natural art items. I take an animal's bone, simmer it in a pot until all the flesh falls off, then soak it in dish soap for a couple of days to degrease it, and then use peroxide to get it clean and white. Of course, I have to do all this in the garage because after my test run, my mom wanted to kill me. The house smelled bad, and the thought of having an animal's carcass in a pot on the stove grossed her out.

I glue the last piece of baby's breath on the wood platform holding the skull of a raccoon surrounded by moss. Coming out of its wide-open mouth is a baby spider plant. I call this piece Scarce, since when food is hard to find, raccoons eat various grasses. Well, at least that's what the internet says.

The back door slams, and seconds later, Boozer barrels into my room and dives on my bed. He shakes himself off, casting a shower of dirty water across my bedroom, dotting the walls. "Mom!" I yell, glancing at the clock. Is it after five already? Poor Boozer, I haven't taken him out since this morning.

Mom rounds the corner and peers over my shoulder. "That's creepy."

I glare up at her. "Boozer just shook wet dog droplets all over my room and on my art."

She sighs heavily. "Well, it is raining out, so it happens. I'll grab a towel and dry him off." Her eyes scan the other nine natural death art creatures lining my desk and dresser—a mouse, rabbit, opossum, even a skunk. "Well, at least there's no human ones," she says with a sarcastic tone.

"Not yet," I say matter-of-factly as she walks out of my room.

The floor vibrates, and there's an audible thud as Boozer leaps from the bed and trots after my mom.

My mind wanders to Mastyx and his actions at the funeral. Why did he protect me? I know inside my head I was asking for help, but he's the last person I imagined coming to my rescue.

Tomorrow is my very first craft fair, and I'm nervous but excited. Either people will love what I've created or stick their nose up at it. It doesn't really matter to me, I'm just happy to get out of the house and spend a Saturday without my parents hovering.

I rub my forehead, a headache creeping its way across my brow. Tonight, we're dining out at a local restaurant. People around town say they have the best fish fry around. I wouldn't know. I don't care for any seafood. I always order chicken tenders or macaroni and cheese. My parents don't mind, since it definitely costs a lot less.

No one talks about what the doctor at the hospital found after performing the rape kit. I imagine they couldn't wrap their head around it, the internal burns, the scarring. Perhaps they don't want to upset me by telling me I will never have children. Sometimes I wonder if their silence is an effort to force me to come to them, to open up to them first. I won't do it.

Ever.

I can't. I'm having a hard enough time holding myself together and maintaining my composure every time I glance at a calendar, trying not to obsess over the next fast-approaching full moon.

My dad pops his head through my open doorway. "You about ready, kiddo?"

I glance at the creation in front of me. "Yep. Just finished."

He disappears back through the opening, and I follow him, the faint sound of the phone ringing downstairs growing louder as I descend the steps. My mom picks up the house phone, and her face shifts from cheerful to concerned to downright irritated. She rolls her eyes at my father, covers the receiver with her palm, and whispers, "It's mom."

He stands in front of her, waiting patiently for her to hang up the phone.

The wrinkle in her forehead deepens as the phone slams onto the cradle and she says, "She's wandered off again. That was the sheriff in the next town over. They found her standing in a cornfield wearing nothing but her robe for God's sake."

I stifle a laugh, and my mom's eyes dart to mine, burning a hole through them. "This isn't funny, Contessa."

Oof. When she uses my whole name, I know it's serious.

"You're going to have to take the car away from her now. The home has shuttles and drivers who can take her to the store and to her appointments when we can't," my dad says, wrapping his arms around her waist. "Can we go eat before we go get her?"

She shakes her head, a tiny smile creeping in the corner of her otherwise stern face. "No, we can't just leave her there. I told the sheriff I'd get her and bring her back to the home myself."

He purses his lips and blows out, making his lips flap together before letting his arms fall to his sides. "Okay, well, I'll stay here with Tessa and order in while you go take her back."

Mom presses her hands firmly into her hips. "Oh, no. We are all going. This is a family affair."

I'm trying not to laugh as my parents have a stand-off in the middle of the kitchen. My grandma doesn't care for my dad, and they are constantly bickering, so I get why he wants to stay home.

Dad and I exchange glances as Mom turns away from us and slides her feet into clogs. She's all dressed up for dinner, wearing a beautiful blue floral summer dress, but her irritation with the situation has her not giving a shit about her footwear.

My stomach rumbles, and I cover it with my hand with widening eyes. I glance at my dad, who covers his stomach and says, "Yeah, me too."

We're both starving. My mom has the appetite of a bird, and we look forward to this one night a week, with no cooking, no dishes, and no healthy meal, to dive into something fried and fabulous. As if she senses our starvation, Mom turns to us and says, "I'll call the restaurant on our way back and get our usual meal ordered to go. We'll pick it up after dropping off my mother."

Like two children getting the toy they both wanted at the store, my dad and I exchange wide-eyed smiles.

She shakes her head and points toward the garage. "Come on, you scavengers. Let's get this over with."

*   *   *

I lean back in the back seat as my dad and mom approach, my grandma wedged between them. She stops in the middle of the sheriff's parking lot to adjust her robe, opening wide for the world to see before closing it again and tightening the belt. My dad's eyes drift to the sky, before pinching closed, no doubt trying to burn the image of my grandma's bare, wrinkly body out of his memory. I couldn't look away. How can boobs get so flat and long as you get older?

The back door flies open, and my grandma drops into the seat beside me, chuckling to herself. "No sense of humor," she says as the door closes beside her. She glances over at me and grins broadly. "Hey, there, Tessa bear, how about a hug for your old grandma?"

I shake my head, declining as I gesture to the front of her with my pointer finger.

She gazes down at her left boob, lying flat against the front of her partially open robe. "Oh, hell, if you've touched one boob, you've touched them all. Hug me."

Her arm hooks around my neck, pulling me against her bare chest, the faint smell of liquor wafting from her lips. "That's my girl."

My mom gazes at her through the rearview mirror. "Mom, why don't you close your eyes and take a little nap before we get you back to the home?"

She releases her hold on me, and I can't help but brush her dead skin cells off the front of my shirt.

Blech.

Her hand disappears into the front of her robe and reappears holding a joint and a lighter.

Where the hell was she hiding that?

My eyes widen as she presses the joint between her tight lips and flicks the lighter multiple times. A flame rises, lighting up her face, and my stomach tightens. Without thinking, I snatch the joint from her mouth, burning the palm of my hand, roll the window quickly down and chuck it out onto the highway.

Grandma June glares at me, her eyes narrowing. "What the hell did you do that for?"

The lighter hovers in her grasp between us, and I peel it out of her tightly clenched fingers, tossing it out the window as well. "No smoking in the car."

It has nothing to do with the car. I could care less. It has everything to do with the flame. I don't want Mastyx to see me, to hear anything we discuss in the car—good or bad. Fire is his gateway, and I refuse to allow that gate to be opened around me, especially after what I saw at the funeral.

Grandma's eyes leave mine and stare through the windshield for several seconds before she looks back at me. "Well, hello there, young lady. Who might you be?"

Fuck. This isn't the first time she's forgotten who I was. My mom's been ignoring the signs of Grandma's Alzheimer's for months now.

"Grandma June, it's me, Contessa, your granddaughter."

Her eyes flit to the outside, watching the trees float by before they return to mine. "How have things been going, Tessa bear?"

And she's back.

I open my mouth to give her a rundown of my summer so far, when her head drops back against the seat and she starts snoring softly.

Let's add a side of Narcolepsy to her Alzheimer's, why don't we?

After returning grandma to the old folks' home, we swing by our favorite restaurant, pick up our lukewarm food, and head back home. I excuse myself to my room, lie on my stomach at the foot of the bed and flip on the television, shoveling forkfuls of mac and cheese into my yap.

Fatigue and a long day weigh my head down within minutes. My life only grows more complicated by the day, and I don't think it will ever be normal again. I close my eyes and listen to the weatherman reporting faintly in the background, his voice growing quieter and further away.

Chapter Eleven
Stranger Danger

My eyes spring open, my sun-lit room sending me
into a panic. Fuck. What time is it? The craft show is
today. I flail out of bed, my eyes crusty and my face
sticky, and glance at the wall clock.

Seven. It's seven in the fucking morning. Fucking
summertime trickery.

The fair doesn't start until ten and runs until five, but
I have to pack, decide what to wear, shower, and start
laundry before I go. I pass my floor-length mirror and
stop abruptly. Attached to the side of my face is a
macaroni-and-cheese noodle. My eyes drift to the end
of my bed where I fell asleep. The bowl I had my
macaroni in rests on its side, spilling all over the
comforter.

Damnit.

I open my bedroom door and yell, "Boozer."

Seconds later, a thundering horde of footsteps
stampede up the stairs. Boozer barrels around the
corner, knocking me sideways into my dresser before
diving onto my bed, his nose grazing across the
comforter until he finds his prize. I shake my head as he
devours the entire thing and excessively licks my
comforter.

The dresser drawer slams open, and I paw through it,
looking for my nude bra and underwear. I yank a faded
light blue pair of capris with tears in the thighs and a

white V-neck t-shirt off their hangers, then snatch up my white tennis shoes and carry everything to the bathroom.

After peeling off my clothes from the day before, I turn on the shower and step in, leaping away as the frigid liquid strikes my chest. "Fuck," I yell, then quickly turn the knob to the left to heat the water. I place my hand under the pelting stream before immersing my face, rinsing the dried macaroni off my cheek.

A soft knock rattles my bathroom door. "You okay?" My mom's voice carries through the partition.

"Yeah, I'm fine."

She must have heard me yell. Ever since the incident, any stress-related sound I've made has made them run to check on me. I guess having so many unanswered questions keeps them on high alert.

I wash myself thoroughly but tenderly over my still-healing calf. Most of the red handprints have faded, with only a few leaving discolored blotches. I'm hoping that one day they, too, will disappear. Until then, I stick to capris instead of shorts so the marks inside my thighs remain invisible to the outside world and to me.

The craft fair will be my first public appearance since the funeral. I'm hoping because it's in the next county over, not as many locals will show up, but I have my doubts. It's a pretty popular fair.

My mom helps me pack Grandma's car after breakfast. She told me before that I couldn't drive for a while, but I think she realizes that letting me drive myself makes more sense than having her drive me back and forth. And since Grandma June's car has been parked in the driveway collecting dust, Mom decided to let me use it for the craft fair only. It's an old Nova, but according to Grandma, it runs like a dream.

I peck my mom's cheek and drop behind the wheel. She stands there holding the door open, her face riddled with worry.

"Mom, I'll be fine," I say reassuringly as I grab the door handle and pull it gently.

She removes her hand, letting me close it, and knocks on the rolled-up window. I crank it down and raise my brows. "Yes?"

Her hand disappears behind her back, and when it reappears, a smile spreads across my face. I snatch the cell phone quickly, tapping the screen like a madwoman. "Is this the new iPhone?"

A heavy sigh escapes her lips as she rests her hands on the open windowsill. "It's only for emergencies and when you leave the house. When you come home, I want it back. I don't want you browsing the internet all day."

"I won't. I promise. Thank you, Mommy."

Mommy is what I call her when I really want something, and she gets it for me, which isn't often. But I didn't ask for this, so I knew there would be strings.

"Don't think about going anywhere but the fair. I have a tracker app on it so I can locate you any time."

I place the phone in the cup holder beside me and smile up at her. "Craft fair and back. I won't let you down." The car rumbles to a start, vibrating my entire body.

Drives like a dream, my ass. It sounds like it's seconds away from bursting into pieces. Mom taps the hood's top with her palm. "And Tessa, no texting or talking while driving."

The car staggers backward as I shift it into reverse, backing slowly out of the driveway. "I won't." I pull the shifter to drive and wave goodbye.

Once I reach the highway, I relax a little. I haven't driven since the day of the accident, and it all feels different somehow. The way the road appears before me, the other drivers on it —everything feels surreal. I slow the car down, something in the distance catching my eye. On the side of the road, there's a cross with white flowers wrapped around it, staked into the ground beside the bridge railing where my car went over. Maureen's name is etched across the front. I gasp as I continue driving by it, realizing I stopped breathing momentarily. I take a deep breath, drawing in a large gulp of air before blowing it out slowly, trying to hold back the tears threatening to form. I blink away a stray one and slap the turn signal up, taking the exit toward the sign that reads "Craft Fair Today" with an arrow pointing to the right.

The parking lot is packed full of vendors and early shoppers waiting eagerly to browse this year's selections.

I find my table and canopy set up and ready to go. I paid extra to have everything prepared, so all I had to do was place my tablecloth on the table and line up my ten creations with my cash box. It's supposed to be hot today, so I brought my rechargeable clip-on fan, clamp it to the table, and turn it on low before sitting in my cushioned metal chair.

Multiple shoppers pass my table without a second glance once the clock strikes ten. I keep checking my phone, waiting for my mom to send me a message checking on me. When I glance down at the phone a third time, a shadow darkens the space before me. "Hi," a man's voice says. "Did you make these?"

I can't help but scan his outlandish and eccentric outfit. His sunglasses are tinted purple, and his bright floral scarf seems out of sorts on such a hot day. He lifts the raccoon skull from the table, his black painted fingernails gripping the edge tightly so as not to drop it. He studies its detail, every inch of it, before resting it on the table. "Wow. I love it." He reaches into his back pocket and pulls out a wallet wrapped in duct tape. "The name, Scarce, is spot on. Great work." He removes a fifty-dollar bill from his wallet and passes it to me. "I'll take it. Do you have a box?" My jaw hangs open. Here, I thought I priced my art too high, but the amount of time it took me to make them seemed appropriate at the time. Now this man's eagerness to whip out his wallet and drop fifty on my dead raccoon has me second-guessing my prices. Maybe I'm better at this than I thought.

"You're my first sale," I say to him, unable to stop my grin as I place the raccoon gingerly in a box.

He pushes his glasses up the bridge of his long, pointy nose and says, "Well, I won't be the last after I show your work to my colleagues."

Colleagues. Is he an art professor?

I pass him his box as another man stands beside him, uncomfortably close. He holds his business card out to me and shifts away from the intrusive customer beside him. "Here's my card. If you want to visit my table, I'm down there." He points to a purple and black canopy with a sign dangling from its opening. "I'm Ethan, and my business name is Ethan's Oddities and Eccentrics."

The card slides from between his fingers as the man beside him removes it and places it on the table. "She gets it, buddy. Now, move on."

Ethan takes one last look at me before storming away, taking his raccoon with him.

"That was rude," I say to the man, placing my hands on my hips as I stand. The man ignores me. I study his face as he picks up every one of my pieces and sets them back on the table. His skin is flaky and dry with acne scarred pits, and he smells like day-old booze and unwashed armpit. The front of his jeans is torn at the knee. His eyes, dark and sinister, creep across the table to me and land on my cleavage. "So, beautiful."

I pull the front of my V-neck up and place my knuckles on the table. "Which one do you want to buy?"

He leans forward, placing his knuckles in front of mine, his fierce and lust-filled gaze piercing through me. "None." He pushes off the table, shaking it. I grip the edge as he slides his hands in his front pockets, purses his lips and strolls away, whistling an unfamiliar tune.

"Fucking creep," I murmur to myself.

A woman wearing a long rainbow dress, her blonde hair pulled back in a matching headband, floats to my table. She picks up the mouse display, my smallest of all of them, and her eyes light up. "I can name him Mr. Jingles."

"You sure can," I say with a smile as she pulls out a crumpled twenty from inside her cleavage and passes it over to me. I unfurl the moist, sweaty bill and shove it to the bottom of the pile in my cash box. After boxing it up for her, I wait until she's far enough away before loading up on hand sanitizer.

The first couple of hours go by fast before I fall into a lull. It's noon, so a lot of people are probably hanging out closer to all the food tents on the other side of the fairgrounds. I reorganize my table and make it look more presentable. A sudden feeling of uneasiness washes over me, and I freeze. I peer up from my table and glance around, seeing nothing out of the ordinary.

I shrug off the feeling as my bladder screams for release. I've been holding the large glass of orange juice I drank this morning in too long. I see the sign at the corner of a building in the distance for restrooms, place my *Be back in ten minutes card* on the table, and head in that direction.

When I round the corner, a row of portable toilets with long lines waiting in front of each one comes into view.

Now, not everyone knows this, but when I was a kid, my parents would bring me to the fair, and they never let me use these toilets. 'They're gross and unsanitary,' my mom would say. They would sneak me into an area that was always roped off and marked as off-limits, where employees and the police department had their own set of cleaner, more private bathrooms. I steer to the right of the line of women and head toward the bleachers that overlook the dirt track where horse racers and monster truck shows are held. Beneath the bleachers, a gate encircles the entire area, except for a small opening with a chained-off entrance and a sign that reads 'No Entry'.

I detach the chain, slide inside and reattach it before scurrying toward the symbol painted on the door for the women's bathroom. The moment my ass hits the seat in the wide-open and spacious handicap bathroom, urine rushes out of me, and I moan in relief. I sit there briefly before smacking myself in the forehead. I left my fucking phone on my table. If someone steals it, my mom's going to kill me. I quickly flush and hike up my capris before slamming the door open. A hand catches it, and my eyes widen as the rude man from my table earlier enters the bathroom, a glass bottle wrapped in brown paper sticking out of his grasp.

"What the fuck?"

I barely have time to get the words out before he backs me into the stall and slams the door closed, throwing the lock into the secure position. He turns to me with a devious smile on his face. "Hey there, beautiful." He wipes his lips with his sleeve. "Want to have some fun?"

His smile widens, revealing a row of yellow-stained teeth.

"Eww. Not a fucking chance." I push past him, my hand just reaching the lock when my head yanks backward, his fingers tightening around my hair, sending pain across my scalp. I dig my nails into the back of his hand, and he yelps, throwing the bottle of booze on the ground, shattering it into a million pieces. I back away from him as his eyes darken to black orbs.

"Get the fuck away from me," I yell, putting my hands up to keep him from getting closer.

He slaps my hands away and presses his body against mine. "You're so fucking beautiful. I bet your pussy smells like heaven." His hand presses between my abdomen and capris. I ram my head forward, striking his nose with an audible crunch. Rage fills his eyes as blood drains down from his nostrils onto his clenched teeth. "You're going to regret that."

I cover my head as he swings, his fist landing sharply against my temple. I stagger sideways and flail over the toilet, the blow sending stars dancing across my eyes.

"Mastyx!" I shout without thinking.

The man's hand wraps around my throat and squeezes. "Who's that, your boyfriend?" His grip tightens, and I slap his arm frantically, trying to gulp even a tiny bit of air as he forces me to the floor with one hand and unbuttons his jeans with the other. "He can't stop the pounding I'm about to give you. They thought prison would change me." He rambles on, his zipper clicking slowly down, revealing stained white Fruit of the Looms underwear. "But all they did was make my appetite grow. Now you get to be my first— my first in ten years."

Oh my God. He's a fucking rapist. A rapist fresh out of prison with nothing but lost time since the last time he took what he wanted from an unsuspecting woman. I grip the top of my pants, holding them tight with both hands. "No!" I scream in his face.

He slams my head against the tile, and the room spins and darkens. I claw at him, hooking my nails deep into the side of his cheek before raking them down. Blood oozes from his face, and a heavy palm stings my cheek. The flame of a butane torch lights up the side of my face, heating it and making me stop fighting. "Now, listen here, pretty girl. I don't want to burn your beautiful, young, and perfect skin, but I will. Now hold still and let me taste you." His hand slides inside my pants, and I cry out one more time. "Mastyx!"

The bathroom darkens, the butane flame illuminating only mine and the rapist's face. His smile widens like the Cheshire cat. "Well, would you look at that, mood lighting."

Darkness rises behind him, darker than the space around us already is. It's like a pitch-black shadow towering into the darkness, swallowing the whole room. My eyes widen, so wide it actually hurts, as I realize we are no longer alone. I thrash on the ground beneath him, fighting in the dark to get him off me, when suddenly, his body lifts off mine, wrenching his hand from inside my pants. Flames rise in Mastyx's eyes, and the man's eyes widen in pure terror before belting out a blood-curdling scream.

Mastyx's tail dives into his mouth, muting his cries for help and his Adam's apple illuminates like a lightbulb inside a lampshade. His flaming tongue wedges between his tail and the man's lips and together they pull his yap wide open, the sides of his mouth tearing with ease like paper. "You want to taste something? Taste my fury. Taste my rage." The man's guttural scream is quickly silenced as Mastyx's two appendages yank the man's mouth violently in two directions, splitting his face in half.

The pieces of the man's face fall to the floor and burst into flames. I cover my nose, the smell of burning flesh nauseating me. The rapist's body slams through the door of the stall, landing on the porcelain sink before dropping to the floor with a thud.

I cover my head, fear coursing through me of what my punishment for allowing another man to touch me may be. A soft set of fingers warms my chin, lifting it to meet his gaze. "Time to go, Little Sinner."

Tears drain from my eyes and dizziness makes my head bobble as I say, "What about him?" My eyes drift to the pieces of my attacker littering the floor of the bathroom.

He touches my face, drying my tears with the heat from his hands before cupping my cheeks with both palms. "Little Sinner, I gave you an order." I unfurl myself from the floor, a sense of trust and reassurance flowing through me as I lean into his palms and whisper, "Thank you."

His cock rises, covered in flames, lava flowing from its tip. I try and pull away, but he holds my face firm. "Don't worry, Little Sinner, it's not the full moon yet." His face shifts to the side, and his nose lightly grazes the space between my shoulder and neck. He inhales deeply, sending chills throughout my body, stopping right between my legs. "Oh, how I've missed the smell of you."

How the fuck can someone who hurt me so bad and scares me so much make me feel this way?

"We are connected now, Little Sinner. You and I are one. You will feel what I feel, long for my touch the way I do yours. You are mine." He releases my face and lifts me to my feet with one swift movement. The fingers of his one hand tangle in my hair before pulling my face to his, so our lips are almost touching, the heat from his chapping mine. His other hand glides down my throat with a gentle scraping of a single nail before stopping between my breasts. "Until we meet again."

I stagger back as he lets me go, my back hitting the bathroom door.

"Go!" he roars, the flames rising in his eyes once more.

The door swings open, and I stumble through it, my palms landing harshly on the concrete before my knees come down to join them. I crawl beneath the bleachers and cower there, weeping into my palms, my head pounding, my soul on fire. It feels like it takes forever, but I know only a matter of seconds have passed before I dare to look back at the bathroom door.

A hint of smoke, like a light fog, curls beneath the door and black block letters smolder on the face of it.

Out of Order.

Chapter Twelve
Desire

I collect my composure the best I can before I stiffly walk back toward my place in the craft fair, my legs barely moving me forward. A few eyes from shoppers and other vendors drift to mine but say nothing. I force a smile so as not to arouse too much suspicion.

"Hey, you." Ethan, the Oddities and Eccentric vendor, calls me. "Sorry, I didn't get your name."

"Contessa," I murmur without looking at him.

He waves a handful of twenties and tens at me. "I sold two of your pieces while you were gone—the Impossible Possum and the Roger Rabbit."

"What?" I gaze at the cash and then at him.

His hand grips my bicep loosely. "Hey, are you alright?"

I snatch the money from his grasp and move quickly around him. How dare he? I mean, who the hell does that?

The box I brought to carry my pieces slams onto the table, and I frantically place my remaining pieces inside, my hands shaking. There's still a couple of hours to go, but I'm already over this fucking day.

Ethan appears in front of me. "Contessa? I'm sorry if I upset you. It's just you were gone for so long, and I didn't want you to miss out on any sales..." His voice trails off.

"It's fine." I wipe a stray tear forming in the corner of my eye and stuff my phone in my back pocket. "I have to go."

He holds up a single finger and says, "Wait one second. I'll be right back." He jogs toward his table as I set the last piece inside the box, place it on my chair, and rip my tablecloth off, wadding it up into a ball before resting it on top of the pile.

An infinity scarf hovers in front of my face, perched on Ethan's open palm. "Here. It's hand-sewn. A peace offering." I take the black scarf with deep crimson roses embroidered into it and run my fingers over the threading. It's tight and perfectly aligned without a stitch out of place. It must have taken hours to create, and it's absolutely gorgeous. I raise my eyebrows. "It's so beautiful and light."

"Nice, right?"

I loop it around my neck, adjusting the length so it's even. "So?"

"It's perfect for you."

He needs to be paid for this; it can't be a gift, or Mastyx may get the wrong idea. I reach into my strongbox and remove a twenty-dollar bill. Ethan pushes it back toward me when I offer it to him. "Oh, no. It's a gift."

"I can't accept any gifts." I slide the scarf off my head and drop it on the table. "Sorry."

The scarf slides over to me. "Why? Will your boyfriend get mad?" He taps the scarf gently with his pointer, his face twisting with a concerned look. "Is that who did that to your face and left those marks on your neck?"

I cover my cheek with a trembling hand.

Ethan takes a step closer. "Is he here? Do you need me to walk you to your car?"

"No." I grab my box and turn to walk away.

"Contessa, wait." He runs in front of me with his hand up, holding the scarf. "Just take it. I'll take the twenty you left on the table so you can say you bought it."

"Fine." I struggle to hold the box and reach for the scarf at the same time.

Before I have a chance to react, Ethan doubles the scarf, slides it over my head and adjusts its length. "There. It hides most of the red marks on your neck, except the one by your jawline." He reaches into his back pocket and pulls out another business card. "Here's my card again. If you need to get away, I can help."

I offer him a sheepish smile. His kindness takes me by surprise, and I hesitate, my hand hovering between us, before accepting the card. "Thanks."

He turns away from me and glances back a few times over his shoulder as he makes his way back to his table. I walk briskly back to my car, set the box on the ground and fight for my life to get the fucking trunk open. Once it pries free, I rest my box inside, push the trunk closed, yank the driver's side door of the Nova open and flop awkwardly into the seat, chattering my teeth and sending a sharp pain through my torso.

"Fuck," I say to the space around me before slamming the door closed. I take a few deep breaths before grabbing the visor and pulling it down with trembling hands. The reflection staring back at me isn't my own. It belongs to someone who appears hauntingly older. My hair looks like I fell asleep after a shower—a disheveled mess—and a piece of what seems to be wet toilet paper wraps around a lock of my hair. I gag and cover my mouth before focusing on the darkening mark on my cheek. It's definitely going to bruise. Red marks dot my upper and lower arms from being manhandled by the rapist. I pull the scarf down gently and examine the ones on my neck. They're going to bruise as well.

My parents will definitely notice.

Shit. What do I do? I rest my arms across the steering wheel and lean my forehead against them, blowing out a frustrated breath. The sound of a siren wailing draws my eyes to the exit. Racing into the lot is a fire truck, followed by two state troopers. They speed down the pathway, blaring their horns at a crowd of pedestrians dotting the road leading to the bleachers. I climb out of the car and stand there holding the door by its frame.

Smoke billows into the sky like black clouds darkening the sun. Craft vendors and shoppers flock to the scene, trying to get a glimpse of the show that's unfolding before their eyes. Little do they know they missed the main event.

A sense of relief and relaxation warms my body, even as the air turns chilly. Mastyx, although a demon and someone who caused me excruciating physical pain, comes with at least one perk.

Protection.

I feel the sheer terror I once felt morphing into something I shouldn't feel.

Gratitude.

What the fuck is wrong with me? After everything he's done to me, I'm actually considering trying to make this work because he saved me?

No. I can't just accept this for what it is, can I? A relationship with a demon is something I can honestly say was never on my vision board for my future—lovely house, fancy car, and a hot husband, yes. But literally a hot demon boyfriend, definitely not.

I close my eyes and shake my head. Images of Mastyx's face in non-human form force my eyes back open. I'm going to have to get him a mask at the very least if he can't keep a human one for every encounter. It's equal to meeting someone with a rocking hot body, but their face is a wreck, so you put a bag over it. I bite the side of my thumbnail, my nerves getting the best of me.

It's not the end of the world, I guess. I mean, our relationship, our agreement, no matter how painful and unconventional it is, could work. What's the alternative after all? Death? Going to hell? I'm already fucking there. Figuring out how to navigate my life with Mastyx is going to be a challenge, but hey, no pain, no gain, right?

A swarm of people, shoppers, and vendors pulling wagons and carrying bags approach the parking lot. The officials must be shutting down the craft fair early because of the fire and smoke. Well, at least I have an excuse now for being home early. The only problem is my face and arms.

My mind wanders to the Dollar General I drove by just down the road. I'll stop there, grab some makeup and buy a long-sleeve shirt. That ought to cover all my bases.

I turn the key, and the Nova rumbles to a start. My fingers curl around the shifter when the familiar feeling of being watched makes the hair on my neck rise. I glance through the windshield and lock eyes with Jayce's mom, a crowd of people filtering around her as she stands stationary, holding a wreath in one hand and a metal chair in the other.

Shit. I forgot she did crafts. I didn't know she was here; there are so many vendors.

She speed-walks to my driver's side window, dropping her wreath and tossing the chair on the ground before pounding on the glass with her fist and yelling through it. "Was this you?" She gestures with her head toward the blackened sky. "Who'd you kill this time?"

I quickly pull the shifter into drive and slam on the gas, my heart pounding, my head spinning with thoughts. Dirt flies up in the air, showering her with debris and rocks as I speed out of the parking lot and wedge into exiting traffic.

"Fuck." I slam my hands on the steering wheel. "Fuck. Fuck. Fuck."

This is bad. This is so bad. She's going to start a rumor, I just know it. I should have said no when she asked me if I had something to do with it before I took off. Now, she's going to tell everyone that I started the fire, or at least that she suspects I did. And when the police find the predator's body, all fingers will be pointed directly at me. I need to get the fuck out of this town, this city, this fucking state, not only for my own sake, but for my parents. I make a quick left into the Dollar General parking lot, ram the car in park and race inside. I move swiftly up and down the makeup aisle, then the clothing section, where I find an all-black, lightweight, long-sleeved shirt.

Perfect.

The pile drops on the counter in front of the cashier, and I drum my fingers on the counter as she takes her time, ringing them up slowly. After paying, I decline my receipt and step outside just as a string of police cars tears down the road, lights and sirens blaring.

My phone vibrates in my back pocket. I toss the makeup I just bought onto the passenger seat, quickly pull my new shirt over my head and rip the tags off before answering. "Hello?"

"Tessa, are you okay? I heard there's a fire at the fairgrounds." Her voice echoes through the phone.

Man, news certainly travels fast in this town. "I'm okay. I stopped to use the bathroom at the store." I lie. I just know she's got her phone in her hand, tracking my movements. "I'll be home as soon as I can get through all the traffic."

Another lie. I really just need to buy a little time to throw on my faux face.

"Okay, sweetheart, I'll be waiting for you." She hangs up the phone before I can reply.

After spending fifteen minutes putting on makeup using my rearview mirror, I turn my head side to side and examine my face thoroughly. The bruising is virtually gone. If I keep my head slightly tilted left, my parents will never see the bruise on my face. The minor swelling may be a problem, but there isn't much I can do about that at this point.

I roll out of the parking lot and join the slow-moving traffic coming from the fairgrounds. It would move faster if everyone weren't rubbernecking and trying to catch a glimpse of the fire.

By the time I reach the highway, and traffic finally thins out, it's been almost an hour since I talked to my mom. I hit the gas and speed home, trying to make up time. When I turn the corner onto our street, I slam on the brakes, bringing the car to an abrupt halt. My core trembles and my knuckles whiten as my fingers grip the steering wheel tight.

Should I run? Just keep driving? I shake my head and blow out a staggering breath. No. It won't matter. Besides, I did nothing wrong. I release the brake, press the gas, and steer the Nova behind the police cruiser parked in front of my parents' house.

Jayce's mom told the police about her suspicions, but since there was no evidence linking me to the crime beyond being at the craft fair with hundreds of other people, they didn't pursue the matter any further.

Mom wanted to call her up and give her an earful, but my dad talked her down. What good would it do? She's always going to look for someone to blame for her son's death.

I open the trash can and scrape my dinner plate, a partially burned candle catching most of the scraps. Ever since the fire and my subsequent fear of flames, my mom and dad tossed out anything that could produce one. They exchanged the gas stove for an electric one, which I appreciate, but also hate. And the fire pit from the backyard sat on the curb for less than an hour before someone snatched it up.

Change is never easy, and although I'm grateful for all my parents have done for me, I've decided to let them know tonight that I'm not going to college right away. My plan is to get an apartment out of town, away from all the rumors and gossip, and work for a while so I can save up for a down payment on a house. I know they'll be disappointed, but until I can get this thing, this arrangement with Mastyx worked out, I feel it's for the best. Besides, how would I explain to my professors my absences that come right after every full moon?

"You okay, kiddo?" Dad asks as he enters the kitchen and sets his plate in the sink.

"Yeah. Just tired, I guess."

More like worried. The full moon is only a few days away, and I want nothing more than to crawl inside the fridge and lock myself inside somehow. I wrap my arms around my dad's waist and hug him tight. "Dad," I murmur into his musk-scented polo.

He strokes my hair with his fingertips. "Yes?"

"With everything that's happened, I've decided to hold off going to college. Just for a little while."

A long, heavy sigh sends the scent of barbecue chicken into my face as he gazes down at me. "I had a feeling." He holds me at arm's length and smiles softly, his eyes kind and understanding. "You've been through a lot this year, and I think that if you were to jump into school this fall, you wouldn't have the focus required to do well, so I get it. Your mother, on the other hand…"

"I know. Can you tell her?"

He snorts and removes my arms from around his waist before breaking out in full-on laughter. "Oh, no. I'm not going to poke the bear. That's all you."

I roll my bottom lip out, giving him my best pouty face. "Please, Daddy."

"What's going on in here?" My mom enters the room and drops her plate onto the pile in the sink.

My dad and I exchange glances, neither one of us wanting to say a word. Dad strolls over to my mom, pecks her cheek and says, "Your daughter has something to tell you." He swings his arms behind his back and moseys out of the room.

Jerk. I think to myself.

"What is it, Tessa?" My mom stands a few feet in front of me, and I can't help but stare down at her tattered slippers, the tip of one of them partially chewed away, compliments of Boozer. Her eyes drift over my face, studying my features, the worry line on her forehead deepening.

"It's about school." I blurt.

She walks away from me, sighing heavily before turning on the faucet and grabbing the sponge. The dishes clank and scrape into the dishwasher as I lean against the counter beside her to finish telling her the big news. "I'm going to wait to start. I need to be fully healed and mentally prepared for college. I'm just not right now. Instead, I'm going to work and save up for a house. Grandma's car's just sitting out there, I figure I might as well use it."

Her hand stops circling the plate she's scrubbing, and her eyes meet mine. "Contessa, I'm only going to say this once. Don't throw your life away on some meaningless job that doesn't pay you squat. You are a smart girl who could go anywhere, be anything. Don't get sucked into a shitty job because you don't have your education."

She called me by my whole name, that's how I know the level of seriousness this conversation is. "Mom, I will go back when I'm ready, hopefully by the spring semester. I just know that as of right now, with everything that has happened, I'm not ready to take on college."

"So, you're staying here, using your grandma's car to go to work and saving up for a house, am I hearing you right?" Her hand circles the same plate that she had already cleaned before dropping it in the dishwasher.

I hesitate before saying, "Kind of?"

She shakes her wet hands into the sink, grabs a hand towel and dries them aggressively. "Well, when you get this job, since you're seemingly taking over your grandmother's car, you can pay for the insurance and gas. Maybe in a year or two, you'll have enough saved and be ready to be out on your own."

I roll my neck. "A year or two? No, Mom. I'm planning on moving out before then. Like in a month or two, when I have the job and enough to pay the first month's rent and security deposit."

"Absolutely not, young lady."

She storms away from me, entering the living room, and I stomp after her. "Why not? Jessie moved out when he was eighteen." I cross my arms, my foot tapping on the floor. I can feel the heat rising in my face. Pushing my mom too far isn't something I usually dare do, but this is something I really want, and I'm going to need her and my dad on board to help me.

My mom points to my dad when he stands. "Sit down." He grimaces and lowers his ass back down on the couch.

Mom turns to me, her voice shrill and rising by the second. "Your brother is not only well-trained in martial arts, but he's also self-sufficient, has been working since he was thirteen, bought his first car by the time he was sixteen, and never relied on us for anything. If he wanted it, he got it himself. You, on the other hand…" She wags her finger at me. "…have had an accident where someone was killed, gone to multiple parties and come home drunk throughout the years, don't have two nickels to rub together and are constantly asking us to help you with this, that and the other. Not to mention you can't even cook grilled cheese without smoking up the kitchen, or boil Ramen noodles without overcooking them. You're not ready, Contessa."

She's right. I hate to say it, but it's true. Jessie has been gone for four years now. He left and never looked back. Now, he lives in Tacoma and works as an engineer, making a ton of money.

"Well, I'm eighteen, and you can't stop me," I rebut. I mean, it's true. I can walk right out the door, the state considering me an adult, and do whatever the hell I want.

If my mom's head could rotate 360 degrees, it would. Her cheeks rise to a shade of red I've never seen, and my dad sits behind her on the couch, his fist covering his mouth, trying not to laugh despite my error.

"Who do you think you are, young lady?" She yells, her finger poking me in the chest. "I brought you into this world, and I can take you the fuck out. If I say you're not ready, you're not fucking ready. Now take your mouthy ass up to your room."

She knows I hate it when she calls me a young lady. When will she treat me like an adult? I clench my fists, my face prickling with blind rage. "Fine!

I turn away from her and storm upstairs to my bedroom, slamming the door. A framed picture of a woman reading falls off the wall and shatters when it hits the floor. It only takes my mom a few seconds to respond. She throws my bedroom door open, her eyes wild. "You want to slam doors in my house; you won't fucking have one." She stomps out of the room, and I hear her thundering steps barrel down the stairs and the tell-tale sound of the kitchen junk drawer clanking open. The steps are heavier on her way back up, the sound like that of a hundred elephants stampeding toward a fresh watering hole. She stops in my doorway, pulls my dad by his sleeve into the room and says, "Do it," before placing a flathead screwdriver in his palm.

My dad lowers his head and nods. She disappears, and the sound of her angry footsteps grows further away as she retreats to the first floor. The screwdriver tip digs into the pin on the hinge, and with a quick pop of Dad's palm, it comes loose. He removes all three pins and pulls the door off its hinge, leaning it against the wall in the hallway.

"Come on, Dad, this is ridiculous."

I reach for my door, and the top of my hand stings with a sudden slap. "Oh, no, you don't. This is your doing, so you're going to accept it and leave the door where it is." He puts the three pins in his back pocket, a small smile playing on his lips. "You know what happens if you mouth back to your mother. Hell, I don't even mouth back to her. Word of advice, let her cool down for a bit, then come down and apologize."

"But, Dad, I can do this. I can be on my own." I open my top dresser drawer, remove the three hundred and eighty dollars I made at the craft fair and slap it on top of my dresser. "Look, I already have almost half a month's rent."

"Where did you get all that?" he asks, picking it up and counting it.

"The craft fair."

He organizes the bills by denomination and returns them to the dresser. "From making those death nature things?"

I drop the money back in my drawer and close it. "Yes."

"Listen, kiddo, if you want to start saving up for a place, go for it. Maybe once you have enough and prove you can be responsible, she'll be open to discussing it again. But for now, focus on getting a job and saving money."

"Fine, I will."

"Good." He turns away from me and steps into the hall. "Love you, kiddo."

"Love you too."

Chapter Fourteen
Sturgeon Moon

After apologizing to my mom and having an hour-long heart-to-heart, she agreed to let me move out, but only after I've saved at least three thousand dollars, preferably five.

My dad hung my door back up a few hours ago, and after a few days without it, all I want to do is leave it open. I chew the side of my thumbnail. Tonight's the full moon, the return of Mastyx, and I'm fucking petrified. I asked my parents to stay home with me, but the stupid neighbor is having another one of his fucking moon parties. He doesn't usually have two in a row, but I guess the Perseid meteor shower could be visible at the same time through a telescope, and it's a big deal.

I mean, it's not like my parents could stop Mastyx, even if they tried. Could they even see him, I wonder? Or would they come in and just see handprints showing up on my body, seemingly placed there by a ghost?

"We're heading out," my dad says, his brow furrowing at my bleeding thumb as he swoops into my room. "Kiddo, you have to stop biting your nails, or I'm going to buy you some of that bitter polish and lather it on like soap."

"I know. It's just, I haven't been alone since the night of the fire." I stare at my floor, not wanting him to see the fear lingering in my eyes.

The mattress sinks as he sits beside me. "We are leaving the cellphone on the kitchen table for you in case of emergencies and will be right down the street. We can be here in less than a minute."

I lean my head against his black-and-white plaid button-up, the faint scent of cheese wafting from his breath. "Did you get into mom's cheese platter for the party?"

He pulls me against his side, a devious smile playing on his lips, and squeezes my bicep. "Oh, I may have had a nibble or two."

"Look who's poking the bear now," I say, glaring up at him.

My body falls sideways with a quick, but playful push of his hand. "Get out of here." He stands, leans down and kisses the top of my head. "Remember, you wanted to prove that you can be out on your own, so staying here alone, without an issue, will certainly boost your mother's confidence."

"I know, Dad. I'm going to work on setting up my Etsy shop and uploading pictures of my natural death creations."

"Okay. Well, keep the doors locked, and we'll be home sometime after two." He walks away from me and disappears into the hall, leaving the door open.

I glance at my wall clock. It's five minutes to eight. Six hours alone. A six-hour window, Mastyx could show and torture me with his flaming hot body. My legs tighten at the thought, and a tremor rises in my abdomen, my anxiety trying to rear its ugly head. I hope he comes as a full man, not a creature or even a partial one. It would certainly make things easier.

My head spins, a part of me wanting to let everything go and not worry about what happens next, and the other part wanting nothing more than to run and hide inside a church, where I may or may not be protected.

I've come to accept he's not going to kill me, and he's obviously willing to go to great lengths to protect what he claims is his, so why am I still so afraid?

My thoughts wander to what I'm going to say to him, and my hands begin to tremor. I rub them together, trying to ease my nerves. Should I ask him not to leave marks where my parents can see? Or ask him how I can help him be more manly and less beastly? How can I even address the issue without sounding insulting? The shaking has traveled from my hands into my entire trunk, rattling my core. Don't be afraid, Tessa, the worst he can do is say *no*.

Fuck, Tessa. What are you even saying? He's a demon. You can't control him. I rub both my sweating palms up and down my upper thighs. I wish they'd stop trembling. My jaw staggers open and close, chattering my teeth. Calm down, Tessa, everything's going to be fine. Deep breath in, I close my eyes and blow it out. I open my eyes and gaze down at the wound on my leg. It has healed faster since Mastyx ripped it open and sealed it back shut. The doctor at my final follow-up thought it was the honey ointment I've been using—says it works wonders. So does the fiery hand of a demon, I thought to myself at the time.

I shake my head, trying to clear it and focus on taking nice photos of my art. Although I didn't sell all the pieces at the craft fair, many people asked about a website to buy from later, which I didn't have. I collected their information on a sign-up sheet, including their emails, so I could let them know when the site was ready.

My bedroom door slams when I hit send on my last email, and I leap to my feet, my eyes like saucers scanning the empty, but dimly lit room. "Mastyx?" I murmur. I stare at my bedroom door for a few seconds, listening for any signs of life on the other side before crossing the room and trying the knob.

It won't open.

I scan the floor first, looking to see if something is blocking it from opening, before I look at the top of the frame. My eyes widen as a blackened handprint burns into the wooden door, an orange outline shining brightly and flaking off, embers floating to the floor. I can't see him, but he's here.

The floor creaks as I back up toward my bed, swallowing hard. I need to try to control what happens next, or at least find a way to make it less petrifying. All I can think of in my crazy mind is accepting what's about to happen. Perhaps if he stays invisible, it won't be so bad. Charred hoof prints burn through my fluffy, white area rug, sending the foul smell of melting polyester into the room.

In the weeks leading up to this full moon, I spent hours researching a way out, but came up short, except for straight-up witchcraft and rituals. Neither of the topics I researched yielded a single answer to any of my many questions.

I've spent almost every night crying myself to sleep in anticipation of Mastyx's next visit and the pain he'll bring with it. One night, I had a particularly ugly meltdown, and an epiphany soon followed. He wants my body, so maybe I can use that to my advantage. Although I've accepted my fate, it doesn't make this any easier, especially when he stands before me, his hooves smoldering through my area rug.

For some reason, he can come at will as long as it's the full moon or when I summon him. Yet, everything I've read about incubus demons states that their victims are usually asleep. Perhaps it was part of the contract I signed with him, but I couldn't read or understand.

Breathe, Tessa. Remember to breathe. You can do this. Offering myself up to him willingly may be the only way to gain the upper hand—may be the only way I can come out of this encounter with less damage to my flesh.

Clear your mind, Tessa. Fucking let it go.

I close my eyes, take a deep, staggering breath and pull my shirt over my head, revealing my breasts to the seemingly vacant room. A tremor vibrates across my core, and my nipples harden to stone as the hoof prints stop moving, stop coming closer to me.

He's waiting. It's working. He wants to watch and see.

I want to stop right here, not let him see anything else, but I know that, for this to work, for me to be in a position to make a request, possibly, I need to sacrifice something first.

My dignity.

I shimmy out of my shorts and underwear, and a hoof print moves closer. My bottom lip quivers, and I put my hand up. "One condition. Please don't leave marks where my parents can see." I sniff my running nose, wipe my watering eyes, and keep moving back until the back of my knees strike my mattress, and I sit down, shifting myself onto the bed entirely. Not a single part of me isn't vibrating with fear, but I swallow it down, hoping beyond all hope he'll grant me this one thing.

The bulb inside my lamp next to my bed pops, and the room darkens at once. The mattress sinks by my feet, and my breath quickens. I gasp for air, fear coursing through my veins, wishing he'd say something or appear. *At least let me know you understand*, I think to myself.

A rising heat floats from my lower legs and moves at a glacial pace to my upper body until it reaches my face. "I understand," Mastyx's low, throaty growl fills the void between us, his hot, scentless breath shifting the hairs on my cheeks.

He's reading my mind again.

Please, tell me how I can make this less painful.

A crushing pain fills my breasts, something gripping them tightly in the dark. It burns, but not so hot that it's intolerable. "I decide the amount of pain you deserve, Little Sinner."

Something drags slowly up my leg, leaving a trail of something hot, wet and thick on my skin. "Open your legs," he orders.

My heart pounds in my chest, so hard it sends a rush through my eardrums. I slide my heels outward, the memory of what happens when I don't do what he wants flooding through my brain and helping my legs open.

A black face manifests above me in the dark, the silhouette of it barely visible in the dim amount of moonlight peeking through my curtains. It moves closer and closer to me, and I press my head into the mattress, trying to keep it from touching me.

He turns his head sideways and rests his pointed ear against my sternum. "Oh, Little Sinner, how your heart pounds for me."

I gaze down at his face, and a hint of the man from the fair flashes briefly through his features, rippling from one side to the next, before returning to all black. My body stiffens, frozen in fear as a pressure, then stretching pain, makes me cry out.

Mastyx's cock makes a slow and torturous entry, feeling larger this time than before. It's hot, but not as bad as our last encounter.

He lets it sit there, not moving, not ramming me with it, just stationary like he's waiting for the right moment to thrust into me. We lie there, in the darkness, me panting in fear and him remaining soundless and relaxed, for what feels like an eternity. His breathing is quiet, almost rhythmic and for a moment, I wonder if he's fallen asleep.

"I never sleep, Little Sinner."

Flames rise in his eyes, casting a hot shade of orange into the room. My eyeballs water and burn, the heat emanating from his coming at me in waves. I scream, and his tongue launches from between his lips, plunging into my throat, silencing me. His cock thrusts into me rhythmically at first, then in short but powerful bursts, sending sharp pains into my core. I dig my heels into the mattress and push up with my body, trying to buck him off, but he's massive, and his weight drops on top of me, crushing my chest. His tongue slithers out of my mouth, and I cough hard, desperately trying to gulp air into my lungs.

His cock yanks out of me, making me yelp. Without warning, he forces my legs apart and extends his tongue between them. It lashes back and forth against my clit rapidly. A tingling sensation travels through my inner thighs and buttocks, and I can't help but moan.

What the fuck is wrong with me?

"This is for you and for me, my Little Sinner."

The tingling suddenly sends a violent wave of pleasure throughout my body. I launch my head back as a blissful and euphoric orgasm drains out of me. His head disappears between my legs, and I grip the sheets, twisting them between my fingers, his audible licking and slurping echoing around us.

If he weren't so hideous, this would be amazing, I think instantly regretting it.

His head snaps up from between my legs, his eyes turning to angry slits in the dark. "You want to see hideous?" His growling voice booms with rage. "I'll show you hideous."

His face changes from a black silhouette with golden eyes to the man from the fair and then to a flaming skull with sharpened teeth. I shriek and pinch my eyes closed, trying not to look at him as I shout, "I'm sorry!"

He grabs me by the arms and lifts me from the mattress, sending me airborne. I land hard on the floor by my door and cover my head, waiting for him to strike me. The clunking sound of hooves grows closer, but I keep my eyes tightly shut.

"Open your eyes and look at me, Little Sinner, or I'll do it for you."

I open my eyes, but stay crouched, keeping them focused on the floor, panting heavily, my pulse throbbing hard in my neck. My lips tremble, and tears stream like rain down my face as I slowly turn to look at him.

My eyes widen in horror. His flaming skull is nothing compared to the rest of him. His chest, like that of a bull, hairy, broad and swole, rises and falls with heaving breaths of fury. My eyes drift to his massive cock covered in ridges, black ooze dripping from its tip. I sit up quickly, pressing my back against my bedroom door. The top of his flaming head blackens my bedroom ceiling as he stands fully. His tail whips around from his back, wraps around my throat and lifts me to my feet. I dig my nails into the coarse, hair-covered appendage, gasping for air.

"Now, I will take you my way, Little Sinner."

My face smacks against the floor, splitting my lip wide open, and the taste of metallic liquid fills my palate. I barely have time to take a breath when his full body weight comes crashing down on my spine, flattening me to the floor. Radiating pain travels through my hips, his clawed hands gripping them tight as he hoists my ass up in the air and enters me violently from behind.

I cry out with every vicious pound, his visceral desire audible, as he bleats, groans and grumbles. The more I try and pull away from him, the deeper the sharp ridges covering his cock, dig into my walls. A puddle grows beneath me, my eyes spilling endless tears of pain and sadness that this is now my life—the life I chose when I signed that contract in blood to save myself.

Boiling lava fills my insides, and Mastyx howls, his rhythm slowing to a painful stop. I drop to the floor, his claws releasing me.

If I could curl into a ball, I would, but the pain inside me is unbearable, and every muscle I have pulsates with an ache I've never felt before. Everything feels weakened, defeated.

I want to die. I should have died.

I shouldn't have taken the deal.

Chapter Fifteen
Oblivious

It takes several minutes for me to realize that I'm alone. Mastyx left me there, lying on the floor, broken.

Defeated.

I push my arms straight, slide my knees beneath me and stagger to a stand. My entire body feels as though it's been run over by a steamroller, and hot soup is dripping on my floor from between my legs. In that moment, I realize that all evidence of Mastyx being there, besides what's currently vacating my body, is gone. There is no char mark on my ceiling, no melted carpet on my floor.

Everything appears normal. I turn to face my mirror and to my surprise, the damage to my body is minimal. There is a little ring of redness around my neck, but it's not burned, and except for a few blistering handprints around my breasts and midsection, the rest of me is intact.

He listened. Despite everything and how badly he hurt me after I insulted him, he did what I asked. He left no marks that couldn't be hidden with clothes. I gather some pajamas and shuffle to the bathroom. Taking a shower sounds painful, so I plug the tub, crank the water to hot, and sprinkle in a cup of Epsom salts. I swirl my hand beneath the water, watching the crystals slowly dissipate before sinking my screaming body inside. Tears escape my closed eyes, and I whimper softly.

*　*　*

A loud pounding startles me awake. The chilled water drifts just under my nose, my face nearly submerged.

"Tessa?"

It's my mom. I glance at the knob, thanking God I remembered to lock it. "Yeah." I frantically stand, grab my towel, and dry myself quickly before stuffing my feet into pajama pants and a t-shirt, my adrenaline pumping.

"Did you fall asleep in there?"

"Only for a sec. I'll be right out." I turn my head side to side in the medicine cabinet mirror. Most of the redness around my neck is gone, and there are no visible signs of skin damage.

When I unlock and open the bathroom door, my mom is standing there waiting for me. "You, okay?"

I nod. "I woke up and couldn't fall back to sleep, so I figured I'd take a bath."

She brushes a wet lock behind my ear. "Okay. Well, get some rest." Her eyes drift to the floor near the door. "And clean up whatever you spilled there. I slipped in it when I came in."

Bile rises in my throat when I peer down at her bare feet. I fight the urge to gag outwardly as she walks away, closing the door behind her.

Mastyx's cum shines on the floor, swiped in an arched pattern, compliments of my mom's sole. My mouth waters, and I rush to the toilet, slamming the lid open before hurling inside. Fucking gross.

The water and vomit rush into the pipes as I flush and let the lid drop. My eyes water, and I wipe them and my mouth on the towel I left on the floor before pulling myself to a shaky stand. My reflection gazes back at me in the mirror above the sink, and I barely recognize the person staring back at me.

Fuck. I'll need to sleep for days to get rid of the luggage I'm carrying beneath my orbs. I splash some cold water on my face, brush my teeth, gargle too much mouthwash, and crawl under the covers.

* * *

"Oh, Jesus Christ," I hear my mom say before the sun suddenly beams into my room as she tosses my curtains open.

"Mom." I cover my eyes with my arm. "What are you doing?"

The blanket launches off my body. "First off, I asked you to clean whatever you spilled on the floor; now it's sticky, and once again, I stepped in it."

My eyes spring open, and a lump crowds my throat, making it hard to swallow. She stepped into it *again*.

"And second, it's freaking two in the afternoon, you can't sleep all day."

I roll onto my side and sit up slowly. My head wobbles a little, and the room spins. I drop back on my pillow. "Argh, Mom, I don't feel good."

Her hand slaps across my forehead, and the wrinkle in her forehead deepens. "Well, shit. You feel hot." She pulls the covers back over me. "Lie back down. I'll make you some soup."

I probably feel hot because fucking Mastyx scorched me from the inside out.

Her bare feet swerve around the sticky goop on my floor before disappearing into the hall. My eyes roll back in my head as I roll onto my back and stare at the ceiling.

My dad pops his head in. "Hey, kiddo."

"You can come in," I say just above a whisper, my throat feeling scratchy.

He holds up his hand. "Oh, no thanks, you can keep your plague to yourself."

My mom wedges between him and the doorframe, drops a bottle of cleaner on the floor with a roll of paper towels, and sprays Lysol around the room. I cough continuously as she empties what appears to be the entire can into my room and bathroom.

"Mom, you're being ridiculous," I whine, the words choking out of my mouth.

"Can't have whatever you have spreading."

"Okay, I get it, but do you have to use so much disinfectant? It looks like a smoke bomb went off in here." I cover my mouth and nose with my comforter.

She sets the empty canister on my dresser, unlocks my bedroom window, and pulls it open. "There. This will help."

"Help what? Disinfect the outdoors?"

"Don't be sarcastic, Tessa. You're ill, and your father and I can't afford to be sick." She squeezes the tips of my toes through the blanket. "Soups on the stove. I'll bring it back when it's ready." She stoops down to the floor, sprays a large amount of cleaner on Mastyx's man juices and scrubs them up with a paper towel, before shooing my dad out of the doorway.

My computer pings from across the room, and I ignore it. Probably spam.

Just as I start to doze off, mom swoops into the room with a tray in hand.

My computer pings again.

"You know," she says, setting the tray on the nightstand beside me, shifting my lamp out of the way. "That's been going off all morning. You should probably check it."

"It has?"

"Yes. Your father and I can hear it all the way downstairs. You know sound carries in this house." She gestures with her hand. "Come on, sit up. Let's get some chicken noodle soup in you."

I sit up and slide back, leaning my head against the headboard. "Will you check for me. I don't think I have the energy to get up."

"Of course. As soon as you take a bite of soup." She holds a full spoon in front of my lips.

"Mom, I'm not a child. I can do it myself."

She raises her eyebrows at me and widens her eyes, staring at me expectantly. I open my mouth and let her shovel the hot soup inside. It singes the roof of my mouth and burns my esophagus the whole way down. "Mom, it's freaking hot."

"You'd bitch louder if it were cold now, wouldn't you?" She places the bowl on my lap. "Eat."

I cup one hand around the bowl and hold the spoon in the other. "I will. Now will you please check?"

An annoyed huff escapes her lips as she turns away from me, leans over my computer and wiggles the mouse, waking the screen. A few clicks later, and she gasps. "Wow."

"What?" I sit up taller and place the bowl on the tray beside me.

"Well, it looks like some of your creepy art has sold."

"Really?" I peel the blanket off me and sit up. My body drifts side to side, and my muscles scream, making me grimace. "How many?"

She turns and looks at me with raised brows. "All of them."

Chapter Sixteen
Fly the Coop

After selling out of my natural death pieces, making over eight hundred dollars in a single day, I immediately went to work making more. In less than three weeks, I reached my mom's required minimum of three thousand dollars to move out.

I found a place only twenty minutes from my parents, closer to downtown, but not so close that I don't have breathable space. It's a small upstairs apartment that came fully furnished. The price was a little more than I wanted to spend, but given how my online sales are going, I knew it was manageable.

It's moving-in day, and as I watch my dad rest another heavy box on the floor of my new living room, I can't help but admire my new home. A set of bookcases flank a nonworking fireplace, giving me ample space to display my art, and an accent wall opposite the fireplace is just wide enough to accommodate my computer desk and chair. The sectional and wooden coffee table fit neatly between them, leaving enough space for me to move freely around the living room without bumping into anything.

"That's the last one," my dad says, dropping a box on the couch cushion beside me. He wraps his arms around me, hugging me tightly, and whispers against my scalp. "We are only a phone call away."

"I know, Dad. I'll be fine." I turn to my mom, who stands tight-lipped and silent by the front door. "I'll come over every Sunday for dinner."

She stiffens her body slightly when I hug her before saying, "What about dinner on Friday?"

I rest my hand on her arm, rubbing it softly as she fights to hold the tears rimming her lids at bay. "How about next week. I really want to take the time to get this mess organized."

She dabs her right eye with the side of her hand and produces a forced smile. "Well, alright."

Her stiff posture and the fact that she's fighting like hell not to cry are telling. She misses me already but will never say it, preferring to stay strong and seemingly unbothered. But I know her, deep down inside, she's melting down.

I grip her biceps and hold her at arm's length. "I won't be far away. You'll still see me."

"Well, the house will definitely feel empty without you."

My dad clears his throat. "Umm, hello, husband here. You won't be alone." He waves his hand in the air.

She shakes her head. "Oh, please. It's not like you're going to watch Lifetime movies with me or go underwear shopping."

He rolls his eyes. "Of course, I will. You just have to ask."

Mom and I exchange knowing glances. We let him come with us once when I needed bras. He kept holding the bras up to his chest and asking us how they looked. It was so embarrassing.

Dad strolls over and stands beside her in the doorway. "Come on. Let's leave her be so that she can get settled."

My mom gives me one last hug and a kiss on the cheek before leaving. Once they are gone, I lock the door and lean against the partition. The small camel-colored leather sectional calls me to it for a nap, but I have so much to do.

I remove two books, Frat Row by Krista Turner Clark and Creep by Brooke Montoya, from the top of the box sitting on the couch cushion and place them on the end table beside the lamp. I only keep two books at a time and don't buy more until I've read and donated the ones I have. Some people think that's weird, but I find, especially in my situation, that it's actually convenient. The shelves can be used for something other than books.

A cloud of dust floats down from the top shelf of the bookcase as I swipe it with my hand.

Gross.

My toes crack as I shift up onto my tippy toes and run a cloth coated in Endust over the wooden surfaces, clearing them of a thin layer of filth. I organize my artwork on the bookshelves by size, with smaller, knick-knack-sized pieces on the top shelves and larger, more detailed pieces on the bottom. After that, I press a row of strip lights on timers around the perimeter of the bookcases on both sides, stand back and gaze at my natural wall of art in awe and wonder.

It's so fucking beautiful.

A few hours later, all the boxes have been unpacked and broken down, making my apartment feel more like home. I sit down with a much-needed glass of water and review my sales for the day. I've sold only one piece, which is fine, but I really want to keep up the momentum and stay ahead on my rent. I pull Ethan's business card for Oddities and Eccentrics from my desk drawer and find his email. After sending him a link to my shop with a quick message, I browse Etsy for anything interesting.

A cool-looking long-nose plague mask pops up on my screen. I click on it. If only I could get Mastyx to wear it to hide his face when it's not human-like. It certainly would make our encounters a little less terrifying.

It's not that expensive. I really shouldn't do any frivolous spending, but you know what? There's a space between my headboard and the wall where the mask would fit perfectly. I click 'Buy Now' and complete my purchase.

What the hell am I doing? Buying a gift for Mastyx wasn't really something I'd ever expect myself to do, but it made sense to me in the three seconds it took my stupid brain to decide it was a good fucking idea.

My computer dings with an incoming email. I click on the icon and read the brief message from Ethan. He's going to share my link and a few kind words with his email list and wants to know if he can send me a list of his subscribers.

Fuck yeah. This partnership will be golden. I attach the link to my people and send it back to him.

I stare at the date in the bottom right corner of my computer screen. The full moon is only four days away. It falls on a Monday of all days. My stomach tremors

and my airway narrows, my anxiety trying to overwhelm
me. I close my eyes, take a few deep breaths, and blow
out a long-winded breath, fluttering the papers on the
desk in front of me.

I've been racking my brain for several weeks, trying
to figure out a way to make our encounters less
frightening. Things didn't go as planned the last time he
came. Perhaps this time I can keep my insulting
thoughts to myself. I stand, stretch my hands to the
ceiling and enter the kitchen, the fridge rattling as I yank
it open.

Nothing looks good, so I pull the bottom drawer of
the freezer out and smile. My dad bought me Bomb
Pops. They have always been my favorite. I peel off the
wrapper and suck the tip of the red, white and blue
popsicle. So juicy.

My computer pings right as I plant my ass down on
the couch. It's so hard not to look immediately
whenever a sale comes in. It pings again seconds later,
and I get up with a huff. When I wiggle the mouse, two
emails are highlighted: one says I have a new sale, and
one from Ethan says, "Did you see this?"

I click on his email and open the attachment. It's a
listing for an authentic ram's head skull on Craigslist.
The person only wants one hundred and fifty dollars for
it. *That's worth way more*, I think to myself. I grab my
phone and call the number at once. The guy on the
other end tells me he bought one, thought it was lost,
and a free replacement was sent. Then the original
showed up. He has no need for two, so he's selling the
extra. I talk him down to one twenty-five, and we agree
to meet in an hour at the local Walmart.

My eyes light up as I end the call. Inside my head, I can already picture how the ram's head will look when I'm done with it, and it's going to be a masterpiece.

* * *

When I pull into the parking lot of Walmart, I spot the guy's hunter green SUV right away. It has gold rims and tinted windows. I scan the parking lot for cameras, and when I find one, I pull beneath it and wave him over. I'm not taking any chances, not after what happened at the fairgrounds.

His SUV slows beside my hoopty, and he steps out, wearing black pants, a button-up long-sleeve black shirt, and nice dress shoes. He's hot as fuck and not at all what I was expecting. His goatee is perfectly trimmed, and his eyes are light gray and kind. The scent of his woodsy cologne wafts into my nostrils as he opens the hatch of his vehicle and curls a lock of blonde hair around his ear. "So, what do you think?"

I blink several times, and my face flushes as I realize I'm staring. Oh my God, so embarrassing. My eyes dart around the lot, looking for a flame. If fucking Mastyx knows what I'm feeling or thinking right now, I'm as good as dead.

"You, okay?" he asks.

I pull the money from my purse and pass it to him. "It's perfect."

He slides the bills from between my fingers slowly, his eyes not leaving mine. "Hey, I'm going to meet a few friends at the bar down the road. Why don't you follow me over so I can buy you a drink?" His eyes flit to my lips, and he licks his own. I feel like he's already tasting me without touching me, and a twitch between my legs makes me giggle awkwardly.

Fuck. There's nothing more I want right now than to follow this man to the bar and bang his ass in the bathroom, but I know it's a death sentence. Fuck my life right now.

He slides his hands into his front pockets and tilts his head, his eyes drifting from my lips to my orbs. "Come on…just one?"

My mouth moves, but words don't form. I break eye contact and stare at a paper straw wrapper sticking to the ground, the end of it fluttering slightly in the cool breeze. "I'm sorry. I wish I could, but I can't."

I feel his eyes scanning every inch of me like he's undressing me inside his head, visualizing what I look like naked. A tingling sensation creeps up the back of my neck, raising my fine hairs.

"Boyfriend?" he asks, passing me the box with the ram's skull and closing the hatch.

"Kind of." I lie, keeping my eyes to the ground.

He spins his keys on his pointer finger before gripping them tight in his palm. "Maybe, another time then. You have my number."

I lift my head and say, "Maybe," with a sheepish smile.

He turns away from me, and I do the same, walking slowly to the driver's side of my car. We exchange a last glance, smiling at each other, before he pulls away, leaving me standing in the lot, my loins starving for attention from a real man.

This fucking sucks. I climb inside the car, rest the ram skull beside me and turn the key. It clicks but doesn't start. I try again, but get the same result. I try a third time. Nothing.

Motherfucker.

Chapter Seventeen
So Many Faces

Over the last several days, I've dealt with a dead car battery, had the shit scared out of me by a mouse in my apartment, had my garbage bag rip at the bottom when I went to take it out, dumping trash everywhere that I had to clean up and now, I just stubbed my fucking toe on my metal bedframe support. I writhe back and forth on my bedroom floor, cursing at the ceiling. "God damnit!"

I don't know why I'm having such a string of bad luck, but fuck, I wish it would end. And the cherry on top, Mastyx, is coming tonight, and I'm not physically or mentally prepared for his arrival.

On a positive note, I finished making the ram's head death art, and it turned out fucking fantastic. The ram's head alone sells for over five hundred dollars online, so I price the piece at five hundred and ninety-nine dollars, which will give me a profit of around four hundred dollars after supplies.

There's a soft knock on the door, and when I open it, a box sits on the floor in the hall, and I catch the back side of a delivery driver jogging down the steps. I pick up the box and grimace, *What the hell did I order?*

I set the box on the coffee table, peel off the tape and open it. Inside, buried beneath a mound of Styrofoam circus peanuts, is the white death mask.

Wow, it came fast. I carry it into my room, set it on my bed and head to the kitchen to search for hanging hardware. Once I find the kit my dad bought me, I set it on the bed next to the mask. I run my fingers over the slightly textured surface of the mask, pick it up, stand in front of my full-length mirror and put it on my face.

So cool. I hold it in both hands before my legs, facing the mirror. "Oh, Tessa, do you really think he'll wear it?" I say aloud. I picture him wearing the mask while carrying me in his arms around hell, protecting me from the flaming hot ground beneath me.

I hold the mask in one hand and slap the side of my head with the other. "Stop it. Stop thinking such crazy things." I toss the mask on the bed, scoop up the hammer, tap a hanging hook into the wall by my bed and hang the mask.

The gray walls provide a perfect background for it. I adjust it slightly to the right so it's completely level. It seems as if this wall was made just for this mask. The spacing, size, and placement all come together perfectly, showcasing it like a piece of art in a museum.

I glance at the wall clock. It's nearly seven. The weather is changing, but not by much. The nights get a little chilly, but it's tolerable. I mean, it is only the beginning of October. I close my eyes and try to think about what to do about tonight. What would surprise me the most if I were a guy or a demon?

My fingers ache from rubbing them together constantly, my nervous energy getting the best of me. I pace the living room floor, trying to figure out how to make our experience less traumatizing. There has to be something, some way to keep him from hurting me so bad, even if it isn't intentional.

How do I stop myself from thinking and dwelling on how much pain he's about to cause? If I could convince him to be gentle, not so vicious, not so animalistic, this might work. It's a big ask, I know, considering what he is. It's like telling a predator not to hunt its prey. I drag my palms over my face and sigh.

Be ready for him. I throw my hands in the air. That's all I can think of. I'm just going to get cleaned up, lather on a bunch of lotion and lie on top of my comforter naked with my legs spread. I don't know what else could be more appealing than that. When I started stripping in front of him last time, he hesitated, didn't just attack. He wanted to take it all in and enjoy what he was seeing. Can't hurt, I guess.

After taking a long, hot bath and shaving every piece of hair I could see on my body from the waist down, I rub a sweet cherry-scented lotion all over my limbs and climb into bed, exhaustion pulling me into a restless sleep.

* * *

Scratchy hands slide up my thighs, waking me from a deep slumber. I gasp as Mastyx tugs my legs gently apart, his face partially covered in skin with fire peeking from the patches in between that stick to his head like skin grafts that shift around when his jaw moves.

Once again, I can see hints of the man from the fair, his flesh breaking down like the cracked earth in a desert landscape, brittle and thirsty.

I swallow hard, trying to keep my thoughts and fears hidden deep inside. His appearance is unsettling, making my abdomen tremor unintentionally. I rest my hand on my midsection, steadying it as his flaming eyes drift to the mask hanging beside my bed and then back to me.

"I…I bought that for you, for when you don't have a face but want one." My voice comes out barely above a whisper, and I can't hide the shakiness in my words. It's not technically a lie. It appears faces are hard to come by since he's reusing an old one that seems to be falling apart.

I grip the sheets beneath me, curling them tightly into my palm, making my fingers ache.

"Close your eyes, Little Sinner," he growls.

I pinch my eyes closed, my pulse throbbing in my neck, doing as he asks, and a hot breath drifts between my legs, making my pussy lips twitch. His hands curl around my legs and without warning, his tongue plunges deep inside me, making me gasp. I scoot back on the bed, my head striking the headboard.

He grips my thighs and yanks me back to him, holding me tight. I rock into him, the sensation too euphoric to ignore. Sucking noises emanate from between my legs as he nibbles and licks every inch of my pussy, inside and out. I feel the tingle; it's racing down my inner thighs. Without thinking, I reach for him, my hands moving toward his head on their own.

My wrists burn as he grips them tightly, slamming them back down into the mattress, forcing his tongue harder between my legs. I lift my hips toward his face, longing for the heat emanating from his fiery lips.

As if he senses my desire, he releases my wrists, spreads my pussy lips wider with his fingers and takes my clit into his mouth, forcing his tongue so far into me, I thought it may pop out of my chest. His tongue slides out of me before he wraps his lips around my clit and sucks hard, really hard, drawing my orgasm out of my body like a syphon. I cry out, filling his mouth with my juices as he moans.

He lifts his head, his eyes partially closed and filled with desire, locking on mine. "My Little Sinner, you taste like a thousand souls entering my mouth at once."

I close my eyes, panting heavily as a single tear escapes my lid. What is wrong with me? How could I have enjoyed that so much? A part of me feels shame, but the other part of me embraces his tongue with open arms as he swirls it around my now sensitive clit. I want him to do it again; the overwhelming feeling of release intoxicates me, clouding my judgment.

He slides from between my legs, stands and removes the mask from the wall.

I scan his body, partly beast and partly human, and for some unknown reason, it's not as vile appearing as before.

Is he somehow shifting the way I perceive him?

He pulls the mask down over his face. "Is this what you want, Little Sinner?"

Lightning jolts through my thighs, the mask on his face unlocking a hidden fantasy—a need, a desire I didn't know was there. The fear inside me melts away, replaced with pure arousal and an overwhelming urge to have my body ravaged, consumed—taken.

He tilts his head as my legs fall open, and I run my fingers along my inner thighs. "Yes, please."

He climbs back onto the bed, the mattress sinking beneath his weight, placing one hoof on either side of my waist, towering over me. My heart pounds inside my chest. The sheer power of him hovering over me forces my spine deeper into the mattress beneath me, and my fingers are back to gripping the sheets. My core tremors slightly, but I push the fear aside and force myself to be brave.

His cock swings above me, back and forth like a pendulum. "Taste me." He drops to his knees, his cock slapping into the space between my breasts.

I hesitate, but only for a moment, before extending my tongue. After what he just did for me, I feel obligated to give him what he wants, not only out of fear of the consequences if I don't, but in hopes that if I do, he will be less likely to hurt me. He holds his cock in front of my mouth, and when I lick the tip of it, it's bitter but not salty, with a hint of smoky flavor, like an overcooked burger burnt on the edges.

"Taste me," he repeats, leaning his hips toward me, forcing his cock inside my mouth. My jaw pops, opening wider than I can naturally open it on my own. He pumps into my face, and I try my hardest to do what he wants, but the size of it makes it difficult to breathe, and I gag. I grip his cock with both hands, pull it slightly out of my mouth, and slide my palms up and down his shaft, moaning softly, the sound vibrating the tip of his cock. He makes a grunting noise followed by a long growl of pleasure.

Time to make a bold, drastic move.

My hands shake as I carefully pull his cock from my palate, slide my palms up his rippled abdomen and push him sideways, slowly shifting him off me.

He snatches my throat, squeezing it harshly for my defiance, the flames in his eyes behind the mask brightening.

I accept his punishment with a soft hand sliding up and down the arm that's currently choking me as a tear slides down my cheek and black spots dance before my eyes.

I'm not fighting you, I think to myself, knowing he can read my thoughts.

His clawed hand melts away from my throat, and I gulp a large breath as he lies on his back beside me, allowing me to climb onto his cock. He grips my ass cheeks hard, and I rock on top of him, my eyes locking on the ceiling, a soft whimper escaping my lips. The pain is intense, like a red-hot poker being shoved deep inside me, singeing my delicate lining. But beyond the agony lies something more profound.

Acceptance.

My body is accepting his cock willingly, and the sheer depth of it touches places no human could ever reach. It's as if everything inside me is shifting to accommodate his length. His cock, molding my internal anatomy, making it a perfect fit, just for him.

It's almost an addictive feeling, like the longing you have for your next fix and finally getting it. You want more of it, need it, despite knowing it's harming you.

His hand wraps around my throat, choking me roughly, and his thumb circles my clit. "Oh, Mastyx!" I call his name out loud.

As I rock on top of him, his hips move in rhythm with mine, and it is as though we are one wave, floating on the surface of the ocean, seconds away from crashing to shore. I can feel his cock ready to burst, and my orgasm is preparing to rupture.

He grabs me around the waist, throws me on my stomach beside him and centers himself behind me. His fingers twist into my hair, scratching my scalp with his sharp claws as he pulls my head back, snapping my neck. He forces his cock harshly inside me, and I cry out as he slams into me from behind. "Do you think you can seduce me, Little Sinner?"

He thrusts into me hard and deep, over and over again. I force myself backward, my face wet with tears, pushing my spine against his chest and climbing onto my hands and knees. He wraps his arms around my abdomen, and I lean back against him, wrapping my arms around his, letting him fuck me hard from behind. I keep my eyes closed, trying not to picture anyone else, only him, knowing that he will feel and see inside my head, hoping beyond all hopes that he understands that this isn't a seduction, it's cooperation.

I'm letting go of my fear, my reluctance, my resistance.

His cock plunges deeper inside me, forcing my knees off the mattress and his arms tighter around my midsection, making it hard to breathe. A piercing pain penetrates my core, and I cry out. His head rests against my spine, and his panting muffled breaths move the fine hairs covering my skin as they float through the mask.

The pain overwhelms me, and I fight like hell not to scream for him to stop. I interlace my fingers with his and let out a breathy plea for mercy. "Mastyx, please." Tears burst from my eyes. "You're hurting me."

He tugs my head back by my hair and whispers in my ear. "Tell me who is in control, Little Sinner." He turns his ear to my lips.

"You are," I whimper through trembling lips.

His tail winds gently around my throat. "Yeeeesssss."

His cock slides out of me, and using his tail to direct my body, he pushes me sideways and onto my back.

He peels the mask off his face, and I close my eyes as he traces the space between my breasts with his lips before they drift to mine. "Open your mouth."

My jaw staggers open, and his tongue floats inside. He twists it around mine, and I slide my hands around his spine as his cock presses inside me. He keeps his tongue tightly twisted around mine, stifling my ability to cry out as his cock pushes deep inside me, then retreats, deep inside me, then retreats.

It feels incredible, and I've never felt so ashamed and confused in my entire life. His rhythm is calm and delicate. If I didn't know any better, I would say he's making love to me, but I know that can't be true. A small part of me wants this feeling never to end, but the other part of me wrestles with how wrong this is, how wrong all of this is, what I have done and continue to do to survive.

My mind wanders into the darkness as his tongue leaves my throat and slides along my jawline before stopping at the space between my neck and shoulder. "Contessa," he whispers my name. "Scream for me."

Before I have a chance to think, to comprehend the words that just left his lips, he plunges his cock inside me hard and fast. I cry out, gripping the textured flesh of his spine, digging my nails into him. The pain surging through my insides is intense and unforgiving, but my body responds to his, and my juices flood every inch of his cock.

"Scream for me," he repeats, ramming his cock into me, forcing the top of my head into the headboard a second time.

"Mastyx!" I scream through blinding tears as hot lava spills inside of me, burning my tender flesh.

He collapses on top of me, the weight of him knocking the air from my lungs. Pain surges through my insides, but it's not like before; it's not like boiling soup being poured inside me, more like a slightly cooled stew—still hot but not scorching.

My stomach pulses against his, and the weight of his pubic bone against my clit, makes me want him when I shouldn't.

I don't want to admit to it, but the truth, no matter how hard I fight it, is more disturbing than I could ever imagine.

That…felt…fucking…amazing.

"Yes, it did, Little Sinner…"

Fuck. I once again forgot he can hear my thoughts. Damnit, I need to be careful about what I think.

I will definitely burn in hell, not only for enjoying what just happened, but also for wanting to do it again.

"Not yet," he murmurs, a playful tone in his voice.

Jesus, I did it again. Clear your head, Contessa. Clear your fucking head.

"Why did you ride my cock? Why did you try and please me?"

Fighting through tears and the pain surging through me, I manage to lift my head slightly so I can look at him. "Because I thought if I did something for you, then you could do something for me in return."

"That's not how this works, Little Sinner." He straightens his arms and hovers over me in a plank position. "But I'm curious as to what you could want in return."

It's too soon. I can't just spill out what I want from him now. "I need to get up," I say, sitting up on my elbows and staring at him expectingly.

He climbs off of me and stands. I cup my hand over my throbbing pussy, the pain reminding me of how badly he hurts me with every encounter.

Mastyx gazes down at me for a brief moment before walking away, leaving the room. I hear the freezer door slide open and close, and he returns to his place beside me, a Bomb Pop in hand. He pulls the wrapper off the popsicle, and I open my mouth, waiting for a bite. His hand wraps around mine that's covering my pussy, and he pulls it away.

My eyes dart to him. "What are you doing?" I squeeze my legs against his arm.

He uses his other hand to pull my legs apart. "Easing your pain." The Bomb Pop presses inside me, and I scoot back, trying to get away from the frigid stick of ice. Mastyx's eyes darken. "Don't back away, Little

Sinner." He presses his hand against my chest, forcing me to lie back on the mattress.

My knees fall to their sides with little effort from his hand, and I close my eyes, moaning as he fucks me with the patriotic frozen dessert, the pain inside me slowly disappearing, and my insides grow numb.

His thumb grazes my clit, triggering an immediate response from me. I grab his hand, forcing the melted popsicle further inside me.

When there's nothing left but the stick, Mastyx removes it and moves his head between my legs before slurping up the sweet treat mixed with my frosted pussy juices, licking me clean. I rock into his face, wanting more, needing more. I want him to taste me again.

His hands grip my thighs tight, a sharp pain penetrating my skin as his claws dig into my flesh, drawing blood. He yanks my lower body up, and I squeal right before his tongue plunges into my asshole. My eyes widen, the feeling like nothing I've ever felt before. His thumb circles my clit in rhythm to his tongue sliding in and out of my other hole. My breathing shallows, my body fighting to release a trapped orgasm.

I need it. I need him to make me cum more than anything in this world. The pain is both pleasurable and torturous. I reach down between my legs, move his hand aside, and press two fingers inside me, determined to set my body free. His eyes land on mine, barely open to slits, before he pulls my fingers from inside me and replaces them with his own. They move in and out of me slowly at first, then pick up speed. His thumb circles my clit, while his fingers slide in and out of me, his tongue doing the same, pressing in and out of my ass.

My orgasm is coming. I feel it racing toward the surface. Mastyx removes his fingers and tongue from my ass and cups his lips around my pussy before sucking it hard. Something sharp enters my asshole and wiggles—his clawed finger.

It hurts, but feels good at the same time, and I don't know how I feel about any of this. I grip the sheets on either side of me and thrust my hips into his face.

"Fuck me!" I yell.

I didn't mean it literally, but that's how Mastyx takes it. He dives on top of me, thrusting his flaming hot cock inside of me. It only takes seconds for my pussy to respond. I burst around him, flooding his cock with everything I have left in me. He doesn't stop when I finish, he continues, thrusting and fucking me harder, faster, desperately. I claw at his spine as he penetrates deep inside of me, filling my insides with a second round of his fluids.

He yanks out of me, growling and panting as he staggers to a stand, his cock drifting side to side, dripping juices on my bedroom floor.

I throw my arm over my eyes, trying to fight the smile that's spreading across my face.

It's not happiness I'm feeling, though; it's pure fucking pleasure, like a fantasy I had long desired finally came to fruition.

After listening to my heart slow from a pound to a quiet thump and several seconds of silence later, I lick my lips and say, "Mastyx, why did you save me?"

There's no reply.

"Mastyx?" I remove my arm from across my eyes and realize he's gone.

Chapter Eighteen
The Longing Inside Me

After Mastyx's sudden departure, I found myself thinking of him often over the next few days. Is that why he did what he did? Is that why he made me feel so much pleasure? Did he do it to make me long for him? Make me crave his presence?

I shake off the thought and continue setting the dining room table for my parents. Mom called me up a few hours ago and invited me over for dinner. Since I was caught up on my projects, I said yes.

It's hot as fuck in here, but I didn't want to wear short sleeves on account of the red marks on my wrists from Mastyx's grip. This shirt has thumb holes, which I like, but it's a pain when it's time to do the dishes.

My dad carries a platter with a spiral ham balanced on top, and Mom is hot on his heels with a massive bowl of mashed potatoes. She sets them down and disappears through the doorway, heading back to the kitchen as my dad sits at the head of the table. He picks up a stray piece of ham that fell onto the tablecloth and stuffs it into his yap. I smile at him as my mom sweeps into the room carrying steaming peas in one hand and fresh-baked biscuits in the other, setting them down on either side of the ham platter.

"I hope you're hungry," Mom says, sitting at the opposite end of the table from my dad. "I made a bunch." She shakes her napkin into her lap and raises her eyebrows. "I made an apple pie for dessert as well."

"Thanks for dinner," I say, reaching over and resting my hand on hers.

She pulls her hand away and waves it in the space between us. "Yeah, yeah, come on, let's eat before it gets cold."

My dad wastes no time, stabbing the pile of sliced ham, picking up four pieces and dropping them on his plate. He stabs two slices and drops them on mine. "There you go, kiddo."

"Thanks." I take the fork from him, pick up a slice, and place it on my mom's plate. She eyes my dad, frowning at the pile of mashed potatoes he filled his plate with before covering them with a pile of peas.

I clear my throat to get his attention and nod toward Mom. "I think she'd like for you to save some food for the rest of us."

My mom sighs heavily. "Actually, I was just thinking about how much salt and calories you just filled your plate with. You know what the doctor said about your sodium."

Dad rolls his eyes. "Oh, come on. If you didn't want me to eat so much sodium, you would have made chicken instead of ham."

He has a valid point. My mom rocks her jaw and extends her hand, gesturing to the potatoes. "Pass me the potatoes before your father hogs them all."

I take a small spoonful and set it beside her. She takes about the same amount as I pass her the peas. We eat in silence for what feels like an eternity before my dad finally says, "So, how's the death art business going? You still making money?"

"It's been great. I'm making more and more every day."

"Good," Mom says, taking a small bite of ham before resting her fork on the side of her plate.

I take a massive bite of potatoes and excuse myself to go to the bathroom.

The door closes softly behind me, and I stare at the mirror above the sink. A flash of Mastyx's face appears in the mirror, and I leap back, clutching my chest. "What the fuck?" I blink several times and realize I'm fucking imagining it. I sit on the toilet and let out a long-winded sigh as my urine stream starts to flow.

My mind drifts to the moment the Bomb Pop pressed inside me, and my legs clamp closed. "Stop it, Contessa," I murmur to myself.

The door rattles with a quick knock. "Tessa, are you okay?"

I swipe my face with my palm. "Yeah, Mom, just using the toilet."

Geez, I can't even use the bathroom for more than a few minutes without everyone worrying. "I'll be right out." I flush the toilet, wash my hands, and gaze at my reflection. I don't look like a sinner, but I'm certainly acting and feeling like one lately.

Mastyx calls me his Little Sinner, and I've grown to like my pet name. Every time he growls it, it sends chills down my spine and a tingle between my legs.

Stop, just stop, I say to myself as I dry my hands and whip the bathroom door open. When I round the corner, I run straight into my dad, clutching his abdomen. "Eat too much, too fast again?" I say, shaking my head.

"Yep." He curves around me, enters the bathroom and slams the door.

He'll never learn.

When I enter the dining room, my mom has already cleared most of the dishes, including the one I hadn't finished, and placed a piece of apple pie in its place, with a fork resting beside it. "What are you waiting for?" she asks. "Dig in."

She's rushing me, and I don't know why. "Mom, what's the rush?" I ask as I take my seat and cut into the pie with the side of my fork.

"Well, there's a new movie on Lifetime tonight, and I thought if we wrapped up dinner early, you would stick around and watch it with me."

Oh, I get it now, she misses me and knows Dad won't watch it with her. I think they don't know what to do with each other now that I am out of the house. I smile at her. "Of course I'll stay."

Her face brightens. "Really?"

"Yes, Mom. You know I can't turn down a fresh and new based-on-a-true-story Lifetime movie."

Dad enters the room. "So, are you sticking around after dessert, kiddo?" He sits in his chair and eyes the pie across the table.

Mom slides it closer to her. "You need to let your dinner digest before you add any pie on top of the pile in your already full stomach."

I giggle, and his eyes snap to mine. "Not funny."

"Tess's staying and watching that new movie with me," Mom says with a smile.

He leans back in his seat and interlaces his fingers on his stomach, rolling his eyes. "I told you I would watch it with you."

"Why, so you can whine the whole time about how unrealistic it is?" She scoffs, stuffing the last bite of her pie into her mouth before standing.

Dad opens his mouth to speak, and I shake my head at him. It's not worth the fight, so he closes his eyes and sighs. "Well, I guess I could run to the gas station and buy some popcorn for you ladies." He glances at his watch. "When's it start? Eight?"

I rise from my seat. "I can go, Dad. You stay here."

He slides his hand into his back pocket and pulls out his wallet. "You need money?"

I mean, the old me would have my hand out in a second, but the new me is much more responsible. "No, that's okay. I got it." I kiss the top of his balding head, grab my jacket, and head out the door.

My car rumbles to a start and staggers backward out of their driveway.

I drive down the street and come to a halt at the stop sign. A small fire billows high above a fire pit in someone's side yard, catching my attention.

"Mastyx," I whisper his name without thinking. The flames shoot sideways from the firepit, making the people standing around it scatter like ants. My eyes widen right before an inappropriate chuckle escapes me. *That wasn't very nice, Contessa,* I think to myself.

A car beeps behind me, making me jump. I pull into the intersection and turn left toward the gas station on the corner. When I arrive, the parking lot is full, so I park along the curb nearby.

The bell above the door dings when I enter, and the cashier gives me a quick head nod as I turn down the salt and sweets aisle. It's not a huge selection, but it carries most everything you could need.

I grab a box of popcorn and turn the corner into the next aisle. A man stands there, holding a woman's arm so tight in his grasp that his knuckles whiten. "You will listen and do as you're told," he hisses in her face. His eye dart to mine. "What the fuck are you looking at, bitch?" The woman puts her head down, not wanting to make eye contact with me or show her face, but it's too late. The dark bruise around her eye tells what he's done and will continue to do if I don't do something about it.

Mastyx has always come to me when I've been in trouble, but I've always wondered if he would come to me just because I call him.

I back up and go to the next aisle, avoiding passing the abusive man and drop my popcorn at the register. I pluck a book of matches from the display and set it on top of the popcorn. When I finish paying, I step outside and wait for the man and woman to exit.

A few minutes later, the door crashes open and the woman stumbles outside, the man shoving her toward the gas pumps where an old, beat-up teal pickup truck is parked.

I fall in line behind them, scanning the parking lot. Most of the cars that were parked here when I arrived have already driven away.

The man pulls the gas nozzle from its holder and feeds it into his gas tank before noticing me. He yells at the woman, who's spinning the thin wedding band around her bony left finger, over the bed of the truck. "Get in the fucking truck, Darla."

She reaches for the door handle, her sunken eyes filled with despair, and I grip her arm. "Run."

"What?" Her eyes drift to his, her face paling. "No. He'll kill me."

"No, he won't. I promise." I pull a hundred-dollar bill out of my wallet and place it in her palm. "Get as far away from here as you can."

She nods, takes one last look at the man, who's staring at the pump watching the numbers go up, turns and takes off in a sprint.

I round the truck bed and stand behind him. A car horn honks, and he turns his head just in time to see Darla, jetting across the street in front of traffic.

"God Damnit, Darla!" He shouts in her direction. "Get the fuck back here."

"Hey," I yell at him from behind. "Leave her alone."

His eyes narrow at me as he fights to remove the end of the nozzle from his gas tank. "You fucking bitch. What the hell did you do?"

He grabs my arm roughly, sending a sharp pain through it.

Fear courses through me, sending prickling adrenaline across my flesh. Inside my head, I wonder if I made a mistake. What if Mastyx doesn't come, and this guy takes me?

"Answer me." The man twists my arm, but despite the pain it causes, the fear lifts from my body and dissipates in the air. It's like my brain and body somehow *know* Mastyx will come the minute I call him to my side.

Does he know I'm in trouble somehow? Is he sending me a message from the sanctity of his dwelling beneath my feet?

"I saved her," I say with a smile, yanking my arm out of his grasp. "And you'll never hurt her, or anyone else, ever again." I open the book of matches, pluck one out and strike it, watching the flames grow before my eyes. "Mastyx." I drop the match between us, and it lands in a small puddle of spilled gas, lighting up the ground at the man's feet.

The nozzle breaks free from the truck as the man tries to move quickly away from the open flame.

I bolt away from him, knowing Mastyx will fan those flames right for the gas pump.

A massive explosion deafens my ears, and a shockwave knocks me to the ground, face-first against the pavement. Blood pools in my mouth as my teeth drive into my lip.

Someone grabs me from behind and hoists me to my feet. "Run," the cashier from inside the store screams in my face, but I can barely hear his muffled voice.

He all but drags me behind him, heading straight for the metal dumpster where he slings me behind it as a second explosion rocks the ground beneath our feet. I peer around the corner, staring wide-eyed at the inferno.

Mastyx briefly emerges from the flames, his claws curled into the man at the pump's chest. The man's face suddenly sinks in, his skin melting off and seemingly transferring to Mastyx as he sucks out his soul before they disappear into the billowing black smoke, the fire raging out of control.

I'm right. Well, at least I think I am. It does appear that Mastyx can take the face of the person whose soul he takes.

I gaze down at my hand, still clutching the plastic bag containing my box of popcorn, with a small tear in its corner. The cashier turns away from me, pulling out his phone and no doubt dialing 9-1-1. I walk briskly to my car, still parked on the side of the building, and climb inside.

The cashier turns around and scans the area beside the dumpster, searching for me. I push the key into the ignition with violently shaking hands, start the car and drive away.

Chapter Nineteen
The Lighting of the Flame

I didn't return to my parents that night after the gas station explosion. When I peered at my reflection in the mirror, I realized it would be hard to explain my fat, bloody lip and the singed hair on the back of my head.

Mom and Dad heard about the fire and immediately called me when I didn't come back. I pretended like I didn't know what they were talking about and acted genuinely surprised. I hate lying to them, but what's the alternative? Tell them the truth?

My excuse for not getting the popcorn and coming back was that I started driving toward the store, then thought about my apartment and some things I needed done, and by the time I realized I had passed the store, I was nearly home. I could hear the disappointment in my mom's voice, but I promised her I'd watch the next new movie as soon as it's released.

I tuck my hands behind my head and stretch out on the couch. When I close my eyes, all I can see is the man on fire at the gas station and Mastyx taking on his face. I thought for sure I would hear the man screaming, suffering the way he made his poor wife, but besides the roaring of the flames and the crackling and crunching of the fire and twisted metal nearby, it was quiet—quiet and hot. I didn't realize how hot it was until I came home and saw my hair. And the smell, God-awful. I had to trim off the singed pieces, which meant essentially giving myself a full-on hair trim to make it look less noticeable.

But that wasn't even the worst part. The worst part is how much I loved the way it made me feel. The sheer power and control of someone else's life, their death, being in my hands, gives me a perceived sense of invincibility. Being able to beckon Mastyx at will is my new superpower.

In that moment, I felt no fear of the flames. It felt more like a flood of endorphins surging through me— pleasant and euphoric.

I imagine it's the same feeling skydivers and base jumpers get when they first leap from their planes and cliffs. No matter how dangerous the act is, the desire to do it again pulls you, nags you, and consumes you. It becomes an obsession.

My heart thumps in my chest, and my face suddenly prickles. My fingertips tingle, and my thumb flicks a match that isn't there.

That piece of shit deserved to die, that's what I keep telling myself anyway. After watching the news report about the incident at the gas station and its brief mention of his rap sheet, no one could ever convince me otherwise.

The one thing I didn't understand about the whole thing was the woman. She appeared on the news, crying and not understanding what had happened. She made a passing mention of someone yelling at her to run, but the sequence of events wasn't right. She thought she saw the flames *before* a young woman told her to run. Perhaps she's just a good liar, spinning a tale that makes sense to protect us both.

Watching her interview, I couldn't help but notice a light in her eyes that wasn't there when I saw her in the gas station.

I set her free. She can live her life without fear and pain. I did that. I saved her. A broad smile spreads across my face.

He was the bad guy, the villain, and I'm the hero.

Her hero. And now all I can think about is how happy I feel about that—about causing the man's death for *her*.

About his dying in general. I mean, is it even wrong when the person is bad and deserves it?

I don't think so.

A small part of me has concerns about Mastyx. Will he punish me for calling him to do my dirty work when I summon him?

I push the idea out of my mind and allow other moments between us to filter in. A flash of his segmented flesh face pops in my head, and I cringe. The mask definitely made a difference with our last encounter, but there has to be more I can do to make his presence less intimidating and more alluring. Having feet instead of hooves and a smooth, hairless body would make things easier, but how do I get those parts of him to change?

I have noticed that the more people die, the more human-like he seems. It makes me wonder if that's the key.

My eyes widen as something I read suddenly comes back to me, popping into my head like a pleasant memory. It seemed so insignificant at the time, I didn't give it a second thought. I roll sideways off the couch, spring to a stand, and hustle to my computer, searching through my browsing history. A few clicks of the mouse later, and I lower myself slowly into my seat, a sense of hope and promise making it impossible to stand.

Ritual sacrifice.

It's been staring me in the face this whole time. My lips move as I read the background on the topic, its risks, and its benefits. I only skimmed this topic before deciding it was too rash.

Ritual sacrifice has been used for centuries for a myriad of reasons. Two of them stand out to me and have me nodding at my computer screen—punishment for a taboo violation and offering a victim to appease a deity.

In some religions, deities were reinterpreted as demons, meaning Mastyx. So, if I combine the violations, sacrificing the men who are sinning and committing crimes, with the need to appease my deity, Mastyx, I will gain power.

And I need more power—a bargaining chip to have some resemblance of control.

I cover my mouth before swiping my face. This has to be the answer. It makes sense, given what I've seen recently—Mastyx's partial humanization appears to correlate with the deaths that precede it. Even though the crimes these men have committed weren't necessarily taboo, they were still punishable violations, right?

My head whips to the calendar. I need to talk to Mastyx. Get him to tell me if I'm on the right track.

It's Saturday night, so there ought to be lots of dirtbags and scum lingering around the local bars.

Local…maybe I should drive to the next town over, where no one knows me.

After taking a quick shower, I pull a red dress over my head and shimmy it over my hips, smoothing it down. It lands just above the knee and barely holds in my breasts. I slide my feet in a pair of black flats, just in case I need to run, and iron my hair straight before putting on makeup.

The lipstick on my lips glimmers back at me as I gaze at my reflection in the full-length mirror. I look sexy as all hell. It's too bad I don't have a real boyfriend to appreciate it.

When I peer out the window, a thin layer of snow covers the top of the Nova. I grab a cropped cardigan sweater and stuff my arms into it before stepping outside. A chilly breeze penetrates my attire, sending goosebumps in every direction and hardening my nipples to stone.

Fuck it's cold.

I run back up to my apartment, grab a heavier jacket and throw it on over my sweater.

The car rumbles to a start, and the tires spin briefly before it barrels backward out of my parking space. If there's one positive thing I can say about this car, it's the heat it gives off. My lips shrivel in seconds the moment the air flowing through the vents shifts from arctic to Death Valley. I tilt the vents down and let the air warm my legs and feet.

The closest bar out of town is only twenty minutes away, and there are multiple roads leading to it. I pull to the curb on the side of the building facing one of the roads leading back toward my town and apartment and blow out a heavy sigh.

This is such a bad idea. Mastyx is going to be pissed when he figures out I'm using him. That is, if he hasn't already. I rub my palms together before reaching for the door handle, my heart pounding. I hesitate to open it, my mind second-guessing what I'm about to do.

"You're playing with fire, Contessa," I say aloud. "Literally."

I draw in a deep breath, grab my clutch, and climb from the car, slamming the door behind me as I bite my bottom lip. There's no sense locking it. I have nothing inside to steal.

A wave of stale air, smelling of body odor and alcohol, hits me when I open the tavern door. I wiggle my nose as I scan the room, and a sudden sinking feeling weighs heavily in my stomach. This is not the type of bar I should be in.

All eyes are on me—lots of them. It appears I've just waltzed into a biker bar.

A jukebox plays a heavy metal song I'm unfamiliar with in a far corner, and a large pool table surrounded by some very scary-looking men sits nearby.

Fuck. Runaway, Contessa. Run the fuck away.

If I leave now, it will be too obvious, but if I stay, everyone will remember who I am and that I was here—too many witnesses to call Mastyx.

A leather jacket hangs over a barstool beside me. The back of it reads "Hell's Hogs".

Hell's Hogs? What a terrible name.

A part of me wants to turn and dash out the door, but the other part of me likes the feeling of how dangerous this is. The only problem is, I'm frozen in place. My legs don't want me to take this any further. It's as if my subconscious sounded an alarm and alerted all my limbs. Now I have to decide whether to hold fast or retreat.

You can do this, Contessa, I say inside my head, trying to convince myself that I'm not petrified and bordering on shitting my pants.

I lift my chin high, trying to appear unrattled and confident, and take a seat on the barstool beside the jacket and drum my fingers on the bar top, waiting for the bartender. He eyes me from across the room and shakes his head, before throwing a white towel on the bar.

"I think you're in the wrong bar, sweetheart," the bartender says with a heavy Southern drawl.

"Jack and Coke," I say, ignoring his intense gaze.

He raises his eyebrows, "Do you have an ID?"

I glare at him, my eyes darkening. "No, do you? Does anyone in here have one?"

His eyes drift past me, and he nods to someone standing behind me before walking away and grabbing the Jack Daniel's bottle from a lower shelf.

Heat from someone's breath drifts across my neck. "Aren't you a sweet little thing?" an older, deep voice says from behind me.

I peer over my shoulder. "There's nothing sweet about me," I say, ignoring the chill that's running through my body.

The man standing dangerously close to me wears the same jacket as the one hanging over the chair beside me. His eyes are an intense blue, and his sandy blonde hair barely covers his scalp. He smiles broadly. "Not so sweet, huh? Does that mean you're a working girl?"

It takes me a moment to realize what he's asking me. *Working girl.* He thinks I'm a prostitute.

"No, just a girl desperate for a drink," I say with confidence as the bartender rests a coaster down by my hand and places my Jack and Coke in a glass on top.

I quickly gulp it down, ignoring the burning pain that travels from my lips down to my stomach, trying to steel my nerves that are threatening to unravel my entire plan. I push my tongue around my mouth, feeling a gritty texture and odd aftertaste. Within seconds, I realize I have made a colossal mistake.

I shoot the bartender a horrified look before an overwhelming feeling of claustrophobia shrinks me down in my seat.

Every patron in the bar has either risen to a stand and is facing me or is now slowly moving toward me. Within the blink of an eye, they've surrounded me, cutting off my exit. Over a dozen pairs of hungry eyes crawl down my body, leaving me feeling more exposed than I would be completely naked.

My head feels wobbly and my eyes heavy. They're going to take me, all of them, and hurt me. The worst part is, whatever they gave me will wipe my memory clean.

I have to act fast.

The man behind me kisses the back of my neck. I push him back with both palms and nearly fall from my seat.

He steps back and chuckles. "You want to go, sweetheart, you can go." He gestures for me to walk a now clear path to the back of the establishment near the pool table. An exit sign blurs and splits into two as I slide my bottom off the seat and stagger toward it. Hands graze various parts of my body as I pass them, and my legs grow tired, heavy, and weak. I can't walk in a straight line, and my body slowly melts to the floor.

Multiple hands grab me and throw me onto the pool table, knocking the balls in all directions. The blurry faces of numerous people surround me.

A lighter flicks nearby, and a distorted flame lights up the face of the man who appears to be in charge, right before he puffs on something white between his lips, and the smell of marijuana floats into my nostrils. "When you're finished with her, take her outside and drop her in the creek along the back of the property."

I try and flail my arms and legs, but they barely leave the felt of the pool table, the drugs leaving me vulnerable and defenseless.

When he tries to take another puff from the joint, he realizes it's gone out.

I chuckle, the loudest I could chuckle, as my body grows heavier and heavier and my eyes fight to stay open. "He's going to kill you all," I murmur.

"What did you say, sweetheart?" The man in charge leans over me, a smile becoming clear on his face.

I shake my head, trying to force it to focus and stay conscious. "He's going to kill you."

The man tosses his head back, laughing at the ceiling. The others join in, laughing as the sound of unbuckling metal rings in my ears. Fuck they're not even going to wait until I pass out.

"Who?" The man asks as he lights his joint, the flame rising high in front of his face, casting it in orange light.

"Mastyx."

The moment the word leaves my lips, the man's face turns pale as if he knows the name. The room heats up around me, and shades of orange block his face from view. My head falls to the side, and my eyes drift closed, the drugs pulling me under as blood-curdling screams slowly fade into the void.

Chapter Twenty
Flesh Suit

Something moves in and out of my pussy, and I force my eyes open. Confusion and a cloudy mind make it hard for me to comprehend what's currently happening to me. My legs tighten involuntarily around a man's head between my legs, and my body trembles as he consumes every inch of me.

The stars above me twinkle, and for a moment, I wonder if I'm dreaming, my body betraying me and loving the feeling of a stranger's tongue.

I lift my arms, trying to reach for his hair to pull his head back, but they are too weak and heavy.

"Please…" I murmur. My head throbs at the temples, and my eyes drift open and closed. "Stop."

The memory of what happened after I set foot inside the biker bar is lost somewhere inside my mind. I focus hard, but all I can visualize are glimpses of the before, and even those are filled with holes and missing time.

A plane flies overhead, and I follow it with my eyes. It disappears behind a wispy cloud, and I blink several times.

The man's head lifts from between my legs, and I freeze, petrified as a long tongue traces up my abdomen, stopping at my neck. When he peers into my eyes, a faint flame drifts inside his pupils.

It's Mastyx.

He's a full-on man. And not just any man. He's one of the bikers from inside the bar. Not the one who gave the orders, but one of the last people I saw removing his belt before I passed out. *At least he picked a relatively attractive guy*, I think to myself.

"I did this for you, Little Sinner." My body shifts upward, the ground digging into my spine as he feeds his massive cock inside me and pumps it in and out slowly.

I accept him inside me willingly, the realization that I'm not dead and that he once again came to my rescue, arousing me despite my drug-induced confusion. "I don't understand," I moan as the rhythm picks up.

"Your gift to me, the souls, they've given me something a human could never comprehend." He growls and thrusts hard into me, making me cry out.

I was right. The sacrifices of so many souls have resulted in my reward—a fully human Mastyx.

As I lie here, my head filled with fog, my pussy on fire, I force myself to remember what happened after I gulped down that Jack and Coke—the sound of unbuckling belts, the flame, the man's face when I called out Mastyx's name, fire everywhere, but none of it burned me.

Did he kill them all?

"Mmm," Mastyx moans. "Yes…every one of them. They were going to hurt you…." His cock presses deep inside me, and I grip his ass tightly, digging my nails into his tender human flesh. His fingers feed into my hair and twist against my scalp. "…and I'm the only one allowed to hurt you."

I scream, the penetrating pain pulsating through me as he slams into me hard over and over and over again. His palm slaps against my mouth, and his eyes stare deep into mine. It's as though he wants to see my fear, witness my pain, reminding me he's the one with all the power—the one capable of taking my life.

He's the only one I need to fear, not the men in the bar, not some sexual deviant in a bathroom.

Him.

I must never allow myself to forget what he is beneath the false skins he wears.

He eases up and uncovers my mouth, his rhythm slowing, becoming tolerable, gentle. The jolting, fiery pain inside me subsides, his cock healing me from the inside out, allowing the pleasure to consume me.

"I've saved your life, Little Sinner. They were going to kill you. I read their minds as I sucked out their souls." His cock slides out of me, and he sits on my abdomen, straddling me. "Now, you will taste them, their sins, my flavor. Open your mouth."

I pant heavily, caution screaming through my ears, but the fear in my veins steadily drifts away. I do as he asks. I owe him after all. Exhaustion has my body relaxed, and my jaw naturally drops open.

He takes his hand and pulls my jaw down further, feeding his massive cock into my mouth. I gag and try pushing it out with my tongue, but he pushes it down my throat. It takes all the strength I have left to raise my hands. I just touch his hips, when his fingers tighten like vises around my wrists, slamming my arms back to the earth and thrusting his cock deep into my throat. I can't breathe, but it doesn't stop him from pumping into my face, fucking my mouth.

Spots dance before my eyes, the lack of oxygen tightening my chest, making me desperate for air. I gaze up at him with wide-eyed panic right before salty liquid, hot and thick, fills my palate and tears stream down my face.

I'm drowning, but he doesn't pull out. He moans and groans as the fluids continue to flow down my throat and fill my mouth, overflowing around the edges of my lips.

"Swallow me," he demands, releasing my wrists from his grasp.

I can't do it, not while his cock is obstructing my airway. I take both hands and push him hard, forcing his cock from my throat. His hand cups over my mouth and nose. "Swallow me, Little Sinner."

My throat tightens, but I manage to force down a small amount of his cum. When he releases my face, I hurl it back up, coughing and gagging. It spills from my mouth, thick and vile. The contents of my stomach retch and hurl until there is nothing left but dry heaves. I gasp for air, taking several deep, heavy breaths that give me a headrush.

He grabs my throat, gripping it gently. "Good girl." His tongue extends from his mouth and laps up my cum filled vomit. It slides across my neck, face, and breasts, removing every ounce, every trace of the vile fluids. "Your turn, Little Sinner."

I can barely move, my body worn out, and still fighting against the drugs I ingested, but that doesn't stop him. He sits back, grabs me around the waist, lifting me from the cold, damp earth and placing me on his abdomen. Before I can even draw in a breath, he grips my ass and lifts my body up and onto his face, spreading my legs wide open. He grips my hips and forces his tongue deep inside me. I rock into him, my mind drifting off to somewhere unknown as my body runs the show. I fuck his face hard, the way he fucked mine, suffocating him, the way he did me.

I like it. No…I fucking love it. All the fear and doubt I once felt floats away from me as my carnal need takes over.

His lips wrap around my clit and suck it hard as he presses a finger into my ass. I ride his human head, under the stars, beneath the wispy clouds, my nipples hardening as another plane flying extremely low crosses over us.

What the fuck? I peer over my shoulder.

We are in a field beside a landing strip. We are fucking, completely naked, on an airfield. Although we are hidden in the shadows, the thought that someone might see us excites me even more, making me lose my last bit of self-preservation. I call out to him. "Oh, Mastyx, make me fucking cum."

His fingers yank from my ass, and without warning, he pushes me off his face. Suddenly, I'm airborne, slamming hard onto my spine, knocking the wind out of me. He dives between my legs, his tongue plunging deep inside me, his tail fluttering rapidly as it enters my ass.

I grip his human hair, forcing him in and out of me as I lift my hips into his face. Tingling races through my thighs, and I burst, my juices squirting across his cheek, glistening in the moonlight, but I don't let him stop. I never want this feeling to end. He tries lifting his head, but I push his head back between my legs, forcing him to keep his head down, licking and lapping up the juices covering my sensitive clit.

Something is seriously wrong with me. How could I possibly like this…no love this? How could I not be afraid of what's happening to me? My body and mind work independently of each other. Everything inside my head tells me this is wrong, but my body longs for him to continue, to ravish me so I can be in this heavenly state for eternity.

Things are changing. I'm changing. I've gone from doing whatever he wants to stay alive to wanting to do whatever he wants so he can do these sinful things to me. I need him—long for him, but my longing, my desire, comes at a cost.

Someone else's life.

A plane skids to a stop in the distance as my body empties my liquid desire once more into Mastyx's mouth. He clenches my ass cheeks and consumes me before pushing me sideways into the grass. We lie there, side by side, staring up at the stars. I pant, my rapid breaths floating in a staggering fog above us, fighting to keep my eyes open. Exhaustion and grogginess from the lingering effects of the drugs weigh my body down.

"Contessa, why did you risk summoning me in such a dangerous manner?" He stands, towering over me, his cock juices singeing the grass beneath him, his eyes scanning the landscape.

He called me by my first name, not Little Sinner. I sit up on my elbows, feeling like a child who's about to be scolded by her parents. "I took that risk for you."

His eyes dart to mine and narrow. "Why?"

My stomach tightens, and I feel my confidence once again fading. I want to crawl into one of the many snake holes surrounding us to hide from him. I lie back, covering my eyes with my arm, and answer like a spoiled brat. "Because."

Because? Because? Jesus Contessa.

"Answer me!" Mastyx's voice booms, echoing across the field and making my eyes spring open.

A tremor vibrates through my core as fear creeps in, threatening to ruin every ounce of courage and confidence I've gained until this point. I frown up at Mastyx, but show no fear. Instead, I turn my attention to the landing strip where the plane just taxied, and at the marshaller standing nearby, his light-up wand in hand, his brow furrowed in confusion.

My head, now suddenly clear, offers him an explanation. "I wanted to see if you retook a person's face, as you did with the guy from the fair and the one from the gas station, and you did. So, that's what happens? You can take the face and use it?"

"Yes," he murmurs before turning away from me.

"Ha, I knew it. I knew that's what was happening." I lie back down and close my eyes with a smile, my confidence returning. "And when you said to me that I've given you a gift no human could comprehend, what did you mean?"

A slight breeze drifts around me, and I rub the chill on my arm before opening my eyes, "Mastyx?" I look left and right, before crawling to a stand, naked as the day I was born on an airstrip, alone in the dark.

Chapter Twenty-One
Heart to Heart

It's been months since Mastyx took the twenty-two souls at the tavern and left me in my birthday suit on the airfield. The incident not only rocked our tiny town, but it also made national news.

Since then, I've only given him one more soul—a man whom I witnessed kicking his son in the back because he wasn't walking fast enough. The child's better off without him, at least that's what I tell myself.

Despite not getting all my questions answered, I did manage to solve one important mystery. Mastyx can use the face of the recently departed after consuming their soul. When he takes a soul, their likeness is absorbed into him as well, and his unearthly body can use it like a human mask or, in some cases, like an entire suit to cover his demon-like form.

The child's father wasn't good-looking at all. In fact, he was borderline grotesque in a meth-head sort of way. A few times when Mastyx made me look at him and the bleeding scabs on his greasy face, bile crept up in my mouth.

I really need to think carefully next time I go looking for someone to taunt into my web so Mastyx can suck the life out of them like a spider. Because let's face it, looks *do* matter.

After another round of research, spending countless hours learning more about who, or should I say what,

Mastyx is, taking me down a rabbit hole of knowledge and dark tales, I found some relevant information. Knowledge is power after all, and from what I've learned, I can steer our erotic relationship in certain ways with how many souls I give him.

The Aztecs once performed public sacrifices to feed the sun god and maintain a cosmic balance. When I think of the sun god, I think about Mastyx. Could that be who the Aztecs really sacrificed to? The devil? A demon?

Mastyx is hot and fiery after all, and the deaths do technically maintain a cosmic balance between good and evil. By picking sinners and men who deserve it, I feel like I'm balancing the scales of society.

I don't have to sacrifice anyone, but the fact that I can lure men to their death on purpose and let Mastyx take their souls gives a gift not only to him but to me. I get a human or semi-human sexual being to fuck, and he gets a notch in his soul belt, so to speak. Not only that, but I also have the power to choose who dies, giving me even more confidence.

It makes sense to me. At least, I think it does.

Keeping a lighter or matches with me is imperative. That way, if someone tries to hurt me, I can have them killed with the simple lighting of a flame, which brings a smile to my face so broad that it hurts. For the first time in a long time, I'm not afraid.

During last month's encounter, I noticed Mastyx's human form was starting to disintegrate. His skin was paper-thin, the flesh on his face stretched so tight it looked like thin wax, and his footsteps sounded more thunderous as if made by hooves.

Today, there's nothing remotely human remaining. He's back to the bloody skeleton, fiery-faced demon who wears the mask to make me more comfortable. He needs a fresh soul.

His hooves clank against my bedroom floor as he stands and gazes down at me.

Our muddy relationship is not only unnatural, but it's also wrong on so many levels. And yet, I look forward to our time together. It was easier to fall into a routine than I thought. I'd never have guessed in a million years that my future mate would be a demon from hell. But here I am, wishing that we could talk freely like a normal couple.

I forget sometimes, when we are lying side by side, that he's not human but a superior being who steers and bends our relationship to his will, not mine. Although he fulfills my needs and desires, sexually, there is no emotional depth, no love or feelings that aren't superficial. He'll never tell me he loves me. We will never be wed or live happily ever after. I have so many questions and feelings that have been building up inside me that no matter how hard I try, I can't seem to shake them. I'm overwhelmed, confused, and feeling lost as of late. It's as though I don't know my place in this world as the lines between good and evil blur.

I'm fighting to feel normal, to be normal, but there's an intoxicating need that gnaws inside of me, creeping into my head and corrupting my moral compass. I want Mastyx in human form all the time. I crave him—the thrill of luring the sinners to their deaths, getting away with it, and the reward Mastyx gives me that follows.

I shouldn't feel this way, and I often wonder if somehow the more I'm with him, the more his evil seeps inside of me, corrupting whatever soul I have left.

I've even had a crazy fantasy after watching the movie Carrie about covering my body in a thick layer of blood and letting Mastyx lick me clean. I can't get the idea out of my head.

If Mastyx would open up to me, tell me everything about him, what he desires, what he needs, perhaps I could use this information to my advantage as well.

I stretch my arms and tuck them behind my pillow. *Just ask him, Contessa. Tell him what you want.*

"Ask me what?" Mastyx sits beside me and runs his calloused-feeling hand up and down my thigh.

"How often do you need a soul for your face not to fall apart?"

His clawed nail bites into the skin on my lips. "That's not something you want from me; that's just a question you want answered." He huffs in irritation. "And it depends. The human's age and overall health play a role." He slides the death mask off his face and sets it beside us. "Why did you want to know this?"

I rub my forehead and frown, trying not to look at his grotesque face. "I don't know. I thought maybe I could help you get a new one more often. You know, so your face stays relatively human for longer."

He tosses his head back and belts out a diabolical roar of laughter. "Little Sinner, someone must die so I can take their soul for me to get a new face. I thought by now you would know that."

What the fuck are you doing, Tessa? Are you really offering to help him get more souls for your own benefit?

A sinister glow lights up in his eyes, and a Cheshire Cat smile spreads across his face. "You want to deliver more lost souls to me to make our encounters more tolerable?"

"Maybe?"

Dammit, Tessa. Shut up.

He leans forward, cupping my face with both hands, his eyes drilling holes through me, a smile curling on his lips. "No, don't shut up, my naughty Little Sinner. Tell me your terms."

Why is he so excited about this idea? *I wonder what's in it for him.*

"I get their souls, and a new face for a while, but what do you want in exchange?"

He's reading my mind again. What do I want? He's letting me have what I want. Something doesn't feel right about all this.

Still, I do often worry that if I have an unclean thought about another man or think about fucking them, he'll react and hurt me, so it only seems like the most logical choice to consider as part of this agreement.

My palms sweat, and I rub them together, pursing my lips as I calculate my words carefully.

"I choose all the marks, fuck them if I want, before I set them up for you. You know, make them sin or reveal their dark side or taunt them or whatever." I clench my jaw and raise my eyebrows. Even as the words leave my lips, I feel my confidence fading, so I explain further. "I mean…it's not like I want to fuck them, it's just, I may want to or need to convince the person to come with me or at least say I'm going to or…"

"Silence," he says, raising his hand, before leaning away, his eyes darkening, the flames in them growing dim briefly before rising again. "And how often would that be?" He grits his teeth, his jaw shifting as it clenches, his jealous side showing.

He didn't say no right away, so that's a good sign. I need to make it more about my need for him than my need to lure a man to his death.

I take a deep breath and bat my eyelashes, a cocky confidence beaming off of me before saying, "Only when my loins long for your burning cock."

My breath remains trapped inside me, waiting for him to respond, a part of me regretting not only making such a bold request but also manipulating the terms in my favor.

He chuckles at first, but it grows louder and louder. "Oh, Little Sinner, we have a deal."

That was too easy. He's way too willing to share me with another man so he can have their soul. They must be of great value to him to allow that to happen.

"But…" He lifts me from the bed and sets me on top of his abdomen. "…you will no longer just lure them. You will need to get your hands dirty as well, Little Sinner." A flaming piece of paper appears in his hand from seemingly nowhere, the edges blackened and red embers floating off from it, landing on his chest. He extinguishes its flames with a quick blow from his lips and places it before me. "Sign."

"But I don't have a pen," I say, furrowing my brows. "And what do you mean, *get my hands dirty?*"

He grips my hand and holds one of my fingers tight between his. With his other hand, he pricks the tip of my finger with his claw, making me scowl. "I mean, you need to draw blood. You need to be somewhat responsible for your own rescue."

"Meaning?"

The bead of blood triggers a heated gaze in his eyes, before he looks up at me with an amused intensity that makes me tremor. "Meaning, you must kill too."

Kill? He wants me to kill men, not just lure them to their deaths. Fuck. That's not really what I wanted to do. I know I've been entertaining the idea that sacrificing to him may be a way for me to gain power and control, but I didn't plan on diving right in to doing it.

"Sign," he repeats as his sharp teeth grow longer—sharper. He places my bloody finger on the old, tattered paper and forces my initials onto the page.

Before I can object, he rolls the page in his hand, lifts me off him, and stands, towering over me. There's an awkward silence between us as his lips curl and he flicks his fingers, the scroll vanishing in a puff of smoke and flames.

Even though the uncomfortable moment only lasted a few seconds, it was enough for doubt to creep across my neck like a crawling spider.

I thought I was in control right up until he smiled at me with that devilish grin and pressed my fingertip against the page. I mean, it's possible he tricked me into thinking I was in charge of this encounter, to get what *he* wanted, making me feel I was getting something for myself.

His hooves clunk heavily across the floor as he disappears around the corner. I smile, wondering if he's going to grab a Bomb Pop from the freezer to fuck me with. After several minutes, I call out his name.

"Mastyx?"

No reply.

Damnit, I hate when he does that.

No goodbye, no see you later, no thanks for riding me like a bull at a rodeo. Just poof, he ghosts me.

It doesn't matter. I got what I wanted.

Sorta.

I mean, I've never actually killed anyone, and I don't know if I'll have the stones to do it, but we have an updated contract, so I have no choice in the matter. Do I?

I mean, what if I chicken out and can't do it? Will Mastyx step in and finish the job so I don't get myself killed? I bury my face in my hands.

What the fuck have I done?

Chapter Twenty-Two
The Monster Within

A week after I sign the updated contract with Mastyx, I step out onto the street around the corner from a bar. It's a few towns away from my own, but not too far where I couldn't quickly make it back. I strut toward the entrance, the chill in the air biting into my bare legs.

My core trembles slightly as I slide my ass onto a cold metal barstool and patiently wait for a worthless soul to cross my path.

When I gaze around the room, I catch a few eyes staring at me, but none of them are good-looking. If I'm going to do this, possibly fuck someone before I kill or at least attempt to kill them, I want them to at least be easy on the eyes.

I wiggle my nose and take a shallow breath, the stuffy air around me reeking of old beer and stale cigarettes.

The young, blonde bartender eyes me from the end of the bar and strolls over, stopping in front of me with raised eyebrows. "What can I get you?"

I gawk at him, blinking several times, words escaping me. His voice doesn't match his appearance. Outwardly, he's barely twenty-one, but he speaks with a deep baritone voice, making him sound like an old soul lives inside of him.

"Ma'am?"

I shake my head. "I'll try the blackberry mojito."

He nods and walks away from me without asking for my ID, which surprises me. Perhaps it's my attire. I picked a long-sleeved, emerald-green dress that falls just above my knees.

A square black napkin rests in front of me, and the bartender sets my drink down carefully so he doesn't spill it. It's full to the rim, so I curl my lips over the edge and take a few sips from the top. Once it's low enough, I pick it up and gulp most of it down before stabbing the blackberry in the bottom with a plastic toothpick shaped like a sword and plunging it into my mouth.

A pink Cosmopolitan replaces the blackberry mojito I just finished drinking. "Wait, I didn't order this," I say to the bartender as he turns his back.

He smiles over his shoulder at me, revealing crooked front teeth, and nods to the other end of the bar. "He did."

A man with dark hair and a small build smiles at me before giving me a subtle nod. An uneasy tremor rises in my abdomen, my nerves rearing their ugly head. I smile back at him before picking up the pink liquid in front of me and saluting him.

Just be calm, I say to myself as I return my attention to the bar top. I run my pointer finger across the wet circle on my drink napkin before crumpling it into my shaking palm.

How can I expect to be calm, really, when this man is going to die, and it's going to be my fault? I didn't expect to want to do this so soon, but I couldn't stop thinking about it, Mastyx be damned.

The man stands from his seat at the end of the bar and walks over to me, his chin high, cocky confidence radiating off of him. "Hello," he says, setting his bottle of beer beside my drink. "Can I buy you a shot?"

I flutter my lashes at him. He's not sexy at all, not really, but he's not a fat slob either. I'd say he falls into the cute-but-plain category. He needs a haircut and a clean shave, and could stand to gain a few pounds, but he seems harmless enough, with his quiet, smooth voice.

"Sure," I say, taking a small sip of the pink drink still sitting nearly full in front of me.

He flags the bartender over with an overly hairy arm, the tail end of a snake tattoo peeking out from beneath his short-sleeved t-shirt. "Get us a couple of those apple pie shots."

"Oh, that sounds good." I push up my sleeves on both sides and lean my elbow on the bar, resting the side of my head against my hand. "So, what's your name?"

"What's yours, sweetheart?"

A lump in my throat makes it hard to swallow, and I look away from him so he can't see the fear rising in my eyes. It's the way he said *sweetheart*, that sends my mind right back down memory lane. The biker bar incident is still toying with my sanity, as I'm still unable to remember every detail.

I swallow hard, take a deep breath, sending my fear back into the pit in my stomach, and turn to him, "Tessa."

"Pretty." He extends his hand sideways to me, his eyes drifting to my cleavage. "Brent."

What a perverted asshole.

I take his calloused and rough hand to shake it, and he lifts mine to his face, kissing it softly. "Nice to meet you," he says, his thin lips lingering on my skin. He runs his nose across my wrist, my arm jerking toward him as his nostrils trace up my forearm. "What is that? It smells so good."

Jesus, this guy's handsy.

"Marc Jacobs," I smirk, trying not to let him see me squirm.

"I love it. It's very alluring." His eyes meet mine, and a devious smile spreads across his face.

"Thanks." I clear my throat before I tug my arm from his grasp.

The shots slide in front of us across the wooden bar top, and we pick them up, clank them, and gulp them down.

"Want to sit in a booth?" he asks, taking a swig from his bottle of Guinness.

"Okay." I grab my clutch off the bar top and stand, realizing at once that I'm nearly half a head taller than him. He doesn't seem to notice as he nods to a booth in the corner and slides in first. I scoot in next to him, my left knee purposely bumping his right. His hand raises to the bartender, holding up two fingers, mouthing *two more shots*.

"So, what do you do for a living?" I ask him as I slide my phone out of my clutch.

"I'm in sales."

Sales.

The way he says it, without elaborating, has my mind coming to one and only conclusion.

Drug dealer.

Still, I play along, luring him into telling me more. "Do you sell anything good?"

His arm stretches over my back, landing slyly across my shoulders. "I can get you anything you want, beautiful." He raises the shot glass the bartender sets on the table and dumps it down his throat. I pick up mine but don't drink it.

"How about you?" he asks, setting the shot glass down on the table.

"I make art out of dead animals." I set my shot down, touch my phone screen and turn it toward him, showing him the finished ram's head skull piece.

His eyes widen. "You made that. Wow." He squints at the screen. "And you sold it for six hundred dollars?" His eyes light up with a greedy glint of amusement.

"What?" I peer down at my phone and realize it does, in fact, say sold. "Huh, it must have sold after I left the house. Nice."

"So, you're good with your hands?" he asks, taking another swig of his beer.

I rest my hand on his thigh, sliding it down to his knee and back up again. "I can be."

He shifts back in his seat, his eyes following my hand as it rubs his leg before I take it away and pick up my shot glass. Everything inside me screams to leave, and I feel like I'm losing my nerve.

A waitress stops at our table, picking up his empty glass on her way by. Brent's eyes linger on her exposed cleavage before turning his attention to her ass, then back to me.

Fucking pig.

I toss the liquid courage, tasting like grandma's homemade apple pie, down my throat and wipe my wet lips. "Want to get out of here?" I blurt.

The tension between us rises, and my stomach turns rigid as he leans toward me and whispers, "Where do you want to go?"

A smile curls on my lips. "Follow me." I slide from the booth, grab my phone and clutch and strut toward the exit at the back of the bar.

I shove the door open, and a chilly breeze tosses my hair across my cheek. I swipe it away, before looking left and right, quickly realizing I'm in the alley beside the parking lot. The door behind me closes with a bang, making me jump.

After several seconds, the door swings wide open, and Brent emerges, carrying a black hooded jacket. "Sorry, I didn't want to leave this behind," he says, holding it up between us. He shakes it out and places it around my shoulders, easing the goosebumps on my arms.

Fuck, maybe he's not an asshole after all. I can't do this.

His hand touches the side of my face before he curls a wayward lock of my hair around my ear, sending chills down the back of my neck. I shrug, shying away from his intimate touch as his fingers graze over my ear and wrap around the back of my head. He steps closer, lifts his chin higher so his lips meet mine, and plants a soft kiss on them before plunging his tongue into my mouth, swirling it around my palate rapidly, taking the intimate moment from 0-60 in the blink of an eye.

I pull away and glance at the alley around us, checking for cameras or other people. There's no one. We are alone in a dark alley that smells like week-old garbage and mold.

"What's the matter? Are you afraid someone will see us?" He steps away from me, finds a piece of splintered wood from an old pallet and wedges it beneath the bar door, securing it closed. "There. Now, come here." He crooks his finger at me, his eyes darkening a bit.

The way he's looking at me, like a lion seconds away from pouncing on its prey, makes my heart pound. "This was a mistake." I turn away from him, my insides shaking violently. "I'm not ready." I walk swiftly away from him, my heels echoing down the alley.

"Ready for what?" He jogs to catch up to me, grabs me by the bicep, and spins me around to face him. "What are you, a virgin?"

His eyes scan mine, waiting for me to answer.

I came here because I have a job to do, but I feel like he might not be the right mark.

"To let him have your soul," I say without thinking.

Holy fuck, Tessa, what is wrong with you? Don't tell him the truth.

His face twists, and without warning, he grabs me by the shoulders and slams my back into the brick wall, my head striking it hard, knocking my clutch from my grasp. "Who? Who fucking sent you, some rival gang or something?"

Stars dance before my eyes, and my knees buckle slightly, but I don't fall.

He lifts me higher on the wall and shakes me hard. "Fucking answer me." His spit sprays across my face as he seethes outwardly. "Who the fuck are you?" His hand wraps around my throat. "Fucking answer me."

His grip on my neck tightens, making it impossible to speak and darkening my vision. I try not to panic, but I can't get to my clutch to light a match or use my lighter. Even if I could, I couldn't say Mastyx's name.

"Answer me," he hollers in my face, his hot breath heating my cheek.

I slap his arms before forcing my arms between his and grab his head, pulling it hard toward the ground. I raise my knee, striking him hard in the face before ducking and twisting away from him, breaking his hold on me.

"Mastyx," I call out before picking up the clutch that I dropped off the ground and turning to run.

My head flies back, his fingers twisting tightly around my hair, pulling me back toward him. "What did you say?" He pulls my body back against his, his one arm tightening around my waist, the other rocking my head back and forth violently, making me dizzy. "You'd better tell me what the fuck this is about."

Jesus. He's going to fucking kill me. I misjudged him.

My body flies forward, the ground stinging my knees as I land on it, knocking my clutch out of my hand a second time, spilling its contents.

A sharp pain rips through my ribs, his boot striking them hard, knocking me sideways to the ground. My arm scrapes against the vile pavement, reaching for the contents of my clutch, searching for the switchblade I placed inside earlier. He drops to the ground, his leg swinging over my stomach, straddling me.

His arm swings back, and his fist swings toward me. I pinch my eyes closed right before my mouth explodes with throbbing pain, and blood fills my palate.

My head falls to the side, and I see the blade just out of reach of my fingertips. I stretch my arm close enough to grip it in my hand and press the button.

"Who's coming for me?" he asks, clenching the front of my dress and pulling my face close to his.

I smile with bloody teeth up at him. "Mastyx." When I swing, he sees the blade coming and puts up his hand. The sharp silver tip glides into his palm, and he shouts, before wrenching it away from me. Blood drains down his hand and arm as he drops the blade beside us, stares at the wound on his hand with wild eyes, before narrowing them at me. "You're going to fucking regret that."

He grabs me harshly and flips me quickly onto my stomach, his full body weight crashing down on my spine as his zipper rapidly clicks down. "When I'm done fucking you, you can go back and tell whomever you work for that you belong to me now."

His fingers twist into my hair, winding their way to my scalp before yanking my head away from the asphalt and slamming it back down, sending a sudden shooting pain through my forehead, the grit of the hard surface digging into my skin.

I turn my head sideways, resting my ear against the ground of the filthy alley, feeling the rumbling of cars driving down the cross street, but I can't hear anything over the ringing in my ears. Blood drains down from my head and drips onto the slimy alley beneath me. I close my eyes and beg for Mastyx to save me inside my head. My dress slides up my thighs, then my ass, and his fingers press inside my pussy. "Nice and wet, just the way I like it."

"Stop!" I cry out through blurry tears.

He pulls my head off the ground by my hair. "Tell me who you work for, and this will all be over."

I remain silent. I already told him who I came here for and why. He just doesn't believe me.

"Fine. Don't tell me. Just remember you asked for this, now you're going to fucking take it." His fingers slide out from inside me, and I feel him positioning himself to enter me from behind.

Something Mastyx said about being *responsible for your own rescue* filters into my head.

I have to save myself.

With every ounce of strength and courage I have left, I reach for the switchblade, pushing through the pain the weight of him is causing me. It's just outside my reach, so I buck my body to keep him from entering me from behind and scoot my hand closer to the knife.

Pressure pushes against my ass, and I realize he's not trying to enter my pussy, he's going straight for the other hole. I rock my body side to side, stopping him from pushing inside me, and a hammering pain slams into my thigh as he punches it, deadening my leg. "Stop fucking moving," he shouts, before licking his palm and swiping it across my asshole, moistening it, and making it pucker.

The tip of his cock harshly breaches the opening, tearing me wide open, and I scream just as my fist tightens around the switchblade.

I swing it blindly over my shoulder, and his cock instantly softens as gargling sounds come from behind me. I shift my body from beneath him as he falls sideways into a deep puddle, littered with garbage. I climb on his midsection and slam the blade of the knife in between his ribs, blind rage taking over. The knife plunges in and out of his arms and hands as he tries to cover his vital organs. His arms drop down to his sides, the fight in him fading. My feet slide against the slippery pavement as I climb off of him, drop backward and stare wide-eyed at what I've done.

His legs slide against the pavement and blood spurts from between his lips.

Something wet dribbles down my cheek. I raise my hand to wipe it and freeze. Dark crimson coats my fingers, hands, dress, legs and arms. Every part of me is spotted or drenched in metallic crimson. The fantasy I had about being coated in blood races back to me, and I realize I'm living part of that fantasy right now.

It's everywhere.

A car horn beeps in the distance, and my head darts in the direction of the noise, breaking me from my trance-like state. I scan the alley around me, my heart pounding. I have to hurry up and collect myself and get out of here before someone sees us.

I crawl across the ground, my hands and knees gliding through the growing puddle of bloody water around Brent and pick up my pink lighter that fell from my clutch. I hold it between us, press my thumb against the flame adjustment, turning it up high and flick it.

Nothing but sparks.

I try again, fighting through blinding tears, but the blood on my fingers makes getting a good grip on it hard. I wipe my hand along the hem of my dress, on a clean part, and try again. A whooshing flame nearly singes off my eyebrows. I take a deep breath, holding it before murmuring one word through staggering lips, "Mastyx…" My bottom lip quivers, and my teeth chatter. "…help me."

The flame shoots higher than it should, and within a heartbeat, Mastyx manifests beside us in the shadows.

I drop the lighter and scoot back the short distance to the wall, leaning against it as my entire body shivers, suddenly feeling too cold.

Brent's eyes drift to mine, pleading with me to call for help, to save him. Mastyx steps between us, and through his legs, I watch Brent's mouth and eyes stretch unnaturally wide in horror. He tries to scream, but blood instead of words coughs from between his lips.

Mastyx peers down at me over his shoulder, his eyes narrowing before snatching Brent from the water, holding him high, and inhaling deeply. Brent's legs dangle and twitch as his soul separates from his body in a blurry haze and enters Mastyx's throat, lighting it up on the way down to the pit of his stomach.

I cower beneath them, too stunned to move. Mastyx's face slowly transforms from a flaming skull to Brent's. By the time Mastyx finishes sucking the literal life out of him, Brent is nothing but a pile of bones with a light skin covering him, completely desiccated.

Mastyx throws what's left of him across the alley, and he lands inside a dumpster, the lid closing on top of him.

The silence that follows is deafening. Mastyx stands beside the dumpster, his eyes fixed on it. There's a hesitation, like he doesn't want to look at me, and it makes me feel ashamed.

His head pivots abnormally slow in my direction, and I immediately put my head down, afraid of what he may do to me—afraid he changed his mind about our agreement and decides to hurt me.

His footsteps echo around me, growing louder as they come closer. I sense him, hovering above me, but still, I keep my head down, remaining submissive.

Fingers glide across the back of my neck before wrapping under my chin, where he presses upward, tipping my face up to his. "Oh, my Little Sinner, what has he done to you?"

A sense of relief washes over me, and I sob, resting my face in his palm, my bloody head smearing across its surface. He catches a tear racing down my cheek with a hooked black claw and sucks my sadness off his fingertip before picking me up and carrying me down the alley.

I rest my heavy head against his hairy chest, nuzzling into him, my eyes barely able to stay open as we turn out of the alley and walk toward the dark, abandoned lot I parked in. When we reach my car, nearly concealed in darkness, he opens the back passenger door and places me inside.

I stare up at him. "What are you doing?"

"You called me here, so your loins must need me. That's what you said. That was our agreement."

My eyes widen. "But—"

He grips my jaw roughly. "This arrangement was your idea, Little Sinner, remember?"

I close my eyes as he pulls me toward him, spreading my legs when my ass is resting on the edge of the back seat—the chill of the night air, spreading goosebumps across my lower body. A whimper escapes me as he makes a slow entry and moves in and out of me quickly but not deeply.

His claws dig into my upper thighs, and he hoists me higher before thrusting hard into me.

I cry out, my legs and body screaming from the violent attack I just endured. Tears drain into my ears on both sides, muffling Mastyx's moans of pleasure.

His body heats up, and my eyes widen as his cock, not ripping my insides to pieces or scorching my tender internal walls, glides in and out of me, massaging my walls with a warmth and tenderness that soothes me from the inside.

How can that even be possible?

He pulls me up to his chest before wrapping both arms tightly around me, holding me there as he stills, finding his release. The fluid inside me numbs the pain, and I find myself slowly forgetting about what I just went through in the alley.

His hand cups the back of my head, holding it softly against his chest, his heat smoothing the goosebumps on my skin.

He holds me at arm's length before reaching between my legs, his warm fingers sliding gently inside my ass. I close my eyes and moan as a tingling sensation travels down my thighs, into my bottom, and through my spine, the tearing pain that was once there, dissipating in an instant.

A staggering breath escapes me as his thumb grazes over my clit, stroking it gently. All the pain I was feeling has been replaced by pure pleasure. Mastyx's head drifts between my legs, and I grip the seat, my body instinctively sliding back as his long tongue extends from his lips and slides between mine, flickering inside me. My orgasm coats his tongue within seconds, and with my release, the last of my energy drains into his palate.

When I feel a sudden chill, I open my eyes, and Mastyx is gone. I crawl from the back seat and stand, swiping my forehead, checking for blood, but feel nothing. The pain throughout my body no longer exists.

I glance at my arms, turning them side to side, but they are clean. The driver's side door groans open, and I sink behind the wheel, pulling the visor down and peering into the mirror. My face looks fine. I turn my head side to side, covering my mouth in disbelief. There's no bruising, no blood, no signs that anything happened to me at all.

He healed me.

* * *

Over the last several days, I've barely slept. Every time I close my eyes, I see Brent's fist coming at my face, forcing my eyes back open. Even though Mastyx healed my physical trauma, the mental and emotional effects linger, making day-to-day activities that I usually enjoy feel more like chores.

I gaze at the unfinished project on my desktop that I started before the incident with Brent. It takes everything in me to sit down and pick up my glue container, determined to finish what I started. Baby's breath, moss and finger bones rest on either side of the plank, waiting for me to decide what to do with them.

After Mastyx left me healed in the abandoned lot, I went back and, using my switchblade, roughly cut off a few of Brent's fingers in a fit of rage. At the time, I did it to take away the appendages he used to violate my body with. But the more I stared at the decomposing fingers, the more I realized I had a better use for them in my art.

A heavy sigh escapes me, blowing the dried flowers across the desk and over the edge onto the floor. I shake my head and set the glue back down. I'm not in the mood. My arms feel too heavy, too tired.

I stand, shuffle the short distance to the couch and flop down on the cushions, throwing my arm across my eyes. Maybe I'll try again later.

Maybe.

Chapter Twenty-Three
Don't Knock

A year has passed since I lured Brent to his death in the bar alley. That night changed everything for me.

I misjudged him, which taught me a valuable lesson. Just because someone acts like a gentleman doesn't mean they are.

Things can change in the blink of an eye, especially when someone expects to get something out of you, and you reject them. I see things differently now when I meet people or see them in public. Even perfect strangers aren't safe from my internal thoughts. Every time I see someone doing something kind for another, I always wonder, what's their motive? Is that guy holding the door for the lady to be friendly, or is it because he wants to get a second look at her ass as she passes through the doorway?

Even when I see two people interacting who seem to know each other well, I find myself focusing on their body language, checking for subtle hints of deception.

After dealing with a wave of ups and downs, going from having a clean house and creating a bunch of art to sitting on the couch and letting my apartment fall into disarray and then back again, I concluded that no one else matters. Other people, in general, are beneath me. They don't have a demon who's a flame away from sucking out their souls for something I perceive as sinful.

I'm the one who has literally gone through hell and back. I'm the one who has been beaten, raped, and drugged. I'm the one who is more powerful because of it.

Because of him.

He sees it too. The way he looks at me has changed as well. Not in a loving way, more like I'm proud of what I created kind of way. It's sinister, and I love it.

Mastyx and I have fallen into a routine. One that, despite the pain it causes and the injuries I endure, I've grown fond of. I find myself longing for him constantly—the heat of his clawed hands on my thighs, the warmth his body brings me on these cold winter evenings.

He never stays for long. I lure my mark, call Mastyx to me, and he takes what he wants from them and from me. Sometimes there's aftercare, which I look forward to, but not always. At times, it seems as though he's in a hurry to return to hell. Perhaps he's eager to gloat about his new face, the one taken by the most recent doomed soul I've brought him.

In the time it's taken for me to go from hating him to our current status, I've saved enough money from my art to put a down payment on a house. I now have thousands of followers on social media and a backlog of artwork requests. With every death I am responsible for, inspiration seems to find me, and the creations that follow have stirred the art world, drawing the attention of a local community arts center, which has requested a full display of my work for its next annual art expo. Their events draw thousands of people from hundreds of miles away and expand over multiple blocks. One of the main streets through downtown remains closed for the three-day weekend event, forcing the public to detour around the area.

When I discovered the house I wanted and bid on it, my parents weren't exactly pleased. "It's too far away," Mom said. "It doesn't have curb appeal or any front windows," Dad said. But because of the unique style of the design, it sat on the market for an unprecedented amount of time, and the price just kept dropping. How could I resist?

I close the door behind my parents and lean against it. Finally, the house I closed on a few days ago is empty except for me. They've been with me all day, unpacking boxes, putting things away, and schooling me on the ins and outs of homeownership. My dad fixed a dripping faucet, tightened a few loose knobs, verified the fireplace was in working order, and made sure it was clean before they left.

The fireplace.

I still remember the first time I toured the house. The minute I spotted the ornate fireplace in the living room, with its carved marble, beautiful oak, and iron insert, something stirred inside me, and my loins screamed for attention. I could feel Mastyx's closeness at that moment, even though the fire inside wasn't lit.

Although the house is small, it's just enough for me, two bedrooms and one bathroom, with an efficient kitchen and a small island. From the kitchen, I can see the living room, my bedroom and office, all at once. A direct line of sight to each room, depending on which way I turn my head. Off to the far right side, a door that leads to a back porch, and on the other side, a small pantry. The second bedroom is set up as my office space and craft room.

My apron dangles from a coat hook near the door. I didn't want to get a job; my art pays for everything, but I knew that, to get a mortgage on this place without my parents' help, I'd need a consistent income.

Once I started working at the deli not far from here, it didn't take long for me to rise from deli assistant to deli manager. Customers raved about my perfect slices and charming personality. Not to mention that when the manager went on maternity leave three months after I started there, they gave me her job temporarily to run things, and I fell into the role as if it had always been meant for me. So, when she decided she'd rather be a stay-at-home mom, I was the obvious choice. And now, here I am, two days before my twentieth birthday, all moved into my first house, with a well-paying job, a beater in the driveway, and a demon for a boyfriend.

Boyfriend. It's weird when I call him that, but what else would I call him?

I'm just happy at this point to not have to commute so far to work. Driving almost an hour back and forth from my apartment was getting to be too much. I would have chosen something closer to my apartment, but Wahalla is where I wanted to be on account of the city's history. They have the highest rate of missing persons than anywhere else in the U.S., so what's a few more?

I had to take a detour on my way to work one day, and it took me right by this house. I knew the moment I saw it that it was meant to be mine. The space between neighbors was ample, almost a whole other house could fit between us, and the front yard has a small fence, a long sidewalk, and, most importantly, it has a lot of character and charm, with detailed millwork around the porch roof and columns. The porch is welcoming but not spacious, just enough room for a chair and a small table if I choose to sit outside. On either side of the steps, red daylilies bloom, drawing attention away from the windowless front. And the door…gorgeous, and heavy mahogany with vines and leaves carved into it.

It almost felt like it was inviting me in—calling to me.

The neighbors have been overly friendly, taking every opportunity to strike up a conversation and even going so far as to find excuses to leave their homes when I step outside. I keep conversations short and uninformative. The last thing I need is to make new friends and have them stop by unannounced. I've literally been their new neighbor for less than twelve hours, and I've had two casseroles and three plates of cookies dropped off. Jesus, do people really eat strangers' food like this around here?

One of the casseroles has a dog's hair trapped beneath the Saran Wrap. I gag and frown. Come on, people, lint-roll your clothes before cooking.

I scrape both casseroles into the garbage, along with the cookies. I'm not a huge fan of sweets to begin with, but raisin cookies are my least favorite.

Blech.

After a day of relentless knocking, doorbell ringing and uninvited visitors, I decided I needed a sign. I paint one of my wooden planks outside, and once it's no longer tacky, I add the words 'Don't Knock' in white paint before setting it on top of the washer in my laundry room to dry. I don't mind the doorbell as much, but the incessant banging on my beautifully carved door will eventually create a wear mark.

I suck in a sharp breath and let it out just as quickly, then kick off my shoes, grab the remote, and sink into my oversized couch cushions, covering my lower body with a throw. The channels flick from one to the next, nothing really catching my attention. I toss the remote over to the coffee table, leaving the news channel on and blow out a long-winded sigh. Finally, I can relax.

A nap sounds nice. Now that the sun has gone down, the neighborhood is quiet for the evening, and I've never been more thankful. Just as my eyes flutter closed, the front door rattles with a sharp knock.

My eyes spring open, and I roll them, letting out a long-winded huff. "For fuck sake." I toss my blanket off me, stomp to the front door, and whip it open. "What?"

A man, hotter than fuck, tightens his grip around a baby in his arms. His jeans sit right at his thin waist and stretch over the bulk in between his legs. My eyes drift from his cock back to his face, and I soak in this God-like man's tan skin and smooth lips. His brown hair, just as soft as silk, begs for me to run my fingers through it.

"I'm so sorry to disturb you," he says, hoisting the baby higher on his chest, the sleeve of his shirt tightening around his defined biceps.

I open my mouth, but words don't come out. He's fucking gorgeous—from his sharp jaw to the way his nose curves slightly to the side, and the five o'clock shadow creeping across his face, everything about him says he's a manly man, not some dainty office worker.

"I live down the street, and I just got out of work, but I wanted to say hi and drop this off for you. It's a list of trustworthy contractors in the area, in case you ever want work done. It's hard to find good help these days." The baby stirs in his arms. It's skin, tan like his father's, and his thick eyebrows and hairline are the same. I imagine he's an exact duplicate of him at that same age. "Oh, umm, this is my son, Timothy. I just picked him up from the sitters."

A small part of me is jealous of whoever made such a beautiful creature with such a handsome man, knowing it will never be me.

There's an awkward silence between us, neither knowing what to say. Just as he opens his mouth to say more, I pull the paper from between his fingers, manage to squeak out a 'thank you', and swing the door around.

At first, I sense him still on the other side of the door. I press my ear against it, listening to see if he says anything else, but all I hear is a sigh, then the creaking of my stairs and footsteps growing further away.

A part of me feels disappointed, and I think it was the first time all day that I wanted someone to ring the doorbell or knock.

What the fuck is wrong with me? I haven't felt like this about anyone, ever.

He made me feel starstruck, as if I were meeting a celebrity for the first time.

I collapse back on the couch and read the paper on my lap. At the bottom of the page, a handwritten message points an arrow to a name farther up the page.

This is me, and here's my cell if you ever need anything.

The arrow points to Bellagio Painting and Repairs.

What I need is to sit on his fucking face and let him fuck me.

No, Tessa. He can't be one of your victims. He's a dad, a neighbor, and a seemingly nice person. Just shake it off and stop thinking about him.

But I can't. I want to, but every time I close my eyes, he's there, taking me into my bedroom and throwing me down on my bed. What am I missing here? I have someone who protects me, fucks me, and lets me fuck others at the low cost of their soul instead of mine, and I find myself sitting here wanting more.

Needing more.

My fingers travel between my legs, and I close my eyes, touching myself but imagining it's him. I clench my fist, taking my hand away from my clit and shaking it off.

I can't think about him this way. Not only because he seems like a family man, working, picking up his baby from the sitters, and caring for his neighbors, but because I know nothing good will ever come of it.

Of us.

Not being able to have him creates a void inside of me. But why? Is it because I'm yearning for a family? To be a mother despite knowing I can never have children. Is that part of why I feel so empty inside? Because I see a family or any sort of happily ever after was taken off the table the minute I signed my life away, giving it to Mastyx?

Stop it.

I push thoughts of him and what my future *could* have been back into the depths of my brain. Fantasizing about David is all I can ever do. I can never have a husband, a family, or anything that resembles true love.

Mastyx would never allow it. Our arrangement is all that matters now. He gets what he wants, and so do I.

Sort of.

A part of me wonders what would happen if I truly fell for someone, someone who makes me feel like breaking the contract with Mastyx is worth more to me than my life. Would he drag me to hell and kill them out of spite?

I can't let that happen. I won't let that happen. I have to keep everything superficial with anyone I meet. My desires for them need to be kept in check. Mastyx will always be the only one for me, like it or not, this is what I signed up for.

* * *

Time can be a fickle bitch.

It's been two years. Two years that I've watched seasons, people, and families come and go, and a small part of me aches for a normal life.

David passes by my house every day, taking his son Timothy for a walk around the block after work and on the weekends, holding his small hand.

I gaze down at my manicured fingers and picture a child's hand clutching them, taking a walk of our own. Sometimes it makes me sad and a little jealous, if I'm being honest, that I will never carry or have a child of my own.

I'm not sure I'm deserving enough to be a parent. Who would want me, a killer, with a demon lover as a mom?

Lovers…that's what we are to each other now after all this time. The day Mastyx called me my Love instead of my Little Sinner, changed things inside me. It gave me a small amount of hope that he cares enough about me that he may not drag me to his fiery lair one day for doing something he perceives as breaking our binding contract.

My red 2005 Audi A4 gleams, a fresh wax job reflecting the sunshine into my eyes. Business has been good. Real good. It's a used car, but it sure beats the hell out of the shit-box '88 Nova. Ever since I started harvesting the bones of my victims, my business has skyrocketed. Who knew there were so many twisted fucks like me in the world?

The elderly neighbor nods and offers a subtle smile as he unloads groceries from his trunk. I don't usually spend much time outside on the porch; it screams, "Come and talk to me," to everyone, and I don't care to socialize or make friends, but it's a pleasant seventy-five degrees with a slight breeze, so I'm soaking up a small amount of unseasonably warm weather for January before Mother Nature decides to send a cold front from Canada down our way.

I take a swig of my coffee, the heat and caffeine, sending a wave of pleasure to my brain and belly. The new grinder coffee maker combo my parents got me for my birthday is a godsend. Until now, I never realized how a freshly ground bean could make a cup of coffee taste so much better. I'll never go back to pods or a regular drip maker for that matter. It's funny how, as people mature, we learn to appreciate appliances over other trivial things.

A woman, swinging arms with a little girl on the sidewalk, slows down at the end of my walkway. She bends down, the little girl cupping her hands, whispering in her mother's ear. The woman glances up at me, smiles, and nods before swiping her palm through her daughter's long, golden locks.

I set my coffee cup aside and stand as the little girl enters my walkway, skipping toward me, a bundle of pansies in her hand.

She swipes a wayward lock of hair out of her mouth and holds the flowers out to me. "My mommy said I can give these to you."

A lump crowds my throat. No one has ever given me flowers before. Not my ex from high school, Jayce, not my mom, even though she grows prized rose bushes in her yard, no one.

I wrap my fingers around the flowers and kneel before her. "Thank you."

My body stiffens as she hugs me without warning. I find myself slowly melting into her the longer she holds me captive in my own yard, her love seeping into me, like a cure. I wrap my arms around her, hugging her back before her mom shuffles down the walkway and reaches her hand out. "It's time to go, Hazel. Let the poor woman go."

Hazel's hands fall away from my neck, and suddenly I feel cold. "Make sure you put them in water." Her blue eyes twinkle in the sun when she turns away from me and shields them from the rays. "Bye, pretty lady," she says before skipping back down the walkway.

I stand, grab my coffee cup, and push my front door open, leaning against it once it's closed. A tear races down my face, and a fresh wave of sadness sucks the life out of me. My back slides down the door until I reach the floor, where I sit with pink and purple pansies resting on my legs.

Chapter Twenty-Four
Reflecting

I'm fucking exhausted beyond belief. I don't know when this depression crept up on me, but here it is, holding me firmly against the couch, covered in a blanket, wanting to do nothing else but lie here.

Halloween is coming soon. It's one of my favorite days of the year since moving to this place. It's so easy to find a victim to bring home when no one knows what you really look like. But I find myself struggling. The number of men I'm bringing home grows less and less, the excitement and newness of it all becoming redundant and wearing me down.

I don't know when my unhappiness started. Perhaps it all started the day the little girl gave me the flowers nearly two years ago to this day.

Don't get me wrong, I love what I have done with Mastyx, our agreement at least. It's given me confidence and made me feel like I have a purpose in this world that I don't deserve.

Men swarm to me now. It's crazy how easily they fall into my trap. It's almost like a magnetism hovers around me, and men who get too close get sucked right into my space, my world.

My web.

I barely have to do more than bat my eyelashes to draw them to me. It got to the point when men who were obviously sinful little bastards became boring, less of a challenge. The married ones, though, now those are electrifying. The sneaking around, the game of seduction I play on them with the promise that their wives will never find out. The way they battle with their inner demons, the whole time knowing how wrong what they are about to do is, but the temptation of being able to fuck some anonymous woman without their spouse finding out is too good to pass up.

Until it isn't.

But then the time came when that didn't even excite me anymore.

Now I've moved on to the not giving a shit who I pick phase. I don't care whether they are good or bad, married or unmarried, single or dating.

Mastyx still comes on the nights of the full moon, and most of the time, I wake up and enjoy his company. But my doctor put me on Ambien, and a few times, I've slept right through Mastyx's visit, not even remembering it happened. If it weren't for the hand marks on my body the next day, I would have thought he had forgotten to come. Perhaps a part of me wants it this way—to forget.

My mom wants me to see someone, to talk about what has led me to feel this way, but I prefer to figure it out on my own, especially since I already know what the problem is.

I found out that my most recent victim has two daughters that he cares for. His wife is in the military, and he went out to the bar for a long-overdue night away from home, thanks to his parents visiting in town.

Now I feel rotten to the core. I don't think it would have bothered me if I never knew about his backstory but it made the news. During the broadcast, the wife pleaded for the return of her husband, and it nearly broke me—the two little girls hugging her legs, tears flooding their faces, wanting nothing more than to have their dad back. I'm a shit bag.

Fuck.

I have no one to talk to except for Mastyx about this stuff, but the only way to get him here is to kill again, and I can't even lift my head right now. The soup I heated up sits on the coffee table untouched. I thought I wanted it; my stomach has been growling nonstop, but I can't find the will in me to pick up the spoon.

A thick layer of dust covers my coffee table, and the smell of stale air violates my sinuses. I should get up and try to clean before my house starts growing mold and attracting more than just spiders. If only I had the energy.

My door rattles for the third time today. Jesus, does no one read the fucking sign? I'm not getting up. I curl the throw around my shoulders and ignore it. Multiple voices filter into my head all at once. One says to answer; one says not to; another says bring Mastyx into the mix and have him take their soul for disturbing your pity party. Another is my mom's voice, asking when I'm coming over for dinner again.

I've built up enough stock of art to last several months, and all my clients have received a message letting them know I'm taking a two-week vacation. And by vacation, I mean sitting around doing nothing but watching television and ignoring my responsibilities.

Let's face it. I'm in a funk.

The doorbell chimes multiple times overhead. Persistent fucking bastard.

I pick up my phone, find the camera app from my security system and peer down at a man holding a clipboard scanning the street before looking back at my door. His hairline is receding, but his beard is well-trimmed, and his tattooed arms send a tingle between my legs.

Don't do it, Tessa. It's broad fucking daylight.

The doorbell rings again, and I cover my ears with the couch pillow. If he keeps this up, it's fucking on.

I listen to the room, hear nothing but silence and pull the pillow off my head. Good, he's gone. I didn't want to have to get up.

Rattle, rattle, pound.

Mother fucker.

I throw the pillow across the room, roll off the couch, stagger to the door and yank it open. "For fuck's sake. What?"

The man stands there, staring at me, looking up and down before clearing his throat. "Umm, yes, I'm from the local solar energy company and wanted to see if you'd be interested in learning more about it?"

His teeth are crooked, but his thin waist and wide upper body tell me he works out. And the smell wafting into my nostrils, one of my favorites, Polo Ralph Lauren. Not the blue bottle crap, the green one. Man, that stuff could make even the ugliest guy tempting to fuck. He slides a hand in his front pocket, tilts his head, and raises a hopeful, thick eyebrow, waiting for me to answer.

I want him. And besides, he knocked. Maybe that can be my new rule. Don't knock or else.

"Sure, come on in," I say with a smile.

He hesitates and nods down to my lower half. "Do you want to put pants on first?"

I glance down at my attire. I'm still wearing a T-shirt and underwear, but nothing else. I've been wearing the same thing for two days. "Well, if you're not comfortable with what I'm wearing, then I guess I'm not comfortable letting you in my house to listen to your pitch."

The door slowly closes as I swing it around, and his hand slaps against it. "No. It's fine. I don't mind."

A slight smile curves on my lips. Gotcha.

He pushes the door closed behind him, and I gesture for him to have a seat on the couch. When his back is turned, I twist the deadbolt on my front door and join him in the living room. "Drink?" I ask him as I seize my half-empty bottle of wine, before pouring myself a full glass and sitting in the armchair across from him beside the fire, crossing my legs.

"No, thanks." His eyes drift from my wineglass to my lips as I take a sip, then hyperfocus on my bare legs. "Umm, so what do you know about solar?"

"Enlighten me," I say, batting my eyelashes before taking a massive swig of wine and then setting the glass on the floor beside me. Fire ignites with a quick whoosh inside the fireplace as I ignite it and uncross my legs.

He opens a folder on his clipboard and begins his speech, his words intermittently staggering as he tries to rattle off the benefits of the sun's power. In my head, all

I can hear is blah, blah, blah. I yawn broadly, quickly growing bored.

Without realizing it, he has stopped talking, his eyes locked between my legs. My hands slide up and down my open legs, grazing my inner thighs with my nails. His jaw drops as I slide my fingers inside my pussy and moan. "Do you like what you see, Mr. Solar Salesman?"

He nods, his mouth still gaping.

"Want to fuck me, big Daddy?" I hook my thumbs around the edges of my panties and pull them over my ass, dropping them to the floor and flicking them at him. They land beside him on the couch, and he stands, his cock growing in his pants. His eyes trace up my bare legs, stopping at the space between them. "Yes," he gulps, swallowing hard.

I don't have the energy to ride his cock, so I stand, walk over to my small island and spread my legs, waiting for him to make the next move. He unbuttons his pants without haste, unzips his fly, and practically trips over his pants as they fall around his ankles, trying to get to me. I smile deviously at him, my lashes fluttering, luring him in before turning my head and focusing on the flames. The salesman wedges himself between my legs, and the fire intensifies as he feeds his short, fat cock into me. His hands tighten around my breasts, and my body shifts back and forth as he rocks into me rhythmically.

"Oh, fuck. Oh fuck. Oooooh fuuuuuck," his head launches to the ceiling, a satisfied smile on his face as his cum floods inside of me.

Two pump chump.

He rests his head between my breasts, holding me against the island, his mint-scented breath filling the space between us.

My hand slides along the kitchen counter until it bumps into the side of the butcher's block holding my knives. I pull it out slowly, the sound of the metal scraping against the wood sending a tingle of excitement between my thighs. "Did you like that, Daddy?"

His eyes meet mine. "Oh, fuck yeah."

I run my fingers through his sandy hair, my lips curling into a smirk. "Do you have any children at home?"

"No." He answers without hesitation, and I know his words are truthful.

I kiss him softly on the lips and say, "Good, then they won't have to miss you." The knife pierces through his right side and into the space where his liver should be.

He yelps and falls away from me, staggering and tripping over his own pants. His hand presses tightly against his wound, his eyes locked on the blood dripping from the tip of my blade. "What did you do?"

"I'm sorry," I murmur as I drop the knife in the sink beside me and gaze into the flames. "But I need to talk to Mastyx, and killing you is the only way."

"What? Who?" The words barely exit his mouth when a hooved foot breaches the flames, landing in front of him. The salesman slides back on the floor, leaving a trail of blood, his face paling from blood loss. I stand there, my eyes unseeing as Mastyx's other hooved foot breaches the flames, his body entering the room in slow motion. The salesman's eyes widen, his mouth stretching into a cartoon-like face right before a blood-curdling scream pierces my ears. Mastyx lifts him from my living room floor, blood dripping like rain onto the hardwood from his knife wound and pulls the man against his chest so they are face to face.

I feel nothing. I do nothing as Mastyx's throat lights up, and the man's soul leaves his body and enters Mastyx, draining him dry until he's nothing more than a pile of loose skin and bones.

The skin-coated bones thud to the floor. What once bothered me no longer matters. Seeing so many deaths over the years has numbed my soul. I'm a heartless monster, just as much as he is.

My eyes drift to Mastyx. "I don't feel like myself anymore."

He narrows his eyes at me. "They're all sinners. No more tears for them. You don't know what they do or think behind closed doors, but I do. I know everything." He walks toward me, forcing me backward into my bedroom. "Now, lie down and let me take care of you."

* * *

After Mastyx had his way with me, which was entirely for my benefit this time, including after care, I have a spring in my step. I feel…refreshed, like everything that was bothering me suddenly vanished, and I feel anew. I have an energy surging through me that I haven't felt in days, and I wonder if he had something to do with it.

Did he clear my mind of what's making me depressed?

This is what he does. He takes care of me.

He makes me forget who I've hurt so that I can focus on the why.

I want to survive—to stay in this life amongst the living.

My eyes brighten as I sit in front of a block of wood, the man I just killed, and Mastyx's juices still seeping out of me. Buying human bones online can be pricey, and their quality and legitimacy are questionable. Using the bones of my victims in my work just makes sense. Why pay such a high price for something I have access to for free? And the best part is, no one will be the wiser. It's not like I'm not already doing well with the animal art pieces; I'm actually doing fantastic. But human ones, buyers absolutely love them, and the price point I can set for them is significantly higher.

The salesman's feet are currently serving as a buffet for my beetles. Dermestid beetles are curious and useful little creatures. I love the way they can take fleshy body parts and devour them in a matter of days, especially with the large colony I maintain.

Once the bones are picked clean and ready for use, I'll attach them to the plank and surround the edges with little nursery pots that I've strategically attached to the plank. I will fill them with mature micro grasses and add bundles of dried flowers. I think I will call this piece Spring in My Step.

The next full moon is not only rare, but one that has the police making announcements and on high alert. People who own black cats are warned to keep them indoors, and they anticipate an uptick in crime and unusual calls. I scan the list of warnings provided by the police department, published in the local town crier, and smile—no warning to local men not to go home with strange women.

I call that a win for me.

*　*　*

Halloween is a week away. I don't like decorating too soon, then I'll end up doing it at the same time as most of my neighbors. I prefer to do it at the last minute. Get it up, enjoy the day and take it down like a week-long pop-up shop that suddenly appears out of nowhere. I secure my skull archway at the end of the sidewalk and plug it into my green outdoor extension cord to make sure it lights up.

My eyes brighten at the sight of multiple skulls in different states of horror, screaming with a glowing backdrop of red lights. It's perfect.

I turn my attention to the rows of marigolds that line the walkway leading to my porch. Water spills from my watering can, giving each one a drink before I kneel in the grass beside them. Cleaning the ground around them may seem pointless to some, but I like the black mulch surrounding them to be pitch-black and perfect. It really makes the blood-red flowers pop at night. I stand, brush off my grass-covered knees, and grab my sign to put at the end of the walkway, just beside the archway, so that everyone can see it.

The rubber mallet bounces in my hand, vibrating up my arm as I tap down the list of rules for Halloween night. I stand and back up into the street, making sure no cars are coming, and gaze at my simple, yet lovely Halloween display.

"Looks good," a voice says from behind me.

I turn to see the old man across the street giving me a thumbs up from his porch, where he's resting his freshly carved pumpkin. I'm not a big fan of real pumpkins; they attract critters to your doorstep. I nod to him and return my attention to my display.

The five-foot skeleton is a little crooked, so I walk over and adjust it until it points perfectly at the rule sign in the yard. I once again back up, and a broad smile stretches across my face.

It looks amazing. A sense of calm and relaxation washes over me. It's been a fantastic couple of weeks. I sold my third human art piece, raking in over two thousand dollars. I could start listing them on auction sites to get the most out of my work, but I prefer to do all the work so I can keep all the profits.

Mr. Solarman's skull, as it turns out, served a better purpose as a centerpiece for a dining room table. I carved a perfect hole in the top of his head and placed a Raven ZZ plant in its center. With leaves that start green and turn black as they mature, I knew buyers would love the color combination. Around the skull, deep purple dried pansies and green moss skirting the borders of the circular, black-painted wooden plank. It was light, gothic, and "stunning" according to the five-star review I received from the buyer, along with several beautiful images she took from every angle.

I feel optimistic about my future, and if the last few sales are any indication of what's to come, I'll be upgrading to a new car in no time.

Chapter Twenty-Five
Trick or Treat

Candy. The one thing in the world that I can live without. But tonight, just this one day a year, I keep an ample supply of it.

The kids flock to my house on Halloween. I am *the house*, not because I have the best candy, even though I do. The children think that's why their parents bring them to my doorstep, but the truth is, I'm a mystery. I've lived here for five years and have rarely interacted with anyone. I leave early and come home late.

Sure, a few random neighbors have caught a glimpse of me scurrying out after dark, but they are few and far between. I'm sure the men who parade the children from house to house also enjoy visiting my humble abode. I am single after all, with high cheekbones and a tall, fit frame, I could have been a model. I ignore and decline the numerous requests to meet this one and that one's brother or friend. I have no use for relationships. My tastes are very singular. Yet, despite all my rejections, they keep trying.

I know what you're thinking. Why not tell them you're in a relationship so they leave you alone? Well, then I wouldn't get so much attention.

And I love attention—crave it even.

It's like a minuscule amount of foreplay before the real show begins. For once the porch lights flicker out, that's when I prowl—prowl anywhere the unexpected, unknowing and gullible men thrive—bars, house parties, even sporting events. No place is off limits as long as the men are drunk and incapacitated. Sober men think more with their heads than their dicks, and I can't have that.

Before I begin my hunt, I need to deal with the children.

I frantically arrange the candy neatly in my cauldron. Every year, I make up two hundred packets filled to the brim with all the best candy secured at the top with a single staple, and almost every year, I run out. I should bump it up to three hundred, but where's the fun in that? I love the desperation in the children's eyes as they line up along my cement walkway, beautifully accented with blood-red marigolds. I don't overdecorate because, let's face it, then I have to take all that shit down and prepare for the next holiday. No, I simply have my archway, my rules and my skeleton pointing to the list.

The weather tonight is fabulous, and I look forward to sitting outside. Last year, wind and rain kept many trick-or-treaters away. Instead, their parents drove them through the sheriff's office, Boo with the Blue drive-thru event, leaving me with leftover candy packets.

I yank the long sleeves of my red devil dress down to my wrists, toss my amber hair over my shoulder and smile down at my filled cauldron. "Five minutes to spare. This must be a new record, Tessa," I say aloud. I gulp down the last of my red wine, leaving red lipstick on the glass, pull the front of my dress up to hide my cleavage, and throw my massive, solid wooden door open, revealing a large line of costumed children and a few random parents waiting in formation.

They've clearly read the rules. *Form a neat and orderly line, do not step on my porch until the clock strikes six, and DON'T KNOCK.*

Check, check and check.

The same sign I posted out front when I moved in reads, '*Don't Knock.*' It's simple and easy to read so you'd think such a singular rule would be hard to break, right?

Wrong.

The very next day, the neighbor next door had friends over for a barbecue. Now, I'm not entirely sure, but I'm pretty certain the neighbor dared a couple of his guests to knock on the mysterious house next door to see what would happen. Alcohol makes people do the dumbest things. Needless to say, the two pranksters mysteriously vanished later that night, and I suddenly became the talk of the town. Whispers and gossip spread rapidly as theories and accusations swirled through the small community of Walhalla, South Carolina. After a year or so, the rumors finally calmed down, and the two men were forgotten. It doesn't stop people from talking or trying to get little tidbits of information. They come to my house as often as it would make sense, no more, no less, trying to dig up breadcrumbs—carolers at Christmas, 'misdelivered mail', being lost and needing directions, even sending their children to my door to sell Girl Scout Cookies.

Halloween, on the other hand, is the only day of the year when everyone in town has a reason to be at my door.

Have there been other mysterious disappearances over the years? Of course, people go missing for various reasons all the time, especially in this town. This has been happening before I moved here, and it continues to occur. It's one of the primary reasons I chose it.

Ever since the men who knocked on my door disappeared, everyone has been eager to speak to the girl who resides in the house with no front windows. I didn't make the house what it is. It is all on one floor, which I love, but for some unknown reason, the previous owners covered the front windows facing the street when the house was sided with new white vinyl. It was a hard sell for most buyers, as they wanted to see who was outside their home. I took it as a unique opportunity. All they had to do was place cameras above the doorway facing the walkway as I did. I can see who's on my porch, walkway and even the old man across the street when he sits in front of his television picking his fucking nose.

A mother clears her throat, bringing me back to this very moment as my watch flicks to six. I sit in my black porch rocker, tug my red dress over my knees, and cuddle the cauldron on my lap before nodding to child number one. She eagerly scales the stairs and rams her fingers into the pile of sweet bundles, ripping one bag open. I seize her greedy little paw and shake my head without a word as my grip tightens enough to make her let go. I'm not allowing that kind of behavior, not from anyone, even if she is dressed up like an innocent little angel.

Her mother gasps at my audacity, clutching her fictitious pearls. The girl slams her hands to her sides. "I'm sorry," she says before glancing back at her wide-eyed mother and twisting a lock of blonde hair nervously around her finger.

I adjust my devil horn headband higher on my head, before fixing the mess she made, making her wait, making them all wait for me to make the pile neat again, a lesson for those who come after. Once the cauldron is reset and orderly, I remove a bag from the pile and hold it over the angel's pumpkin treat bag. She holds it open, waiting for me to let go, but I don't. I haven't heard the words she's required to say; they are all required to say them. I hold the bag with all but one finger, circling my pointer finger around and around like a buffering television waiting for a signal.

Her mother murmurs a reminder to her and rocks back on her heels, a lack of comfort plaguing the air around her. The girl's blue eyes land on my hazel ones before she spits out, "Trick or Treat," louder than necessary.

"Trick or treat," I reply, dropping her treat inside the bag and giving her a dismissive nod.

She whispers shyly, "Thank you," and speeds down the steps to her mother. Other children and parents roll their eyes and shift their hips, irritated that the child wastes their precious time.

I shrug as one of my favorite single dads, David, wearing a fitted pair of faded blue jeans and a black t-shirt that reads, 'This is my costume,' ascends the steps. His six-year-old son is dressed like Batman, holding his hand. He first came to my home when his son could barely walk, a newly single parent after his wife left him for another man. At least that's what the busybodies around town were saying.

He asked me out once, and I turned him down, saying I'd just gotten out of a relationship and the time wasn't right. I had to lie for obvious reasons, but since I left the "I'm single" window open, he's asked me to go out for coffee just as friends and invited me on a walk with him and Timothy, both times, turning him down with a flirtatious smile.

His eyes, an extremely dark brown that nearly blacken his orbs, are shadowed by long lashes that flicker repeatedly as the material of my dress rolls up my pale legs as I cross them, revealing a massive scar on the top of my thigh. I gingerly cover my legs, hiding them from him and the prying eyes of everyone standing behind him.

That ought to give everyone something to talk about. How'd she get that scar? Did someone do it to her, or did she do it to herself? Maybe aliens abducted her, and they put an implant there. I wonder what they will come up with next.

"Good evening, Tessa," David's voice staggers out as his eyes break free from my legs and land on mine.

I nod and flash him a small, sly smile as his son waits patiently just behind his thighs. Everyone in town knows my name, but I barely know any of theirs, except for this hot specimen standing before me. I made a point of remembering his. I hold a bundle of candy out to David's son, Timothy, and he glances up at his father, waiting for permission to accept a treat from a stranger.

Timothy has a shy way about him that I appreciate and understand. It's hard to trust someone who intimidates you. I, too, have someone who makes me feel like that, but in a different way. Mastyx makes me shy in the bedroom, and I cower beneath his commanding presence.

Two women whisper back and forth, their eyes locking in on David's ass before they break out in hushed giggles. David runs his fingers through his brown hair, my porch light revealing hints of gray creeping through the strands, and sighs heavily. I get the sense he's tired of being one of the topics of the town gossipers. "Happy Halloween."

"You too, David," I say, wishing I didn't have such strict rules as my face heats up and my underwear moistens with desire.

Later, Tessa, I say internally to myself as David hesitates before turning and walking off the porch, his firm ass calling to me as he strolls away.

I close my eyes and take a deep breath, pushing all inappropriate thoughts of David deep inside myself. I need to make it through this evening so that I can hunt for a suitable replacement.

After an hour of endless trick-or-treaters, my cauldron drops the last bundle into a teenager's bowl. Several children and parents grumble that a teenager is getting the last piece, falsely believing they're undeserving. However, if they have made the effort to dress up and stand before me, following the rules, I may add, they are just as deserving as the next person. Besides, they could be doing worse, like egging or toilet papering someone's house.

I turn toward my door as the remaining trick-or-treaters bow their heads, sadness plaguing their faces, and grumbling their discontent. Perhaps if their parents had made my house a priority, their children wouldn't be so glum. Then again, there was never going to be enough. Secretly, I'm hoping one day to see a brawl of children and parents battling it out in the middle of the street—a band of minions fighting to be one of the lucky two hundred.

My front door creaks open, and parents and children alike crane their necks, trying to get a quick glimpse inside. I block the open door with my body, and with a quick flick of my fingers over the light switch, the porch light darkens, dispersing the disappointed crowd. I close the door behind me and lean against it as my grandfather clock strikes seven, echoing through the house until it reaches its number of hours. I finished a whole hour early. How lovely. I kick off my black satin flats and stroll to the kitchen.

On the countertop rest three bags of candy corn. Every year, my mother mails me a few bags of the orange, yellow and white candies, thinking incorrectly that I love them. And every year, I say nothing, so she keeps buying them.

I have a new use for the waxy candies now.

The double boiler my brother bought me for Christmas a couple of years ago sits empty on the electric burner, waiting to be used. I fill the bottom pot halfway with water, rest the other pot on top, and dump in two bags of candy corn. I turn the burner on low and rest the lid on the pot, hiding the candy from sight.

My red-painted fingernails, filed into sharp points, tap the handle, drumming it like an introduction to a show, a drumroll of sorts—a prelude for what's to come. Melting the candy down is something I've perfected through trial and error. Timing is key. Once it reaches the perfect consistency, it will become something useful, something glorious, something sinister.

Chapter Twenty-Six
My Sacrificial Lamb

The candy corn swirls in the pot, smooth like butter.
I rest the wooden spoon on the side of the stove on a
small black floral plate and sigh.

It's time.

I enter my room, strip off my conservative
Halloween attire and paw through the box in my closet
labeled 'Costumes'. Hmm, I think I'll go as a vampire
this year. I lift the black-and-red low-cut dress from the
box and shake it out. Dust particles float into the center
of the room and settle on the hardwood floors. I feed
my fingers through the bottom, pull it over my head,
and shimmy the dress down my curvy hips,
straightening it out as I go.

It's a tight dress, landing just below my knees,
showing off my soft, bare legs. The silky material glides
beneath my fingers as I slide my palms across my
covered breasts and adjust the black lace trimming,
skirting my partially exposed cleavage. I lift my hooded
double-sided cape, throw it around my neck, black side
out, and secure it to my throat with a single snap. Some
people prefer the red side facing out. Not me. I like
how the red flutters behind me like a background from
the front, and the black conceals everything in the dark
from behind. When the hood is up, I could flatten my
body against a black wall face-first, and the only thing

you could see if you were to drive by is the whites of my ankles.

Using my big toe, painted black with a little red rose, I flip open the shoe box, revealing my satin red spiked heels. My heart skips at the sight of them, and my lips twitch at the small rust stain that tarnishes the side of one of the heels near the point. These are my lucky shoes. I've worn them on almost every hunt. So versatile, so beautiful…so deadly. You wouldn't believe how cool it sounds to stomp the tip of one of these suckers into someone's eye, especially a dirty, rotten scumbag who tries to take advantage of you, thinking you're intoxicated. The joke was on that guy. Pop goes the weasel. That was a couple of years ago. I've become more reserved and careful since then.

After turning off most of my lights, I lock my front door and climb behind the wheel of my 2024 Cadillac CT4. It's not brand-new like I wanted, but it had fewer than a thousand miles on it, and I got it for a great deal from an elderly woman whose husband had recently passed, not long after he'd bought it for himself. Mr. Solarman's entire bone structure was sold within a week after his skull, netting profits of over ten thousand dollars. I sold my Audi, used the funds from that and a small loan to purchase this midnight black beauty of a ride. Every time I sink into the luxury leather seats, it brings a smile to my face.

Clemson is just over twenty minutes from my house, and a Halloween bar crawl is going on, so it's the perfect opportunity to find someone willing to come home with me. As I drive out of town, parents lingering on the sidewalks, watching their children scurry from one house with their lights still on to the next, stare at me with judgmental eyes.

I shoot them a sinister smile and continue on my adventure. They don't know me, not really, and they never will.

College Avenue is Clemson's main strip, and it's currently alive with ghouls, goblins, and Waldo's dressed to the hilt, entering and exiting bars and restaurants. I pull to the curb down the street from a group of bars participating in the crawl—a trifecta of opportunities lying before me.

My window vibrates as someone smacks it with their palm, startling me. I turn my head, and a man wearing Scottish attire, carrying a set of bagpipes, lifts his kilt. My eyes widen at the tip of a small cock, barely visible from within the pile of hair surrounding it. I shake my head at the man, a truly handsome man indeed, but one not blessed with a dick worth riding.

His friend, dressed like the Grim Reaper with a skeleton-painted face, slaps the plaid-wearing drunk's kilt down and waves at me through the window, mouthing an apology before continuing down the sidewalk. I hope there are more suitable choices inside, or I might be in trouble.

I begrudgingly climb from my car, shut the door softly, and stalk toward the bar straight ahead of me.

My heels click quickly across the street as a woman dressed as Xena Warrior Princess sees me coming and holds the door for me. I murmur a pleasant thank you and enter the darkened space.

It's humid and stuffy inside, likely due to the overcrowded environment. I can barely move through the sea of costumed patrons as I make my way across the room to the bar. Lights from a disco ball cast glittery, colorful specks around the room, dotting patrons' faces like sprinkles on a soft-serve twist. I weave around a group of people standing in a circle, talking, and wedge myself sideways between a couple of men at the bar so I can order a drink.

The scent of armpit singes my nose hairs as the bartender leans toward me and places a coaster by my hand. "What can I get you, sweetheart?"

His sweetheart comment sends a painful ping to my abdomen, a reminder of what happened at the biker bar rushing back briefly before I shove it back into the depths of my mind where my trauma lives.

Nose plugs for starters, I think to myself, recovering quickly from my intrusive memory. I look away from his prying brown eyes and the unibrow over them, glance at the specials board on the wall, and shout over the crowd, "Blood Thirsty Martini, please."

I mean, it's an obvious choice.

The bartender nods as I drop a twenty-dollar bill on the dark walnut bar top, scratched in various places from years of abuse.

It's kind of like me in a way. Etching and scars mark my body subtly here and there. Most of my tarnished skin is unnoticeable, hidden from the public eye by the clothes I wear, but others, like the gnarly scar from my car accident long ago, could only be reduced in size by plastic surgery. I don't mind it anymore, though. I come up with all kinds of ways it happened when people ask, avoiding the truth.

Bob is carved into the once-smooth finish of the bar top. I trace my fingertips over the three letters, feeling their texture as a dark crimson drink clanks beside my hand. The bartender winks and covers the money I gave him before stuffing it into his pocket. I don't bother waiting for change; I know better, as I've been here before. You don't get change unless you specifically request it. Otherwise, the assumption is that the remaining balance is their tip.

Greedy fuckers.

I sink into a tattered and torn leather seat in the corner and toss my cape over the silver metal back. A green-tinted lantern above me, with a little plastic skeleton decoration hanging from it, swings back and forth, ever so slightly, every time the front door of the bar swings open. A slight breeze swoops through, carrying the hot, stale air out the back exit, held open a few inches by a rock.

It's become a habit of mine to always sit near a way out—an open window, a door, a thin wall I can bust through like the Kool-Aid man.

There's nothing worse than being trapped inside an enclosed space when a bunch of drunks decide to brawl with each other.

My mind wanders back to the past, taking me on a journey that leads me to this moment. I've come so far in five years. From being a high school graduate making a deal with the devil to save my soul and living with my parents, driving my grandma's rickety old Nova, to becoming a successful artist and homeowner who drives a Cadillac and wears name-brand clothes instead of Walmart specials.

A prickling sensation dances across my cheeks, the pleasant thoughts of where and who I am now—powerful, confident, and alluring melt away any doubts I have about my future endeavors.

My next move is an isolated mansion filled with fireplaces where I can lure multiple men under false pretenses to give my lover the face he deserves, even if it's only for a short while.

I cross my legs, lifting the end of my dress above my knees, and immediately catch the attention of a familiar face. The Grim Reaper, whose friend showed me his minuscule penis a short time ago, tilts his head, his eyes locked on my legs as his Scottish-dressed friend speaks loudly in his ear. His dark eyes drift from my legs to my eyes, then linger on my lips as I raise my drink by its stem and take a small sip. I smack my lips together, relishing the sweet yet strong beverage as the Reaper hops off his wooden barstool and strolls over to me, confidence radiating off him like the vibrations of a speaker at a concert.

He sets his beer beside my martini, the chair scraping harshly against the floor as he pulls it back and drops into the seat across from me. Condensation races down the side of his Coors bottle, creating a wet circle on the table. He lifts the drink, and I watch as he takes a massive swig before smacking the empty bottle down on the table with a loud *clank*.

"Can I buy you a drink?" he asks, his eyes set on mine.

I tap the side of my glass with my pointed nail and say, "I have one."

He leans forward, moving his empty bottle from between us and rests his folded arms on the table. "Well, drink up, Buttercup, so that I can buy you another."

Buttercup?

Just what I want, someone calling me an invasive flower species as a pet name. Well, it's not like I'm picky anymore. At this point, the unibrow bartender could easily be my victim, but people would miss him.

I take two fingers, resting the stem of my glass between them, and slide it out of my way before leaning forward, my face nearly touching his. "Want to fuck?" I ask, getting to the point.

There's no time for pussyfooting around. I need to hook him like a worm and catch him like a starving fish. The longer I linger in this place, the more likely someone will remember me.

His neck recoils, and he sits back in his seat, dumbfounded. He glances over at his drunk friend, hanging on a cackling, drunk blonde with blue skin dressed like Smurfette at the bar before looking back at me and saying, "If you're offering, I'm accepting." His hood pulls off his bald head with a quick swipe of his hand, the light above us glistening across its Mr. Clean surface. "What's your name?"

"No names." A playful smile creeps across my face, prickling with amusement as I say, "Air drop me a dick pic, and I'll give you my address if you're worthy."

He leans forward, his legs rocking the table as he undoubtedly opens and closes them, his excitement growing by the second. After a few seconds, he flashes me a crooked smile and asks, "Worthy of what?"

Oh, I'm so glad he asked.

I always strive to be honest with everyone, regardless of the risk that someone may one day take me seriously. His eyes follow a bead of sweat as it races down my throat and disappears between my breasts. I rest my palm on his hand, pulling it toward me slightly as I look deep into his brown eyes and say, "To be my sacrifice." I release his hand and sit back, the coolness of the chair startling my bare skin as I grin at his suspicious, squinting eyes, before they soften and he laughs outwardly.

He doesn't believe me.

Men. Always so gullible.

"Sure," he finally says as he digs beneath his Reaper robes and fishes out his cellphone. "But, you should know, I like to play rough."

Fantastic. I love a challenge.

I reach into my cleavage, remove my phone, and set it in the center of the table.

He hovers his phone beneath the table, smiles as his phone flashes in his lap, and a swooshing sound follows soon after. I drum my fingers, a seductive smirk playing on my lips, waiting for his photo to reach my cell. My phone vibrates against the table, and a quiet but audible ping alerts me that his image has arrived. I lift my phone, accept the image transfer and smirk at the dick pick on my screen. Even soft, it's a nice size. Here's to hoping it works without a little blue pill.

I tuck the phone back into my red lace bra, pluck a paper napkin from the dispenser on the table, and a two-inch pencil for playing the lottery from its holder. I scribble my address on the napkin and push it across the table to him. "Two conditions and one rule. Condition one, don't come until midnight, and two, come alone."

My dress rises higher as I scoot forward and stand, the slight hint of my red lace underwear peeking from between my legs as I stare down at him. He wraps his rough palms around both my thighs before grabbing my dress hem and tugging it down, glancing around to make sure no one else saw his soon-to-be prize. His eyes drift from the space between my legs to mine before asking, "And the one rule?"

I run my fingertips over his smooth, recently shaved bald head and say, "Don't knock."

Chapter Twenty-Seven
Waiting

An alert dings on my cellphone. I flip it over and tap the banner notification, alerting me that someone's been spotted. I touch my keypad to awaken my computer screen so I can see what's on the camera on a larger scale.

Here comes the Grim Reaper. Let's see how long it takes him to grow frustrated. I drum my nails on my maple desktop as he rings the doorbell. I can't help but chuckle as he adjusts his manhood, clearly uncomfortable and needing a release.

This won't take long.

He glances up at the camera in the corner and waves his hand in front of it. "Hello? I'm here." A car horn beeps as they pass, making him glance over his shoulder. He stares at my closed door with a tight-lipped look, deep in thought.

I hold my breath as his hand balls up, and he reaches over to knock, but stops midway, thinking better of it, remembering my rule.

A puff of dust floats away from my computer screen as I exhale my held breath and uncross my legs, leaning forward and zooming in on his grimacing face.

Just a little longer.

He presses the bell again and scans the front yard and driveway before rechecking the address I gave him.

"Fuck it," he finally says and steps off the porch.

Huh, I thought for sure I had that one.

He strolls away, tossing his Reaper robe hood off his head, making up his mind to leave.

Or so I thought.

He stops halfway down the sidewalk, and I pan the camera to his face as he cautiously turns toward my door. His mouth moves, but his words are indiscernible. Caught in an internal debate between what he wants and what he was told, he struggles to decide.

My desk chair squeaks as I rotate away from my computer, stand and make my way to the door with a spring in my step. I lean against the wall beside it and wait, tapping my painted nails on my crossed arms. The floor vibrates beneath my feet as he hops back on the porch, and the door rattles with an irritated knock.

That's a good boy. Come to mama.

I whip the door open and slide my right hand up the frame, cocking my hip sideways. "Tsk tsk." I wag my finger at him. "You broke the rule."

He reaches up, his Reaper robe sleeve sliding down, exposing a thorny tribal tattoo that wraps around his forearm, starting at his wrist and disappearing beneath his sleeve at the elbow. His fingers lightly touch the skin of my raised hand and seductively travel from the base of my thumb to my armpit, sending goosebumps across my flesh like a wave crashing to shore, before dropping his hand casually beside him. "What are you going to do about it?"

I snatch his robe quickly, twisting the front of it in my grasp, and yank him harshly into the room before slamming the door and locking it behind me. He smiles playfully, backing up carefully as I stalk toward him.

"I'm going to secure you to that altar behind you and torture you."

His head pivots toward the elevated wooden altar, its surface lit by candles, with chains and leather cuffs dangling over the edges. My wood-burning fire crackles over his shoulder, sending bright orange embers up into the chimney and waves of heat into the room.

Mastyx is here. I can feel his warmth through the flames of the fireplace. A few times, I've come home, and the fire was out, making my blood and body feel chilled to the bone. The room feels vacant and lonely when the fire isn't lit. It's our connection, mortal to immortal; his flame heats my flesh, igniting and fueling our contractual relationship. Without it, our bond may be severed.

There's a slight hesitation in the Reaper's mannerisms, in his movements, in his thoughts as he battles with his overwhelming desire to fuck me and the fear of me tying him down so he has no control. He turns to me, wanting to question me further about my plans, so I do what I always do: make my offer irresistible.

I reach up to my throat and unsnap my cape, letting it fall silently to the floor, kicking it aside with my heeled foot. Before he can open his mouth to speak, I grab the bottom hem of my vampire dress and pull it over my head, tossing my hair side to side before combing my fingers through my locks and resting them gingerly over my shoulder on one side. His jaw drops open, hanging slack like it's waiting for a fly to buzz in. I run my thumbs along the inside seam of my red lace bikini underwear, tugging them slightly down, revealing a fading tan line from summer. He approaches me with fire igniting in his eyes as he scans my body from my face to my toes and back again. "You're so fucking hot."

Hot? He has no idea what real heat feels like.

But he will.

I grab the zipper of his Reaper robe and tug it downward, listening to it click slowly, one tooth at a time, until it opens completely at the bottom, allowing him to pull it off, revealing his naked body underneath. I drag my painted nails over his chiseled, tattooed abdomen from his sternum down to his happy trail, leaving bright red streaks, marking my territory before twirling my fingers in the pubic hair just above his rock-hard, sizable cock as he groans.

He pushes his outfit against mine on the floor, slides his palm behind my neck, pulling me in closer and plants a harsh kiss on my lips.

Does he think this counts as being rough?

How boring.

I grab his face with both hands, crushing his cheeks with my palms and thrust him backward into the altar. He quickly grasps the wooden edge, stopping himself from falling to the black fuzzy rug beneath his feet. "Oh, we like it *really* rough, do we?"

My hand thrusts against his cock, gripping his shaft tightly as I squeeze and stroke it. His body bends back as he perches on his tiptoes, trying to escape my iron grip to no avail. "Easy now. Don't rip it off," he pants with heavy breaths as his ass slides up and across the surface of the altar.

"Lie down," I order, releasing my hold on him.

He does as he's told, as I reach to my Wiccan altar table at the head of the altar and gently stir the small batch of candy corn, still warm and melted in the copper Tree of Life-handled pot resting above the tealight candle. It swirls beneath my wax-seal spoon, its consistency smooth and ready to use.

"What's that?" he asks, sitting up on his elbows and trying to look behind him.

I press his forehead back against the altar with my pointer finger and rest my painted nail against his lips. "Shhh." I walk my fingers across his chest and down his arm. "Have you heard of wax play?" I ask as I gingerly grab his wrist and tighten the first restraint around it.

His eyes light up at the thought. "Oh, hell yeah. It's my jam."

Aren't I the lucky one?

I sway my head, moving it side to side to the quiet music of Bryce Savage playing in the background, humming along to Curiosity as I mosey to the opposite side of him and seize his wrist. He yanks back, pulling my hand against his chest and holding it there. "Don't hold back. I live for this shit."

As he releases my hand, a broad and sinister grin spreads across my face as I giggle and say, "Oh, don't worry, darling, once I begin, you will beg me to stop."

He chuckles as I grip his ankle and smirk at a tiny broken heart tattoo peeking just above his low-cut socks. Using the end of the altar for support, he kicks off his sneakers, letting them drop to the floor with a thud. I reach for his socks, and he pulls his foot away from me. "I got this." He takes his big toe, curls it inside the top of his sock, peels it off, and then repeats the same process with the other toe.

"Spread your legs wide," I say, planting both my palms on his thighs and tugging them harshly apart. He gasps as I wrap the leg restraint around his ankle, then glide over to the other one and do the same. I stare at him briefly before walking to the head of the altar and tossing a strap across his forehead, securing it to the other side, and forcing his head flat against the table, keeping him from moving.

His chest rises and falls rapidly as I shimmy out of my underwear and climb onto the altar, straddling his legs and pinning them down as I rub my bottom lip with my fingertip before tracing my finger down the front of me, my hand disappearing between my legs. I rub my pussy, moaning and rocking on his bare legs, feeling the moisture inside me building as I close my eyes and pleasure myself.

He shifts beneath me, and I force my eyes open, gazing down at him as I remove my fingers from inside me and slide them into my mouth. "Mmm, do you want to taste me?" I ask, my throat humming.

He nods rapidly. "Oh, fuck yeah," he says, opening his mouth wide.

I plant my hands firmly on his chest and scoot my pussy lips across his cock, inching my way over him, leaving a trail of moisture in my wake, until my ass sits almost on his neck, before lifting my body and lowering myself down on his face. His tongue plunges inside me, sending lightning through my thighs as it twirls about searching for the juices it longs for. I rock into his face, rubbing my clit across his nose as I lean fully forward, reaching for the handle of the pot above his head. I bring the hot candy corn closer, resting it just above his scalp on the altar as I slide backward off his face.

"What are you doing?" he asks, his face glistening. "I want you to bust in my mouth."

I grip his cock tightly, stroke it and press it inside me, forcing its entire length into me. His eyes roll back as I rock into him hard and relax, hard and relax, hard and relax until I feel the tell-tale tingle of my orgasm racing to the surface. "It's coming. Close your fucking eyes and open wide," I say as I continue rocking.

His eyes pinch close, and his mouth flies open, waiting to receive my pussy juices. I sit on his face, letting him taste me. It's something that I usually don't allow. Mastyx is the only one who is allowed to taste me—to eat me. But I'm caught up in the moment and press my luck, trying to have another man taste my pussy juices for the first time.

I slide off his face, his lips, and the area around his mouth, glistening with my fluids, his mouth still hanging open with a smile. I grip the pot of hot candy corn, plug his nose, and pour it into his open mouth. His eyes fly open as he tries to scream, but the molten candy bubbles in his throat, choking out his cries for help as it slowly begins to harden. I rest the pot back above his head, and lean forward, grabbing my wooden candle wick and plunging it in the center of his orifice, holding it there gently as it dries around it. Tears drain down both sides of his face as his body trembles beneath me. I grin broadly and say, "Now, you be a good boy and hold still. This will only hurt for a moment." I release the wick, grab my Jack Skellington Zippo from my table, and light the wick as I stare into his eyes, blown wide open in shock as he suffocates.

My pussy swells and tingles as I drop the Zippo and rub my clit in a circular motion, bursting onto his face as I cry out, "Oh, Mastyx, my incubus, I fucking need you. I call you here on Halloween night, beneath the light of the full moon. Come to me, my lover, accept this offering as a symbol of my devotion."

The fire flickers higher and brighter as my lover receives my message from the pits of hell. I grab the wax spoon, plunge it into the thickening candy corn, close the dead and empty eyes of the Reaper beneath me, and pour a spoonful onto each of his eyelids. A bubble rises and pops in the pot as I rest the spoon inside and pick up my wax stamp, pressing its golden end evenly into each of the Reaper's eye sockets, leaving the impression of a rose with a half skull peeking from its stem. I rest the stamp beside the pot of candy corn and smile down at my masterpiece—candle flickering inside his mouth, eyes sealed closed, soul ready to take when my lover makes his appearance.

I've had this planned for months, telling Mastyx that this night will be something special I've put together just for him, and I can't wait for him to see. The flickering flame inside the Reaper's mouth gives me another idea for a future art display. A jawbone candle holder. Yes, that will be lovely.

I swing my leg off the man beneath me and lower myself to the floor. It's funny how the sight of a dead man in the middle of my living room never gets old— another benefit of having no front windows. I shrug and saunter to my double bedroom doors, throwing them open and rattling their transparent windows. My fingers glide across my black satin comforter as I crawl across its cool surface, lie face down, and close my eyes with a smile.

Chapter Twenty-Eight
Mastyx

The room heats up as he manifests beside me. I don't move, don't open my eyes, don't breathe.

I'm still on my stomach, facing away from him on my bed. The floor creaks, and his footsteps grow distant as he walks away from me and into the living room.

A few seconds later, a whooshing sound tells me he's sucked out the soul of the Reaper on the altar, accepting my gift. The room grows eerily quiet, and the heat on my back feels like the scorching sun reflecting off the ocean on a blazing day. It's almost unbearable to the point where if I were on the beach, I'd have to go inside or take cover under an umbrella to avoid sun poisoning.

Only this isn't a poison affecting me, it's Mastyx, crawling onto the end of the bed. The heat from his body warms my feet, then my calves, and finally stops on my spine as he hovers over me. My shoulders tense up as his claws graze my bare flesh and drag their way from my upper spine down to my ass, where he squeezes my cheeks tightly, crushing them in his grasp before gripping my thighs and violently yanking my legs apart. "You've been a bad girl, my Little Sinner."

I gasp but don't move. He hates it when I try to squirm away from him. And by bad, does he mean like what I did was naughty by leaving him such an extravagant display, or is he referring to letting another man taste me?

I pinch my eyes tightly closed, not wanting to see his face—not wanting to know if he's speaking out of anger or lust. Although he wears the mask I bought for him, sometimes he keeps it off until he's finished having his fill of me.

The wet lash of his long tongue whips my spine, and I recoil against its sting as he licks his way over my ass and thrusts it inside my pussy. I creep forward, my toes digging into the mattress, trying to escape the burning pain and pleasure of his tongue swirling inside me, holding in my screams.

He snatches my hips, his sharp claws hooking into my skin and his hands scorching my flesh like leather seats on a hot summer day as he removes his tongue and says, "Keep still, my Little Sinner," he orders in a booming voice that sends chills down my spine and trembling through my core.

I bite my pillow as he rams his tongue back inside me, slurping and licking every inch of my insides that he can reach. He lifts my bottom off the bed and slowly pulls his tongue out of me as he pulls me upright, my spine against his chest, his hot cock pressing into the space between my legs, and murmurs in my ear, the heat from his breath like a furnace firing for the first time. "You're so fucking delicious. I could eat you every day for the rest of eternity and still feel famished."

My throat closes as he wraps his tongue around my neck, holding it firmly, and my pussy pulses with anticipation, dripping wet and ready for him. I gasp for air as he rams his hot cock inside me, sending my body upward like a fire was just lit beneath me.

I don't know how to describe how he feels inside me. If I tried, I'd say it would be a cross between orgasming and having your clit tattooed while getting railed by the best dick of your life. It's excruciatingly pleasurable in a vicious sort of way. I've grown accustomed to what to expect from him. Sometimes he's gentle, warm, loving and soft, kneading my body with his heat and pleasuring me for me. Other times, like this, when I've gone too far sexually with my sacrifice, he gets jealous, territorial, visceral. He doesn't like it when I share my juices with anyone else; they are for him and him alone.

I knew that before I sat on the Reaper's face, but in the moment, I didn't care.

Now, as my head grows dizzy, and I feel my strength fading, a wave of regret washes over me.

I relax my body, forcing him to hold me upright as he spills his hot lava inside me, coating my interior walls and singeing my tender lining with his soft flame, making it too painful to allow anything or anyone else to enter or touch it, even me. He releases me onto the bed; my body thoroughly soaked in sweat from his touch. I lie there, gulping precious air as his tongue recoils away from me. "You've been a naughty little freak." His tongue lashes hard against my ass like a whip, tearing my skin. Something wet trickles down the side of my ass cheek, and he swipes it with a clawed nail. He flips me over with both hands in one quick movement, so fast and sudden, my eyes flash open and lock in on his face as he straddles my thighs.

He's wearing the white death plague mask, his fiery eyes flaming with desire through it. His tongue slides out of the bottom of the half mask's narrow nose and extends to his long, pointed fingernail to lick the crimson from it.

My crimson.

I scan his muscular chest, so perfect, so flawless, and dig my nails into it, raking them down the front of him. He hisses as the wounds rip open and black fluid pours down the front of him, dripping on my stomach like melted onyx wax, setting my blood on fire with desire. He chuckles as the wounds close on their own and return to perfection. "Silly Little Sinner, you know you can't hurt me," he says as he rests the full weight of himself on top of me and heats his body to a barely tolerable burn. "But I can hurt you—kill you even."

I flicker my long lashes at him, staring right into his flaming eyes as I say, "But you won't, my love."

He huffs through his nostrils like an angry bull and runs his claws through my hair before wrapping it tightly around his fingers and holding my head firm as he takes the mask off with his free hand. I shut my eyes, not wanting to remember how he looks in his true form.

"Open your eyes," he orders.

I peel them open, and my breath quickens as his skeleton-like face stares back at me with red, bloodshot eyes, fire retreating behind them. "Kiss me, my Little Sinner. Not the masked man. Kiss me."

I steady my breathing, remembering how he makes me feel ninety percent of the time. This is my punishment for allowing my juices to flow into the Reaper's palate. I close my eyes and open my mouth, letting his massive tongue slither inside. I try to push his tongue back, keeping it from blocking my airway, but he wraps it around mine like he's twisting a cherry stem, holding it as it heats up, scorching the inside of my mouth. I scream inside my throat and buck beneath him, slapping and clawing his chest. He unwraps his tongue from mine, backs away from me, and stands.

I can't move. I mean, my eyes can, but that's it. I can barely talk or think. Every muscle in my body feels weighed down by some unseen force. It's like he's injected me with a paralytic.

He disappears, leaving me spread-eagled on the bed, helpless and unable to defend myself. Seconds later, he returns, the grisly skeleton face gone and now resembling the man I just killed, stealing his likeness to make me more comfortable. His body fully human now, he climbs back on the bed and kisses each of my breasts with tender lips, releasing me from my state of stasis. Every inch of me is on fire, burning like a blistering sunburn as he holds a bottle of green gel he grabbed from my refrigerator in one hand and squirts a large amount on my chest. It startles me with its cold as he rubs it gently across my skin, massaging my burns and blisters. He moans, his human cock rising, coming to life as he becomes aroused once more. "Oh, my Little Sinner, look what you do to me." I reach for his shaft, and he drops the aloe gel and grabs my wrists, forcing them above my head. His knee wedges between my legs, separating them quickly as he positions himself to enter me once more. "I'll be gentle," he whispers as he grabs the aloe gel, squirts it the length of his shaft, and slides it inside me.

A squeak escapes me, and I reflexively move away from his cock as the slow rhythm and chill of the aloe does little to kill the pain of the internal burns. He reaches beneath me with both hands, holding me tight against him, forcing himself further inside me and keeping me from pulling away again. I groan softly, starting to enjoy myself, when suddenly he stops and peers down at me. "Is this what you like?"

I nod my head, not thinking about the repercussions of enjoying him in human form—enjoying the memory of the Reaper inside me, tasting me.

His eyes turn black, and his human cock pulls back slightly as he roars, "Then let me give it to you as you deserve, my little whore."

Pain floods through me, shooting daggers into my abdomen as he forces himself hard and fast inside me. I grip the comforter beneath me, my heels digging into the mattress as I move my body back and away from him. He grips my shoulders, pulling me back to him as he rams me hard, too hard. Nausea creeps into my throat, and a sharp but brief pound from his cock makes me cry out for him to stop as he strikes my pubic bone, sending a crushing pain through it.

He stops. Without hesitation. Without a word. Without asking why. He knows my limits. If I tell him to stop, he knows I've had enough of this torturous game we play.

His eyes dart to mine. "You're mine and so is this." He grabs my pussy lips tight, crushing them in his grip. I wince as he glares at me. "Every ounce of your juices belongs to me, Little Sinner. Don't forget your place."

I nod, and he unfurls his clenched fingers from my pussy lips, letting the blood flow return to them.

My punishment could have been so much worse, but the benefits of our relationship outweigh the sin I've committed in his eyes.

He needs me, despite it all. I'm more of a benefit to him alive than in hell.

"I'm sorry. It won't happen again, " I say with a coy smile.

His eyes scan mine briefly before asking, "Would you like your treat, my love?"

I close my eyes, breathing heavily, trying to regain my composure. Everything inside and outside of me hurts. I want to crawl beneath my covers, curl up into a fetal position and sleep for a few days. Being the submissive of a sadistic incubus is exhausting, painful and intoxicating.

It's not like I don't deserve the punishment for what I did…what I've done. That's what brought him to me in the first place. Similar to the accident I caused, it felt great at the time, but the consequences after are like a recurring, torturous nightmare—the headaches, painful scar, and memories of that night, coupled with the searing burns of his touch and desire for me, blur everything together and somehow make me feel a small amount of absolution.

The sad thing is, I love it. I love the way he hurts me and cares for me when it's over. I love the way the pain brings me right back to the moment he sends an orgasm racing out of me. And although he terrifies me and I know at any moment he could decide to take me to hell for my sins, where I truly belong, I find it worth it to feel again, if only for a short while.

I clear my mind, wipe the moisture from my head, and force a smile, stretching beneath him, tucking my hands under my pillow with a satisfied grin, "Yes, please."

He kisses my abdomen, and the bed rises as he climbs off and saunters away, the tight ass of the Reaper looking back at me. Too bad Mastyx couldn't keep the body of anyone I offered him forever. He returns seconds later, sucking on a red, white, and blue Bomb Pop from my freezer, melting it partway. "Open wide, my love."

I spread my legs as he kneels on the bed and slides the popsicle inside me, moving it in and out of my traumatized pussy. I groan and rub my clit as he swirls it around and around, inside and outside of me, before plunging it back inside his mouth. "Mmm…it tastes so much better with you coating it."

He pushes it back inside me. "Now for the trick to your treat…making it disappear." I giggle as he uses his thumb to push the popsicle off the end of the stick, and it vanishes inside me. He tosses the wooden stick over his shoulder, spreads my lips apart with both hands, and dives between my legs, searching for the patriotic pussy pop that's already melted into me. I grip his bald head, wrap my legs around his back, and dig my heels into him, closing my eyes as I fall into the abyss of euphoria that only Mastyx can provide.

Chapter Twenty-Nine
Blisters

Pain draws me from a deep state of unconsciousness. I stare up at my ceiling fan, whipping faster than I have ever seen it. It wobbles unbalanced, ready to launch from the ceiling at any moment. Mastyx must have turned it on high before he retreated to the place he calls home.

Hell.

I've never been there myself; mortals aren't allowed. I can only imagine it. A place where fires burn constantly and sinners are tortured with red-hot chains thrashing across their backs as they maintain the hellscape. I roll to my side and sit up slowly on the edge of my bed, my head spinning, my body traumatized. Mastyx did a number on me this time. I touch the blistered handprints where he held my legs and shift the liquid inside the bubbles.

"Fuck," I murmur as I stand.

My legs fail me, and I drop harshly to the floor, my shin smashing into the sharp edge of the bed frame, splitting it open. "Son of a bitch," I yell, holding my knee to my chest and examining the cut on my shin as blood pools in the crack and trickles down my leg. "Grr," I grumble as I rock back and forth, covering the cut with my palm before forcing myself to a stand. My weak legs shake as I hobble to the bathroom, warm blood dripping down my shin to my foot, and sit on the edge of the tub. A blood trail dots the floor, leading from my bedroom into the bathroom. I reach up, slide the sage green hand towel off its ring and press it into the cut, keeping the pressure steady.

The cabinet beneath the sink creaks loudly on its hinges as I yank the door open and pull out the black wicker basket underneath with medical supplies. I paw through the pile of random wound care products, looking for the first-aid burn cream and Bacitracin I swiped from my parents' house when I visited last. My dad always has an ample supply of these things since my mom is clumsy as hell and always burns herself.

After successfully harvesting all the stems from an aloe within a month, my father decided to buy a supply of cream to keep on hand instead of further torturing the poor plant.

I dump the wicker basket by my feet and frown. I'm all out of burn cream. The scorched skin inside my mouth dangles from the roof, and my tongue stings with every bit of movement as I open and close my jaw. I guess it's ice chips and cold milk for breakfast.

My eyes flit to the living room visible through the open bathroom and bedroom doors. Sitting on the altar are the skinless remains of the Grim Reaper, his chest and stomach torn wide open. How kind of Mastyx to take all his skin off and remove his vital organs. All I have to do now is dispose of the meat-covered bones. I sigh heavily, peel open a large band-aid with my teeth, remove the tabs, and smear Bacitracin inside before sticking it over my cut. The wrappers crunch in my hand as I ball them up and toss them in the direction of the trash can. They float over the can, landing behind it in the corner. I shake my head. So, this is how my day's going to go?

I use the sink for leverage, stand and gasp at my reflection in the mirror above the vanity. My lips look like a child in the winter who's been licking them too much, and now they are red, blistered and peeling around their perimeter. A blistered red ring with purple bruises circles my neck, like a piece of jewelry, compliments of Mastyx's choking tongue wrapping around it, and the front of my chest is an angry shade of red from the heat of his body, scorching it slightly.

Damn it. I open the medicine cabinet, pull out the bottle of Percocet I was supposed to dispose of for my mother, toss a couple of the pills into my mouth, and turn the faucet on, sticking my mouth under the falling water to wash the pills down. They scrape their way through my swollen throat and land harshly in my empty stomach. I step back into my bedroom and examine my entire body in the full-length mirror.

My entire body is covered in first and second-degree burns. I turn around and peer over my shoulder. The back side of me looks similar to the front, except for a deep gash across my ass from Mastyx's tongue lashing it. I didn't realize how deeply the sharp edge of his tongue penetrated my flesh until now.

Fuck, fuck, fuck.

I'm going to have to go to the emergency room for that one. I can't exactly treat that with superficial cream, even if I had any. Thankfully, I took the week off from my job as a deli manager, so I have time to recoup.

I need to come up with a good cover story. How do I explain the burning gash across my ass? Did I back into a hot gas grill? That might work. It's not like I owe anyone an explanation. My eyes lock in on the aloe sitting nearly empty on my nightstand. I'm going to need to buy that stuff in bulk. I remove my plush robe from the hook beside my mirror, slide my arms in it carefully, and pull it over my shoulders before tying it loosely around my waist. My legs tremor as I enter the kitchen, reach under my island cabinet and get out the meat saw and a few heavy plastic drop cloths.

After spreading the drop cloths around the altar, I plug the saw in, grab the wrist of the Reaper, and make my first cut. Just over an hour later, I have the hands, feet, jaw, legs, which are each cut at the knee, and the arms ready for my beetle colony. The rest is in my freezer, ready when my bug babies need feeding again. Removing most of the flesh speeds up the cleaning process.

I fold the plastic around my first round of beetle food, grimace as I hoist it over my shoulder and carry it to the room that's supposed to be the pantry off the kitchen. Once inside, I pull the chain of the red bulb dangling above me, sending a soft, red glow into the room. The beetles don't care for bright lights; they startle and make them less inclined to eat. I remove the screened lid from each of the two massive plastic containers on the floor and slowly set the jaw, hands, and feet in one container and the legs and arms in the other. They scatter at first, then converge on their meal, diving in as it's been a week since I fed them last. I fill their quencher bowl, so they have plenty to wash down their meal, close their lids and head back to the altar. I drag the heavy torso through the kitchen and onto the back enclosed porch, where I keep my padlocked chest freezer. I unlock it and heave the skull-tattooed torso inside. I'm exhausted and my skin begs for treatment that I don't have, but I have to finish cleaning before I leave, so when I get home, I can collapse into a coma.

Another hour later, I'm partly pain-free, out of my robe, dressed in black sweatpants and a Metallica t-shirt, standing by the front door, staring into the living room where the altar glows before a low-burning flame from my fireplace. Everything appears clean and in order. It's not like I have any company; I never invite anyone here unless I plan to kill them. But just in case my parents come to visit unannounced, I want the house to look its best. They've given up on wondering why I don't have any furniture in my living room, just my Wiccan and *'massage tables'*. I tried to explain to them that having four barstools at my kitchen island is more than enough for entertaining. I wouldn't want anyone to get too comfortable. As far as they know, I do massages for extra cash at home, and that's why there are candles everywhere.

Satisfied, I lock my door and head to my car, where I climb inside and flop carelessly behind the wheel. My ass leaves the seat quickly as the stinging pain of the cut on my bottom, no doubt splitting open a little, sends a quick reminder. I swipe my butt with my hand, and a smear of red covers my palm when I look at it, the wound seeping through my sweats. I squeeze the steering wheel, whitening my knuckles and gritting my teeth as I lower my ass back down gently this time. A bead of sweat races down my temple and lands on my breast as I take a deep breath and blow it out, scattering dust particles across my dashboard.

The car glides backward down my driveway. I back blindly into the street and flash a quick smile at the neighbor who's now staring at me with her dog in her arms from the sidewalk, her horrified face letting me know I almost ran her and her tiny terror of a Chihuahua over as I drove backward without checking my mirrors first. I don't apologize, why would I, after all, being as she lets her little troll from hell shit in my yard and never cleans it up.

When I arrive at the emergency room ten minutes later, a screaming toddler's cries pierce my eardrums the minute the double doors open, and I step inside the crowded waiting room. The child's face is beet red, and she's pulling on her ear as big crocodile tears soak her face on her irritated mother's lap. I'm sure she's been waiting for hours.

I step up to the window of the reception area, where a woman, wearing all purple with a body resembling McDonald's Grimace, peers over her readers at me. "Can I help you?"

A nurse exits another set of doors holding a clipboard and shouts over the wails of the child, "Bianca Tremble."

The mother of the toddler sends a quick prayer to God at the ceiling and shuffles quickly across the speckled tile floors over to the nurse as the toddler throws herself backward, and the mother nearly drops her.

"I said, can I help you?" Grimace asks in a huffy voice, drawing my attention back to her.

Her glasses now dangle from a multicolored bead chain around her neck, stopping between her sagging boobs. I frown at her and say, "Yes, I have some first and second-degree burns I need to get medicine for and a wound I need to be checked out."

The woman stuffs a set of papers and clips a pen to the top of a clipboard, practically shoving it into my hand as she says, "Fill this out and bring it back to me when you're done."

I lean against a wall off to the side, as far away from as many germ-ridden patients as I can, and fill out the forms. It gets to the question of how the injury occurred, and I stop writing. Well, I can be honest, or I can lie as I planned. Fuck it. I'm sure they've seen a lot worse in this place. I write my answer neatly in cursive, excluding the part about my dominant being a demonic, sadistic incubus, sign my name at the bottom of the consent to treat, and take the clipboard back to the woman behind the glass. I slide it beneath the partition separating us, and she takes a quick look at it before setting it in a green sticker-marked holder on the wall to her left, color-coded by urgency, no doubt.

"Take a seat," she says to me, waving at a patient standing behind me, dismissing me and calling them to her, "Can I help you?"

Four hours later, a petite nurse, with a hint of amusement in her brown doe-like eyes, finally calls my name, "Contessa Salavatori?"

I never cared for my full name, especially knowing my parents chose it after a romantic trip to Venice, where I was conceived. Maybe if they had never told me that part of the story, I wouldn't mind, but knowing they named me an Italian name after a wild night in Italy made me cringe. Parents shouldn't tell their children *everything*.

When I stand, the nurse waves me into a sterile, clean-smelling room. She shakes her head, noticing the red ring around my neck that I hadn't bothered to hide, as she takes my blood pressure and checks my pulse before handing me a gown. The curtain clanks closed behind her as she exits without a word, giving me privacy. I kick off my black Nike sandals, carefully slide down my sweatpants, underwear, and all, and toss them on the bed in front of me. I don't need to remove my shirt, because my issue is mainly from the waist down, but what the hell, I was already honest on the forms, I might as well let the doctor see everything.

Chapter Thirty
Unclean Thoughts

The nurse peeks around the curtain as I sit carefully on the bed and asks, "A first-year resident is available to see you now if you don't mind."

They have to get their training somehow. "It's fine," I say, shrugging.

She disappears behind the curtain, and a sudden feeling comes over me as feet appear beneath the curtain. It's not the well-shined shoes and their expansive size that trouble me; it's the hesitation. Just come in already, I think to myself, growing impatient as the pain medicine slowly wears off.

A short sigh is audible through the curtain right before it moves aside, revealing a Godlike creature unlike any other.

Man, I thought David was hot, but this man looks like he should be on the Times Sexiest Man Alive cover.

His kind eyes are bright blue orbs beneath long lashes that stand out even more against his jet-black hair and slightly tanned skin. I can't help but find myself getting lost inside his baby blues. They are like magnificent galaxies that only exist in stories and dreams. He can't be much older than me, twenty-five at the most, but at least a whole foot taller.

The nurse steps between us, blocking my view and breaking the eye contact that the doctor and I are currently locked in. Something inside me senses her jealousy. Perhaps they are in a casual relationship, and she's trying to protect what she perceives as her territory. I send her a warning look that says, 'get the fuck out of the way, you're blocking my eye candy.' The nurse seems unfazed as she shifts aside and leans against the wall, arms crossed, supervising.

The Godly-looking man extends his hand to me, revealing a hint of a tattoo I can't make out beneath the sleeve of his white lab coat. "I apologize for the wait, Miss Salavatori. I'm Dr. Joshua Zuniga, but you can call me Dr. Z."

I take his hand in mine, and his touch is magnetic as we shake hands, formally meeting for the first time. It's a strange feeling when you hold the hand of a stranger, yet you have the peculiar desire never to let them go. I can't look away from him. It's like one of those circus tents you pay to enter to see the wonders of the world. I shouldn't go inside, but I can't help it, I'm curious.

The nurse clears her throat, and Dr. Z and I blink several times, breaking our eye contact as she reminds him to let go of my hand and not linger too long. Wouldn't want anyone to think he was making inappropriate contact with his patient. Although I certainly wouldn't mind.

As his hand falls to his side, I look away from him, not wanting him to see how ashamed I am of what he's about to see. I shouldn't feel this way. I have never experienced this feeling before, so I'm not sure what it is about him that's making me so self-conscious. I think about leaving, just grabbing my clothes and running out the door, but I need treatment, so I have no choice but to stay. Usually, I just let the doctors examine me and listen to their lectures about safety and being more careful. *Your skin is the body's largest organ, so you need to take care of it*, they say. But this time, with Dr. Z, it's different. We have a connection; I can feel it pulling me toward him.

He holds the clipboard containing my information closer to his face and scans through it before setting it on the portable table beside the bed. "Contessa, show me where he hurt you."

I gaze up at him, confused by his statement. He not only addressed me by my first name, but he also didn't ask me to show him my wounds or where I'm injured. He asked me to show him where *he hurt* me. Was I too honest on the form I filled out? Did I mention it was a man who did this to me, because it could have easily been a woman, too? I can no longer remember exactly what I wrote.

The nurse steps away from the crisp, white wall. "If you aren't comfortable showing him, I can have a female doctor come in, but you'll need to wait for her to be free."

"No," I say abruptly, surprising myself. "It's okay. And it's Tessa," I say, correcting him. "I don't want to wait anymore." The bed rises as I come to a slow stand and turn around, letting the back of the baby blue gown I never tied fall open, revealing everything from my neck down to my heels to Dr. Z.

The nurse pulls a pair of large, purple gloves from an array of sizes and moves out of my line of sight, standing behind me with the doctor. The gloves snap against his hands as he puts them on, and his breath moves the fine hair on my back as he sighs. "I'm going to touch you, is that okay?" he asks in a calm and reassuring tone.

"Yes," I murmur.

There's a delay before he touches me, almost like he's afraid or worried he's going to hurt me. After several seconds, he finally says, "Ready, Tessa?"

His voice and the way he utters my name in a deep, low, reassuring growl make my toes curl, and my heart flutter. I close my eyes, feeling my body go from tense to relaxed, and nod my head, giving him the go-ahead to touch me. And with my next breath, his fingers touch my bottom, examining the gash across my ass cheek. I try to hold still, try to let him touch me as much as possible, not only because I want him to, but so he can do his examination as thoroughly as possible, but when he places a second hand on my backside and spreads the wound slightly to check its depth, my butt cheeks clench together.

I recoil away from him, turning around quickly to face him, my eyes welling with tears. The pain of his touch, sending me right back to the minute Mastyx lashed his tongue through me, cutting me open.

He holds his hands up in front of him and takes a step away from me, giving me space and a moment to collect myself. His eyes are glossy and full of remorse as he says, "I'm sorry. I didn't mean to hurt you; I need to examine how deep and damaged the tissue is to see if it needs debridement."

The nurse stands before me, hands on her hips. "Why? Why in the hell would you let it go this far? Don't you and your man have a safe word? I know I have one, and I use it all the time."

"Angela, don't," Dr. Z says, glaring at her for oversharing as he moves her aside and comes closer to me, continuing a visual exam without touching me. He puts his hands in front of my face and slowly brings them to my neck, gently touching the bruised, red rings around them. "Can you swallow for me?"

I swallow hard, and he nods before saying, "Open your mouth." He pulls a pen light out of his front pocket as I open my mouth slowly, a single tear sliding down my cheek as the corners of my mouth, dry and blistered, crack and bleed.

The nurse peeks around the doctor's arm and looks inside my mouth as he slowly withdraws the pen light and turns away from me. "Jesus, even the inside of your mouth is burned. Like, how does that even happen? Let alone the perfectly burned handprints on your thighs? What did the guy do, wear metal gloves heated over an open flame to torture you?"

"Angela, that's enough," Dr. Z says sharply, his face growing dark and irritated. "She doesn't have to explain the who, what, and why if she chooses not to. She's here for treatment, not to be interrogated or judged."

The nurse puts her hands up and steps back against the wall. Dr. Z's face slowly changes from angry to soft and caring. He pulls a couple of tissues from the box beside me and hands them to me before saying, "I'm going to have another nurse come in and dress the wound on your buttock and then come back in and speak with you. It's too wide for glue and not deep enough for stitches, so I'll have her clean it, apply cream, and put a bandage on it."

I dab my eyes gently and wad the tissues in my grasp, holding them tightly.

Dr. Z keeps his eyes on me, pulls the gloves off his hands, tosses them in the trash beside Nurse Angela, and looks at her before saying, "Outside, now."

Her face pales at once. She looks at him, at me, and then back to him, before nodding her head and moving the curtain aside, disappearing behind it, leaving Dr. Z and me alone. He rests his hands gently on my shoulder, his thumb grazing it softly. "I'm sorry about her. She thinks she owns everything in this building."

I smile softly up at him and say sarcastically, "Including you, I guess."

He lets his hand fall away from my shoulder and says firmly, "No one owns me."

I grip the back of my gown, holding the sides together behind my back with one hand. "Must be nice."

A breeze floats over my barely covered backside when I turn away from him.

"Don't move," he orders, making me freeze in place. "Let me help you."

Help me? Help me with what, my sadistic incubus boyfriend? That'll never happen.

"With what?" I ask shyly.

His feet shuffle against the tile as he steps closer to me, the scent of mild cologne filtering into my nostrils. "With your gown." He grips the strings around my neck and ties them loosely before stepping backward and asking, "Is there something else I can help you with?"

I turn on my heel to face him, and I can't tell whether he means medical or something else. God, I want to touch him in so many ways. He has to feel it too, how can he not? I open my mouth to reply when the curtain clanks open.

"Are you coming? You have another patient to see in the next room?" Angela asks hurriedly.

Without looking away from me, he answers, "I'll be right there." He picks up the clipboard with my information on it and tucks it under his arm before vanishing behind the striped curtain.

I release a long-winded breath, I didn't realize I was holding before sitting gently down on the side of the bed, listening to the cheap wall clock tick with every second that passes.

It feels like forever for a different nurse to come back and dress my wound. After she finishes taping a gauze dressing on my buttocks, she plasters ointment on my neck, the various blisters and red marks on my body I can't reach and then passes me the rest of the tube to spread the treatment on the places I can. After she leaves, I get dressed, take the edge of the curtain and move it aside, so they know I'm decent, and jump back when I nearly collide with Dr. Z's chest.

He doesn't move, our closeness making my heart skip a beat. He holds a bag in his hand in front of him, separating our bodies slightly, his eyes gazing intensely into mine. I back up into the room, putting some space between us. He walks forward, closing the gap, staring at me, his mouth partly open as though he forgot why he's standing before me holding a white plastic bag filled with supplies.

The nurse who dressed my wounds enters and advises Dr. Z that his other patient has returned from

X-ray and is ready to be seen. He clears his throat, glancing away from me briefly to thank the nurse before turning his attention back to me. "After speaking to the attending physician about your injuries and my findings, the best course of treatment for your burns is Silvadene ointment used twice daily. As for the wound on your backside, it's not deep enough to need debridement, but you need to have it reexamined in a few days to make sure it's not getting infected and is healing. You can't get a clear view of it in its current location. Keep it covered and change the gauze as needed. Take showers instead of baths for now. Is there someone at home or someone you can call that you're comfortable with who can check it in a few days to make sure it's not infected?"

That I'm *comfortable* with. The way he said it tells me he's concerned about me, which I understand. I shake my head, because who am I going to call? My mom? My dad?

He extends the bag to me, and I take it as he removes a business card from his front pocket and passes it to me. "Take this. It has my number and extension here at the hospital. Call and leave me a message in a couple of days, and we can arrange a quick recheck here in the ER of your wound without you having to wait for hours."

I take the card, my fingers grazing his as I slide it away from him and tuck it into the pocket of my sweatpants. "Thank you," I say softly as I tilt my head down and stare at the floor between us.

There's something about him that makes me feel intimidated and shy, which isn't like me, and I'm not sure how to act around him. A part of me wants to bury my face in his chest and beg him to help me, and the other part wants to stay far away from him. I glance up at him, my eyes staring at his lips as he licks them and swipes them with his thumb. I look away, wishing my life weren't so complicated and that I was deserving of such a handsome creature.

"Contessa," he says barely above a whisper, causing me to look up at him.

Usually, I get irritated if, after I tell someone to call me Tessa, they still call me Contessa, but not with him. When he says it, it sounds seductive and eerily natural, almost like I've heard him say my name many times before, which is impossible under the circumstances.

He takes a small step back as the nurse reenters the room, checking the status of my discharge so he can move on to the next patient. He smiles down at me and says, "If there's anything else, anything at all we can do to help you, call or come back, okay?"

His eyes, so honest, so humble, so sexy. I quickly look away from him. A shudder travels through me, making me outwardly tremble.

"Contessa, are you alright?" Heat rises in my cheeks as he reaches for me, sending a wave of passion and desire to my core.

What the fuck is wrong with me? If Mastyx found out I had these thoughts about someone, he'd be furious.

"Thank you," I say again, without looking at him, pushing all the thoughts and how he makes me feel out of my head and quickly moving around him, my sandals squeaking loudly.

I make my way to the exit, my body screaming, needing to go home and plaster more of the medicine samples Dr. Z gave me on my skin. The nurse put on an ample amount, but I feel like the more I have on, the better.

Dr. Z's face flashes through my head, his eyes full of concern and those soft, inviting lips begging to be kissed. I find it hard not to think about him.

Fuck. I shake my head rapidly and take a deep breath, pushing him out of my head once more.

Outside, as I approach my vehicle, a man walks toward me, flicking his lighter to light his cigarette. He tries again after the first flick fails to ignite. Without warning, the fire from the lighter shoots straight up, higher than his head, lighting his face up orange.

He quickly tosses the lighter away and yells, "What the fuck."

I stand there, dumbfounded, staring at the lighter on the ground and the flame still burning high above it. The man shakes his head at me, walks past, and heads for the emergency entrance. My chest heaves, my breathing growing rapid. The lighter's flames grow higher, as if someone is forcing all the flammable fluid into its wick, fueling the flame's height and sending a message.

Sending me a message.

My thoughts turn to Mastyx, and I wonder if he somehow heard my thoughts about Dr. Z and is now sending me a quick reminder of what awaits me if I cross or betray him. Perhaps it's just a coincidence, and I'm overreacting. I exhale loudly, clench the hospital bag tighter in my grasp and move cautiously toward the flame that stands between myself and my car.

As I close in on the flame, it slowly grows smaller and smaller until, finally, it puffs out its last spark and dies.

I stop in front of it and whisper, "Mastyx?" not wanting anyone to hear me talking to a lighter on the pavement.

Nothing. No high flame rekindling, no sparks, just a dead lighter, resting on the blacktop of the hospital parking lot. I return to my car, unlock the doors, and sit softly in my seat, closing the door behind me.

It's hot for the first day of November. Sweat rapidly beads on my skin as I sit in my car, seemingly stuck in the moment. I blink several times, exhaustion overwhelming me, and dismiss any thoughts of Mastyx's presence playing a part in the lighter fiasco. My key ring rattles against the steering column as I insert the car key into the ignition and turn it. The radio blasts Evenspeak's Little Sinner at full capacity, and the heat in the car suddenly rages at top speed into my face. I quickly cover my ears, muffling the blaring music, before frantically reaching for the volume and heat dials and twisting them off.

My heart pounds hard in my chest and blood races through me, sending violent tremors to every part of my being.

He's here. I tuck a wayward lock of hair behind my ear with a trembling hand, before gripping the steering wheel tightly, my eyes wide with shock.

The window beside me rattles with an insistent knock, making me jump and grab my chest. I twist my neck to face the window and gaze up at Dr. Z, who's no longer wearing his lab coat, carrying a leather bag over his shoulder.

"Are you okay?" he asks, his voice muffled by the partition dividing us.

I don't answer. I put the car in reverse, speed backward, crank the wheel, put the car in drive, and slam my foot on the gas, sending the vehicle flying out of the parking lot and into the street, just missing a man walking to the cancer clinic across the street. He's waving his cane at me when I peer into the rearview mirror.

The car in front of me stops abruptly at the red light, and my foot slams the brake to the floor so I don't rear-end them. Another vehicle pulls up to my right in the turning lane, their window rolled down, their head bobbing as they play drums on their steering wheel to Highway to Hell by AC/DC.

Message received.

Mastyx has made it clear to me that the next time he sees me, our encounter won't be a pleasant one. Perhaps I'll stay awake for the next several full moons and not call him to me with any sacrifices. Full Moons are the only time he can visit me freely. Although incubus demons can only have sex with sleeping women, our relationship is a little different compared to most. We have a contract, one that, if I break, I will receive the punishment I deserved years ago.

A one-way ticket straight to hell.

I can't move.

Not because Mastyx is punishing me for my lust toward another man, but because I collapsed in bed when I came home from the hospital on my stomach, and my neck was propped awkwardly on my pillow, rendering everything from the neck down useless until I can un-contort my head from this painful, distorted position. I take my hand and move it to my face, where I push my head back in alignment with my spine and press my hands into the mattress, forcing myself onto my hands and knees, my body groaning with every muscle I flex. I sit on all fours, like I'm waiting to get railed from behind and rock my body to and fro, loosening my tight and uncooperative muscles.

Jesus. I'm a mess, I think as I slide a foot off the mattress and onto the floor. Surprisingly, my legs cooperate and let me stand without failing. I stagger to the kitchen, take a couple more Percocet and two Tylenol, wash them down with a half-drunk bottle of water I left on my butcher block counter, and wander to the pantry. The beetles make occasional noises, but for the most part, they eat their feast in the quiet solace of their dark totes. I yank the chain dangling above me, kneel slowly to the floor, and peek inside my beetle colonies' habitat, one, and then the other. The bones are nearly picked clean. It won't be long now. I close the lids to the beetles' house and meander to the kitchen. I yank the fridge door open, gazing inside—orange cream wine coolers and milk.

Well, milk doesn't sound as good as a wine cooler at the moment, so I grab a cold cooler and head to my office, where the six-foot table that sits across from my office desk waits for me to plant my ass on the stool and start building my creations. The stool creaks as I sit carefully and twist my body toward my four-drawer, plastic tower, pulling out a few cedar planks from one drawer, glue from the next, and dirt from the bottom. I spread out an array of moss and small plants that have been propagating in water onto the tabletop and select a small black nursery pot.

In my mind, I envision how I want this piece of wall art to look. The centerpiece will be the Reaper's jaw, with the plastic pot resting on its side, a variegated string-of-hearts plant pouring from its center. Around the jaw, an array of dried flowers and bright green moss that have been treated with glycerin for preservation. I'll leave the edges clean, so the cedar acts as a frame around it. Originally, I planned to do a candle but decided against it. Plants look more pleasing to the eye.

I pick up my ruler and pencil and draw straight lines one inch inside the perimeter on all four sides. These lines will be the edge of the moss once it's time to place it carefully. I still have to clean the bones I'm using with hydrogen peroxide and water to make them nice and white, which takes about twenty-four hours, but I have time.

I always take extra time off for the annual Oddities Market in Downtown. It always falls on the first Sunday after Halloween, which is convenient for disposing of body parts. No one bats an eye at the bones in my art. Other people use animals, and I create a few pieces with those as well, but now I prefer to work with human bones.

After measuring the bottom of the plastic nursery pot, I pick up my hole saw and install the bit that's slightly larger than the hole I need. This will allow the pot to sit partially inside the hole. Because a string of hearts doesn't need to be watered too often, the buyer must take the art piece down every one to two weeks in the summer or every three to four weeks in the winter and thoroughly water the little pot over the sink. Once it stops dripping, they hang it back on the wall in their house, which receives direct sunlight for part of the day. The variegated string of hearts features dashes of pink and purple, along with white and green, making it an excellent centerpiece for the dried baby's breath and the scattered pink and purple pansies.

Now that the square cedar plank is adequately prepared, I move on to the round piece of cedar. This one is a foot in diameter and will make the perfect centerpiece for a table. I take a nine-inch-high, four-inch-round vase and gently place it in the middle. The sizing is ideal, leaving a four-inch work space around the perimeter of the glass. I grab my clear epoxy Gorilla Glue, lift the vase from the center of the plank, squeeze the goop in a spiral pattern from the center, radiating outward, and quickly press the vase into the plank. Now I'll let that sit for twenty-four hours to ensure the vase is thoroughly attached before I start adding dried flowers to the perimeter. The Reaper's hand bones will be wrapped neatly around the glass vase, and once it's ready, I can fill it with spring water and plop in the peace lily plant that has been sitting in water.

Two days and several energy drinks later, I have several large and small pieces pre-made, ready for when the bones are ready to be mounted. I grab my brown price tags by their jute strings and lay them out before me. The cost of purchasing real human bones is exponential, so my prices are high, too high for some people's wallets, but I have a few loyal clients who are always looking for unique items they find worth the cost. The human hand vase will be priced the highest, and the jawbone piece will be mid-range. Everything I carry under $100 is made of animal bones only. Occasionally, I'll create a special piece using small pieces of human vertebrae, but it's rare.

My phone vibrates on my desk. I rotate away from my workstation and roll over to view the screen.

Unknown number.

I don't answer those, so that little mystery will go unsolved. I roll back to my workstation and begin the task of cleaning up my workspace. Once I remove the bones from the beetle colony, I'll place them in the hydrogen peroxide bath I've prepared and let them sit overnight to whiten. Then I'll submerge them in a sink filled with warm water and Dawn dish soap to remove the peroxide smell. Once they dry, I can glue all the human parts onto their pre-made planks and pack the pieces neatly in boxes to take them to the market.

My phone vibrates again. I stand from my chair, remove my rubber gloves and gaze at the screen.

Private number.

Still not answering. Bill collectors will try anything to get you to answer the phone.

The doorbell rings as I step out of the room to empty my trash in the kitchen. I freeze in place and turn my head slowly to the Felix the Cat clock ticking loudly on the wall, his tail and eyes swinging back and forth. It's seven in the evening. Not too late for visitors, but later than my parents would arrive if they dropped in unannounced. I walk back into the office and peer at the computer screen. Staring up at the camera on the front porch are the bright blue eyes of Dr. Z. He's wearing gray jogging bottoms and a University of South Carolina t-shirt. He looks away from the camera and rests his hands on his hips, twisting his waist back and forth as if he's stretching his lower back muscles. His cock stands out like a sore thumb from his gray sweats, making it difficult not to notice its size.

He rings the doorbell again. A part of me wants to answer, and another part of me is afraid.

But why is he here? Did I forget something at the hospital?

I glance down at my attire. I've been wearing the same Courage the Cowardly Dog shirt for two days and haven't showered either. There are even Cheeto crumbs on my pink shorts. Once I get in the zone, everything, including hygiene, tends to take a backseat.

I take my hands, quickly swipe the orange specks off my shorts and amble toward the front door. In my head, all I can think is don't fucking knock, don't fucking knock. It's my only rule, and if he breaks it and I don't follow through with his sacrifice, Mastyx will know I feel something for this man I barely know.

The minute my bare foot slaps the floor in the living room, the flames of the fireplace grow high and hot, making me stop dead. My core trembles relentlessly. I take a step back from the front door, and the flames die down to barely a visible flame where they once were. The pulse in my neck pounds as the doorbell chimes again and the faint voice of Dr. Z. calls out, "Miss Salavatori?"

I can't move; fear keeps me from taking another step, but I have to. I have to save him. The flame in the fire rises and lowers rhythmically as if being fueled by Mastyx's breathing.

My head snaps in the direction of the office as my phone vibrates off the desk and bounces noisily onto the floor. It has to be Dr. Z.

The flames of the fire burn lower and lower, indicating Mastyx may be retreating to the Earth's core, where hell awaits. I straighten my t-shirt, take a deep breath, and take two quick steps toward the door. The flames of the fire grow high, and this time, a hot, flaming tongue lashes out of the fire and singes the floor inches from my black-painted toes. I curl my toes under as the tongue slowly recedes behind the fireplace flames. Mastyx can't come into the human world without being summoned by me, but he can use fire to send me a message, one that again I just received loud and clear. I step slowly away from the charred mark on my hardwood floors where his tongue scorched the wood.

The doorbell rings again.

I know what Mastyx is doing. He's trying to keep me from the door, hoping the doctor will knock. I close my eyes and chant internally for the doctor to go away. I go back into my office and close the door. The doorbell sounds louder for some reason. Perhaps it's Mastyx taunting me to try and answer again. I cover my ears and glance at the computer screen. Dr. Z steps off the porch, one hand in his pocket and the other holding his phone to his ear.

The hardwood vibrates beneath my foot as a private number pops up on my phone, still resting face up on the floor. I squat down to pick it up, and the lightbulb in my desk lamp pops violently, shattering across my desk and keyboard, making me leap away from it and fall to the floor, landing on my ass. I sit on my bottom, my breathing rapid in the dark, my heart racing, stunned.

The phone switches to voicemail and goes dark. I peer up at the computer screen, the only source of light left in the room, and there's no one there. The doctor has vacated the premises and not knocked.

Safe for now.

The computer screen goes black before the white bouncing ball of my screensaver kicks in and bounces around the screen. I wrap my arms around my knees and draw my legs up against my chest, taking several deep breaths in and out to steady my racing heart. Several minutes go by before I feel brave enough to

stand. Although there is nothing with me in the dark—
no rising flames, no Mastyx—I find it eerily quiet; too
quiet, as if all sounds have been sucked out of the room
so Mastyx can not only hear me breathe, but he can also
hear my heart go from pounding to a barely audible
thump.

I exhale loudly and grip the edge of the desk with one
hand, then pick up my phone from the floor with the
other before pulling myself upright.

My phone vibrates and lights up, the banner across
the top letting me know I have a new voicemail. I tap
the banner and read the message Dr. Z left me.

*Miss Salavatori, I apologize for stopping by unannounced. I
haven't heard from you to recheck your wound and grew concerned.
Please call the hospital and schedule a recheck appointment.*

There's a noticeable pause, as if he's contemplating
his next few words.

*Also, I don't know what made you take off so quickly when
you saw me in the parking lot, but rest assured, I never meant to
scare you. If it was something, or someone else who frightened you,
I…I mean, we…the hospital has resources available to you.
Umm, have a good day.*

Click.

*Something or someone else…*The doctor is on to
something. It's something more than someone who
frightened me. I leave the phone on my desk and head
into the living room, where the fire is barely lit, the

wood inside glowing a bright, reddish-orange; the intensity waxes and wanes, as if it's asleep and breathing peacefully.

As I pass the front door, heading to the closet to retrieve my foldable wagon to put in my car for the market, the door rattles with an unnerving knock. I freeze, my hand extended to the closet door handle, my head cranking slowly to the heavy partition separating me and whoever is on the other side. It rattles again, the knocker not giving up on someone answering. I peer over my shoulder at the fireplace.

Nothing, no high flames, no lashing tongue, and I crank my neck further toward the office, considering if I should look before I open the door. If it's the doctor and I try to answer, Mastyx will stop me. My hand falls away from the closet door as I turn my body in the direction of the front door, take a deep breath, quickly jog over, and yank open the door with the next persistent knock.

A heavy sigh of relief floats down and shifts the hair of the little boy in uniform, who is holding an order form with both hands and staring up at me. Behind him, standing on the sidewalk, is his mother, her arms folded, the toe of her blue canvas sneaker tapping on the ground, and an impatient look on her face. When the little blonde boy looks back at her, she unfolds her arms and says, "Go on. Ask her."

The boy peers back at me, then immediately stares at his feet as he quietly says, "I'm selling popcorn for Boy Scouts. Would you like to order some?"

"Of course I do," I say with a shaky smile, taking the order form and paper from him. I fill in the line for four boxes of salted caramel corn for my dad, who loves it, and select a kettle corn for me before handing the form back to the boy. "Give me one moment, let me grab some money for you."

Paying $100 for five boxes of popcorn may seem ridiculous, but I remember when I was little and in Girl Scouts. Having so many doors slammed in my face and so many rejections made me feel as if it were my fault. But when just one person places a significant order with you, it makes you feel worthy and successful.

When I return to the door, the boy is smiling up at his mother, who is also smiling. My guess is they've been at it for a while with little to no orders. Now maybe they can go home. I stand in the doorway, holding the money out to the little boy who eagerly scales the steps, grabs it and shoves it into a manila envelope with a glowing smile. He thanks me confidently and leaps off the porch, running to his mother, who has already proceeded down the sidewalk without a word to me.

As the door clicks quietly closed behind me, my eyes get stuck on the low fire that has rekindled in my absence. It slowly grows higher and higher as Mastyx calls to me, eagerly needing to see me in person.

He wants to hurt me, punish me for my thoughts and my desire to save the doctor's life. The contract between us allows him to see me only when there's a full moon; otherwise, my sacrifices to him and my decision to bring him to me are my own, not his. And right now, after what he pulled today, I chose to let him stew until the next full moon to see me. Like the doctor's calls and the bell he rang to summon me to answer my door, Mastyx's messages and requests for my company will go unanswered.

I know I will regret this decision, and the pain that awaits me with the next full moon will be significant and unrelenting, but to me, it's worth it to show him that despite being his submissive, I still have some control over my life. At least, I think I do as I enter the living room and lean against my sacrificial altar, staring inside the fireplace.

The small flame inside suddenly vanishes, the fire burning out completely, no glowing embers, no smoke, nothing. It's fully extinguished. An emptiness grips me that I didn't expect.

I kneel before the dark, porous wood and poke it with the fire iron.

Nothing. Not even a hint of heat remains. I reach in and touch the burnt wood, and it's cold to the touch as if it were never lit. He's gone. Mastyx is gone. I sit back on my heels and stare into the darkness before me, a smile creeping across my face.

Perhaps he read my mind and is backing off, worried he won't get any extra sacrifices or visits from me. I don't feel him or sense his presence, releasing a build of anxiety that has been festering inside me. My stomach unclenches, relaxing into this unexpected feeling of freedom. I rock my head back and forth, my smile broadening, before my face grows serious. My feelings are my own, and Mastyx can't force me not to have them.

"I control my feelings, not you," I say with newfound confidence to the dead space between me and the soot covering the brick back of my fireplace, knowing he can't hear me.

There's a brief moment of peace that quickly succumbs to dread that overwhelms me. I exhale a staggering breath, and fog escapes my mouth as the room turns stone cold, casting goosebumps across every inch of me. My face prickles and drains of color as flaming clawed hands launch from the fireplace, trying to grab me. I leap back, scream, and turn to run, but a fiery grip tightens around my calves, singeing my skin and dropping me face-first onto the hard floor.

Metallic liquid fills my palate, and I swallow it down before digging my nails into the hardwood, splitting and breaking them as I gouge it frantically.

Mastyx's tongue tangles around my throat, cutting off my airway and silencing my desperate cries for help. His flaming body drops on top of mine, singeing my spine through my clothing. I thrash beneath him, frantically trying to escape his grasp.

My feet, then my legs, heat up as he drags me backward into the flames of hell, where the fire consumes me until there is nothing left. Nothing but darkness and silence.

Chapter Thirty-Two
Falling

I'm falling, and he's letting me, the fire down below growing closer by the second—the walls around me, black with grooves leaching lava.

What was I thinking, running my mouth as if I actually have control over my life? I scream at Mastyx, "Please, stop. I'm sorry." Tears sting my cheeks.

He shrieks above me, "Don't forget, you belong to me, my Little Sinner."

My back arches beneath the painful slap of multiple sharp objects digging into my spine like glass. Without warning, my direction changes from heading toward the flames of hell to a bright light.

I pinch my eyes closed, the brightness burning my orbs. A diabolical, low, throaty laugh echoes around me and slowly fades. A beeping noise forces my eyes open right before I slam to the floor beside my bed, sending a lightning-like pain scorching through my arm. I roll onto my back, the pulsating throb in my appendage making me cry out.

"Fuck," I murmur and blink away the tears blurring my vision.

My phone alarm blares above me from the nightstand. I reach over my head, slide it off the surface and turn it off.

The back of my shirt is wet and sticky. It makes sense after the nightmare I just had. I turn my head and gawk at my forearm. It's twice the size it should be. I can't believe this. I haven't fallen out of bed since I was eight and dreamed that I fell off my bike and woke up on my bedroom floor. At least back then, it was carpeted, and the distance I fell wasn't as high. I roll onto my side and sit up, wincing as a painful burning spreads across my spine.

I twist my face in confusion. My head spins along with the room as dizziness takes over.

"No," I say aloud to my empty room. "It was just a bad dream."

The mattress sinks as I press the top of it and push myself to a stand, my legs like jelly, wiggling. I stagger across the room, stand in front of my mirror and slowly turn around. Blood spots stain the back of my Courage the Cowardly Dog shirt, where Mastyx grabbed me with his razor-sharp talons and redirected me.

It was real.

He dragged me to hell, and before I fell into the bottom of the flaming pit, he snatched me up and threw me back to the world of the living.

I drop to my knees and stare at my distraught reflection, my face red with anger and slightly burned by hell's heat. He's teaching me a lesson, a lesson of critical importance, a reminder that he can take me at any time, for any reason, per our contract.

I'm his. He owns me.

For the last five years, our relationship hasn't been perfect, but given who he is, what he is, things could be so much worse. He saved my life, and I owe him my unwavering devotion and loyalty. But as my arm throbs and my back stings, all I can think about is Dr. Z.

Mastyx has made it clear to me that I'm not to have contact with or even think about him. But how? My arm is clearly broken and needs to be casted.

I wipe the moisture from my face, rise and pick up my phone. It's only 9:00 a.m., and I'm broken, burned, and cut, in no condition to go to work. I type a quick message to my boss, letting her know I'm going to Urgent Care for a possible broken arm.

My phone pings a few seconds later. Here comes the barrage of questions. *How? Are you okay? Is it your dominant side?*

Really?

I'm not answering that question. They want to know if I can still come in and work with one hand. Fucking ridiculous. I could be fresh out of surgery, and my employer would ask if I'm coming in later.

No. Hell no.

I reach over my shoulder, grip the fabric of my shirt and pull it over my head. It drops silently to the ground as I stand back in front of the mirror and turn around. Tears burst from my eyes. Ten distinct puncture marks mar my back and will no doubt scar. Mastyx's claws dug deep into my flesh, like a cat clinging to a drape. A drop of blood drains from one of the holes, clearly deeper than the rest. This will be hard to explain to a doctor. The only thing I could think to say is that I was practicing body suspension when my equipment failed.

Makes sense. It will explain my back and arm, so that's what I'll go with.

The smell of armpit wafts into my nose. I haven't showered in a few days. I've been too preoccupied with projects. Now, my throbbing arm pushes my overwhelming desire to shower to the back burner.

After fumbling into a pair of gray sweats and a black t-shirt, I step into the living room. On the floor by the fireplace is my hospital discharge paperwork. I kneel to pick them up, when the front door flies open, carrying leaves into the room and a draft that blows the papers into the low-burning flames. The fire rises, lighting up my face and heating the room as it burns the papers hotter than it should.

A clawed hand rises from the inferno, landing on the ashes. The remnants slowly disappear as Mastyx brushes them away like dust on a table.

His hand slowly retreats into the flames, leaving fresh claw marks in its wake. My eyes get stuck on the fire as it decreases in intensity, Mastyx returning to his fiery abode.

Dr. Z flashes through my mind, and the fire rises higher. My shin stings at the sudden lash of Mastyx's tongue. I leap away from the snake-like appendage and stare wide-eyed as it regresses to the fireplace and crimson soaks into the fabric of my sweats before trickling down my leg onto my foot. I peer through the hole in my pants. It's not a deep lashing, but it's enough to send a wave of regret over me. My eyes drift to my wall calendar, and an uncontrollable tremor washes over me. The next full moon is brightly marked with a red heart.

He may kill me this time—take what he wants from me before ending my life and consuming my soul. This is what I signed up for when I allowed him to save me from certain death. I love my life most of the time, but I find myself wondering if I made the right choice. Cheating death never ends well for anyone in the movies, and I expect one day I'll end up in hell, where I belong.

There's no sense in helping the universe by being reckless and having unclean thoughts. I empty my mind and focus on the task at hand, getting my ass to Urgent Care.

I drop my Ugg boots to the floor in front of me, sit in my armchair and pull them on one at a time. Exhaustion suddenly plagues me, and when I stand, my body sways a little, fighting to stay upright.

Is Mastyx doing this? Trying to keep me from leaving?

My fingers curl around the doorknob, and I swing the front door open, my heart leaping into my throat at the sight of Dr. Z ascending my porch steps.

Chapter Thirty-Three
The Fire Inside

I quickly swing the door around, trying to shut it in his face. His foot wedges between the door and the frame, stopping me. "Oh my God," he says as I release the door and back up into the house. "What the heck happened to your arm?"

My mouth moves, but nothing comes out. I rotate my head to the fireplace, the flames licking into the room as they grow higher. "You have to leave, right now." I push him out of the open doorway.

Once we reach the porch, he stops moving, refusing to take another step. "No. Not until you tell me how you hurt your arm?" He takes my arm in his hands and applies a gentle pressure, examining it. I can't stop the tears that come next, not only from the pain but from the fear of what's to come. Heat floats through the opening in the door, striking me in the face.

Dr. Z feels it too. He lets my arm go, grabs the door handle and slams the partition closed. He gazes at the glowing light beneath the door and takes a step back as my legs give way, collapsing at his feet.

"Please, I'm begging you. You have to leave." My bottom lip quivers as I stare up at him with tear-filled eyes. "Please."

He kneels to the floor, gazes deep into my eyes with a bright, penetrating stare and says, "I can't do that; you need medical attention."

I fall forward, the palm of my uninjured hand biting into the hard surface, a violent tremor racking my body.

His hand touches my spine gently. "Come with me to the hospital."

"He's going to kill me," I whisper after several seconds of silence.

"Who?" He takes my shoulders gently in his grasp.

Mastyx may kill the doctor, too, if I don't get rid of him. I have to stop this. I launch to a stand, nearly knocking him over. "I said leave!" I yell down at him.

He nods, his eyes fixed on my shaking hands before saying, "Okay."

Slowly, he rises, his eyes never leaving mine, before backing down the steps and turning to walk away. As he takes a step toward his car, he glances down at his hand and stops. His head whips in my direction at the sight of blood on his palm. "You're coming with me."

He's not asking anymore, he's telling. I back up against the door as he charges up the steps two at a time and sweeps me off my feet, carrying me swiftly down the steps. I thrash in his arms, but he holds me firm. "You're going to the hospital, Contessa," he orders. "You're bleeding."

I stop fighting him, my eyes widening at the anger I hear in his voice when he calls me by my first name. And with that outburst came something else—a presence and a feeling of something wrapping around me like a warm blanket or an embrace. It was like the feeling you have after a refreshing shower or crawling under the covers after an exhausting day. There's a familiarity to it that makes me feel safe—safer than I have in a long time.

He sets me in the passenger seat of his vehicle and wraps the seatbelt around me before closing the door softly.

The driver's side door opens after a brief hesitation, and he sinks into his seat. He sits there, his thumb grazing his bottom lip.

A quiet has come over him. It's as though he has said or done something he shouldn't have and now regrets it. He glances at me briefly with a half-hearted smile before turning the key. I peer out my window and see a small puff of smoke escape the underside of my front door as if someone huffed out a cigarette beneath it.

I shrink into my seat, hugging my body with one arm and resting my injured one on my leg. The air turns cold, and goosebumps cast across my flesh.

Dr. Z presses the heated-seat button on my side and turns the heat to low.

"Tell me about your arm," he says quietly as he turns the low-playing radio off.

I keep my eyes forward and say, "I fell out of bed."

It's not a lie. I did, in fact, fall out of my bed. Why I fell is another story.

"And your back? Did you hurt it when you landed?"

Telling him the truth will just make me look crazy, and I'll end up on an emergency psych hold. He wouldn't believe me anyway.

No one will.

We roll to a stop at a traffic light, and I lean my head against the window. A car pulls up beside us and sparks draw my attention to their window. The color drains from my face as the flame from their lighter flashes across the driver's face onto the glass and scorches a one-word message in fire.

Mine

I grab my chest, my heart pounding, and the air becomes too thick to breathe. Dr. Z reaches for me as I choke on the invisible smoke that's filling my lungs.

"Breathe," Dr. Z says. "In and out, nice and slow."

The car shakes violently, chattering my teeth as we bounce over multiple potholes, the doctor speeding up, the hospital sign in the distance. "We're almost there," he says reassuringly.

Mastyx is too. He's following us, jumping from one flame to the next. My head bobbles on my shoulders, dizziness overwhelming me as the doctor cranks the wheel into the hospital parking lot. Sweat trickles down my spine, burning as it enters the holes in my flesh. Spots dance before my eyes, and my body suddenly feels weighted and numb.

The door beside me flies open, and the sun, exiting from behind a cloud, blinds me. A flashback of Mastyx entering my burning car years ago sends me over the edge. I scream, pushing the doctor out of my path before falling to the ground and crawling across the pavement, trying to flee. He wraps his arms around me, and I cry out, "Let me go!"

His fingers thread through my hair, and his palm cups my scalp, sending prickles through me from head to toe. An overwhelming calm I can't explain follows as he folds me in his arms, lifts me from the cold ground, and carries me inside.

As we pass the lobby fireplace, the flames rise, and I know Mastyx is here. My eyes roll in their sockets, and my body goes limp, my energy draining, losing the battle with my anxiety attack.

* * *

I wake up in a dimly lit room, the television high up on the wall in the corner, playing a Lifetime movie. A blue cast covers my right forearm, and an IV bag hangs beside me.

"Good morning," a voice says, startling me.

A man in a black uniform sits in the corner across the room, a magazine on his lap. "I'll go grab Dr. Z for you."

He sets the magazine aside, rises and leaves the room quietly, closing the door behind him.

I peer around the room. It's decorated like an old person's bedroom with gold-framed paintings of nature and a small table lamp beside the armchair the man was sitting in.

The door opens partway, and I catch a glimpse of Dr. Z speaking to someone on the other side before he enters the room fully, followed by a nurse's aide. He pushes the door shut behind her and carries a large manila envelope to a white box on the wall at the foot of my bed. The aide leans against the wall by the door.

He flicks on a light, pulls an X-ray from the envelope, and slides it under a clip, illuminating the image of my arm. "You have a simple ulnar fracture." He points to the split between the bones with his pinkie. "Luckily, your radius is intact." The light flicks off, and he returns the X-ray to its envelope. "You'll be in a cast for about five weeks." He passes the envelope to the aide, who sets it on the counter beside her. "You also have two stitches in your spine to close the hole that kept bleeding, but it's going to scar along with the other nine puncture marks." He turns to me. "How did this happen, Miss Salavatori?"

We are back to being formal. It must be because we are at his workplace and the nurse is here.

I look away from him, the lie passing flawlessly through my lips. "Body suspension failure."

A chuckle escapes the aid, and I glance at her. Dr. Z's eyes darken, and he flashes her a dirty look, wiping the smirk off her face at once. I pick at the end of my cast with my fingertips, growing nervous as his intense stare pierces through me, not believing my explanation. "Where am I?" I ask, waving my hand around the room, changing the subject. "And why is it decorated like an old folks' home?"

This softens Dr. Z's demeanor. He relaxes his shoulders and says, "It's the Palliative Care Unit."

My eyes blow wide open, and I sit up quickly, making my head spin. "Am I dying?" I ask, my eyes darting from his to the aid and back again.

Dr. Z shakes his head. "Of course not. We didn't have any other available beds."

"So, someone died, and you gave me their room?" I ask, dropping back against the pillow.

He steps around the end of the bed and stands beside me. "Don't worry, we cleaned the room and changed the sheets."

His attempt at humor makes me smile briefly, but doesn't ease the nervousness lingering in the pit of my stomach.

A soft knock on the door directs our attention to it. A young man, probably in high school, carries in a tray and places it on the table beside my bed. He nods to the doctor, waves at the aide and leaves. My eyes drift from the tray to my casted arm, and a long-winded sigh escapes me. I'm right-handed, so feeding myself is going to be a bitch.

As if he read my mind, Dr. Z nods to the aide. She rolls the tray table to the left side of my bed and removes the lid. Mashed potatoes, pudding, cut-up carrots, and ham—everything that can easily be spooned or forked without landing on me if I'm careful. The nurse grabs a cup of ice, opens the apple juice and pours it inside. She presses on a lid and jams a straw in the top before rolling the table across my lap. "Cream and sugar for your coffee?" she asks in a squeaky voice.

I shake my head, and she asks, "Do you want me to stay and help you eat, or do you think you can manage?"

Stay and help me eat? I keep forgetting what floor we are on. She's used to feeding those who can't. "That won't be necessary," I say politely.

She turns on her heels, grabs my X-ray off the counter, and exits the room, leaving the door open.

My hand trembles as I pick up my fork, stab a piece of ham and push it between my lips. It's dry, salty and flavorless. I hate it. I set the fork back on my tray and stare at the television, ignoring the doctor's inquiring eyes. After several heartbeats of silence, he finally says, "I can't help you if you don't tell me the truth."

Without looking at him, I say, "The truth doesn't matter if it sounds like another lie."

He takes a step closer to me and says, "Try me."

"I'm tired." I close my eyes. "Can you please leave?"

Telling him my injuries are from my incubus lover isn't something I'm ready to share with the good doctor at this very moment.

His posture shifts, and I open my eyes as he leans over me, his face blocking my view of the television. "Contessa," he whispers. "Look at me."

I blink multiple times before saying, "I am looking at you."

He shakes his head and brings his face even closer. "No, really look at me—my face, my eyes, don't you remember me at all?" I furrow my brow at him and shake my head slowly, utterly confused. His palm rests softly on my face, and he whispers, "You're going to be okay."

I draw in a deep breath, holding it as the night of the accident races through my mind. He was there. Dr. Z was there. His younger face becomes clear as he hovers over me, calling to me to keep my eyes open, telling me I'm going to be alright. Then came the pain, my scar burning as the memory of him saying I'm sorry over and over again as he applied pressure to the hole in my leg, slowing the bleeding. Then he was gone; the paramedics arrived and took over. I never knew who he was or where he came from, and he never came forward. Until now, his face was always a blur, a silhouette in the dark that arrived on the scene and forced Mastyx back into the flames.

That's why he makes me feel safe. That's why I'm not afraid when he holds me. My mind has associated the doctor's presence with Mastyx's retreat into the fire the night of the accident.

His fingers glide across my cheek as he stands and says, "Get some rest."

I sit there, my mouth hanging open, tears spilling over my lids as the door closes behind him, leaving me alone.

I wake up with a start, my heart pounding in my chest. Moisture seeps into the sheets beneath me, the memory of falling into hell still fresh in my subconscious, trapping me in what seems like an infinite nightmare. I blink away tears and stare out the window at the dark and ominous clouds.

It took forever for me to fall asleep, my mind stuck on the consequences of my actions, the doctor's actions. It's not my fault. I wanted to stay home, to get rid of the doctor, and bide my time until the next full moon before facing Mastyx.

If I could have renegotiated the terms of our contract and relaxed the rules slightly, it would have benefited both of us. But now, thanks to the doctor's insistent actions and my impure thoughts, Mastyx will find any excuse to drag me violently back into the abyss. And the fact that Dr. Z was there, and until he told me so, I didn't remember, makes everything that much worse. Was it Mastyx who made me forget him?

Rain races down the window with heavy drops. Sensing a presence in my room, I turn my head toward the entrance and clutch my chest. An elderly man stands just inside my doorway, completely naked, his face shrouded in darkness. My eyes pinch closed, not wanting to stare at his sagging and shriveling balls unintentionally. I reach for my call button only to discover it's fallen off the bed. As the man shuffles closer to me, I pull the call button cord, slowly bringing it up from the floor. Liver spots plaster the man's entire body, and his face, now visible, is ashen with dry, flaky lips.

"Umm, I think you're in the wrong room, sir," I say with a soft smile.

A clunk noise comes from the side of the bed, the call button getting stuck between the mattress and frame. The man shuffles a little closer, his bare feet making a scraping noise along the way. I pull the call button harder, trying to dislodge it.

He inches closer, close enough for me to see his eyes and the flames rising inside them. I open my mouth to scream when the old man's long, bony fingers wrap around my throat and squeeze.

His mouth opens wide, and Mastyx utters one word that echoes from somewhere deep inside him. "Mine."

I kick my legs and dig my nails into the old man's forearm with one hand and pound his head with my cast with the other, but he tightens his grip.

"Mine!" Mastyx shrieks, a heat haze flowing from the old man's mouth as it stretches wide open.

Spots float before my eyes, and I release my grip on the old man's arm, frantically searching for the call button cord. It touches my fingers, and I grab it, yanking hard, unwedging it from its trapped space. I slam my thumb into the button multiple times as the room grows darker and darker, Mastyx's eyes shining bright with amusement through the old man's hollow orbs.

"Jesus!" a nurse yells, entering the room and grabbing the man from behind, but he won't let go. "Help!" she shouts, her eyes and face growing frantic. "Mr. Baldwin, let her go!"

The pounding in my head grows harder by the second, my body fighting hard for oxygen. Urine floods out of me, the fear of dying becoming a certainty.

Dr. Z charges into the room and grabs the old man's wrists. Mr. Baldwin's eyes lose their flames, and his mouth chatters closed against the doctor's touch before suddenly releasing my throat.

I gulp the air, heaving in large amounts, trying to replenish my body as Mr. Baldwin drops to the floor in a heap.

"Miss Salavatori, are you alright?" the nurse asks.

Dr. Z kneels to the floor, placing his fingers on the side of Mr. Baldwin's neck. I lean over the edge of the bed, ignoring the nurse and staring down at Dr. Z and Mr. Baldwin. He doesn't have to tell me, doesn't have to say a word; I already know. He's dead. Mr. Baldwin is dead. He was dead before he came into my room. Mastyx stole his soul and wore his body like a scuba suit into my room to kill me. I'm not safe here. I'm not safe anywhere.

The doctor's eyes lock on mine, and he swallows hard before saying, "He's dead."

My legs kick the blankets off rapidly, and I rotate and leap out of the opposite side of the bed. "I have to go."

I wrap my hair around my ears on both sides as the nurse places her arms on both shoulders. "You can't leave now. We have to check you out." She glances at my neck and touches the marks that I'm sure are already forming.

My good hand grips her one arm tight before tossing it away from me. I walk swiftly to the door, but Dr. Z. stands in front of me, holding up his hand. Before he can say anything, I notice he's wearing a polo shirt and khakis. I didn't see his casual attire before; he must have been on his way out. On his arm, a tattoo runs from his elbow down to his wrist.

Redemption through forgiveness.

He reaches for me, his arms wide open. "Please. You have to stay." He points down to Mr. Baldwin and says, "He's always been a little off. He didn't try to hurt you on purpose. His mind was gone, has been for a while now."

If he only knew that Mastyx was controlling Mr. Baldwin like a puppet, he wouldn't be saying such things. I back away from him, afraid of the consequences. "Move," I say, my eyes growing dark.

Another nurse enters, her hands immediately covering her face, her eyes wide open like a cartoon as she gazes down at Mr. Baldwin. "What's wrong with his eyes?" She gazes at us. "And his body?"

In our brief interaction, no one noticed Mr. Baldwin's eyes retreating completely inside his head and disappearing. There's nothing left where they should be except black holes with oozing sludge dripping out of them. His body, flat to the floor, like a corpse missing its muscle and fat, leaving nothing but skin and bones.

Fried from the inside out.

I dart around them and make a mad dash down the hallway, my mind a buzz with uncertainty and options. My bare feet slap against the tiled floor as I round the corner and slam into a man wearing all black with a clerical collar. He holds me firmly, extending his arms, creating distance between us and gazing deep into my wild eyes.

"Child, you're frantic. Come with me," he says, tugging me to a room to our left.

The minute we enter the space, I shriek at the sight of multiple candles burning. "No! He's going to kill me! He travels through the flames."

Candles burn before an altar, set against multiple rows of pews, but they don't rise; they don't lash out with the devil's tongue; they flicker peacefully beneath the cross that holds Jesus Christ.

The chaplain grabs my head with both hands, squeezing gently. "Not here, child," he says firmly. "Not in this room." He plunges his hand into a basin of water beside him and makes the sign of the cross on my forehead. "You are protected."

His words offer me no comfort. Mastyx has breached them before at Jayce's funeral when his father was screaming in my face. Mastyx may not be able to enter the sanctity of these four walls temporarily with the application of holy water on my head, but I can't stay here forever.

A shadow appears through the frosted glass on the door. It swings open, and the nurse from my room heaves a heavy sigh. She shouts down the hall. "Found her." She reaches inside the room and takes me by the elbow. "Come on, Dr. Z is looking for you."

I pull away from her, backing further into the room. "No, he has to stay away from me. It's not safe."

The chaplain nods for the nurse to leave, and he gestures for me to follow him to a pew. We take a seat in the front row, and he gazes up at Jesus. "My child, you are in the house of God. Whatever you are running from, whatever you are afraid of, I can help you—he can help you," he says, pointing up at the statue.

I stare down at my fingers, poking out of my cast, and say, "My fate is sealed—has been for years."

He rests his hand on mine and says, "No one's fate is ever sealed. You can change it through him." His eyes float to Jesus on the cross. "He can save you; you just have to give your life to Him."

I've never been a religious person. Perhaps it's because the devil saved me at the ripe age of eighteen, and I owe him my loyalty. I slide my hand from under the chaplains and whisper, "Making a deal with God to save me for my sins voids my contract with the demon who saved me." I stand and frown down at him. "My life isn't my own—hasn't been for a long time."

He stands abruptly, reaching for me as I back away from him and say, "No one can save me after what I've done." I turn away from him and walk solemnly to the exit.

"Where are you going, child?" he asks, jogging in front of me.

I put my head down, ashamed to look in the eyes of this man of God and murmur, "To face the flames."

When I exit the chapel, I look up and down the empty hallways, searching for the first exit sign I see. It glows at the far end of the corridor, and I run to it, desperate to get away before Dr. Z sends another search party after me.

Darkness envelops me when I step outside and the air chills me to the bones. I wander around the parking lot for several minutes, wondering where I parked my car before remembering that I didn't drive; Dr. Z did.

Fuck.

I slosh through a puddle on the sidewalk that runs parallel to the hospital. Tears blur my vision and sting my face. I wipe them away and press forward, determined to walk all the way home. I stop walking and stare ahead. Home. Do I really want to go there?

Where else can I go? I can't call my parents; they wouldn't believe me. It's not like they could protect me anyway. Not from this. Not from Mastyx. Water soaks my feet with a penetrating cold, curling my toes. Goosebumps race up my arms and stop at my neck. I rub my upper arm above my cast, trying to generate friction to warm it. Raindrops trickle down from the sky, landing softly on my head. I continue walking. The faster my legs move, the harder the rain falls. A lightning bolt dances across the sky, before traveling down to earth, and I swear I see Mastyx's face in the black clouds.

A car passes me, and the faint sound of a single word unnerves me. "Mine." I watch as the car continues down the road and the driver flicks the end of his cigarette out the window, dispelling his ashes. Soon, that's all I see. One car after another drives by me, the word 'Mine' filtering from each person who holds a cigarette in their grasp.

"Help me," I murmur.

Mine…Mine…Mine…Mine.

The cars keep coming. It's like I'm stuck in an infinite loop.

"Mine!"

A cigarette butt flies through the air and lands in front of me, the end of it still on fire. I stop in my tracks, staring down at it as the tip gets brighter and darker, brighter and darker as though it were breathing.

"Miiiiiine."

I scream and run through the park beside me, darting around the slide, slapping the chains of the swings out of my path, sprinting into the dark, far away from the street. My feet barely feel the ground beneath me as I veer right, adrenaline and fear guiding me who the fuck knows where. I just know I can't stop. I have to keep running, staying in the dark, keeping to the shadows. I keep veering right until I run into a row of buildings. I jog along until finally the row of buildings vanishes, and I realize I'm standing in the hospital parking lot, right back where I started.

Shit. I just did a complete fucking circle.

"Contessa!" Someone calls my name.

I spin around and see Dr. Z idling by the curb, waving his arm out the window. "Come on, get in my car, you're soaking wet."

In that moment, I realize how heavy my clothes feel, the weight of them, pulling me toward the soggy, wet grass. I shake my head slowly, turn away from him and take off in a sprint.

Man, I wish I had grabbed my boots before I left the hospital room like a crazed patient escaping the psych ward.

Tires peel, and I know he's chasing after me with his car. I work my way back to the park, staying once again out of the illuminated spaces, trying to find my way back to a familiar place so I can make my way back home. When I reach the street, I see his car fishtail round the corner and barrel toward me through a curtain of rain.

Fuck it. I stop running, sit on the curb and hold my knees, sobbing. He's just going to follow me all the way to my house.

His car skids to a stop, and he pulls to the curb, his headlights blinding me. An umbrella pops open over me, and he grabs my bicep, pulling me off the ground. "Get up, Contessa. Your cast is getting ruined."

I pull my arm away and put my hand up, keeping him at a distance. "You can't be here, Dr. Z. It's not safe."

"Joshua," he says, taking a step closer. "Just call me Joshua."

"Fine, Joshua, whatever, you have to stay away from me." I take another step back as he moves forward.

"Contessa, why am I not safe? Who keeps hurting you?" He holds the umbrella out toward me, letting it hover over my cast arm.

Tears burst from my eyes. "Please, Joshua, just let me go home. It's the only way to keep you safe. I have to face him—let him take me."

"Who?" He drops the umbrella, letting the wind take it across the street, where it smacks into a storefront window. "Tell me…" he says, grabbing me by both arms and pulling my face close to his. "…so, I can protect you."

I drop my head, ashamed to gaze into his eyes. He wants so desperately to help me, but being involved with me threatens his life, and I can't have that.

"Why?" I ask, my eyes meeting his. "Why are you so fucking determined to help me, to save me? Don't you see, I'm trying to keep you safe, trying to keep you from getting hurt or worse?"

"Safe from who?" He places a palm on each side of my whimpering face. "Tell me."

I slap his arms away from my cheeks and yell, "Mastyx!"

"Mastyx? Who's that, your boyfriend?"

If I'm ever going to get him to leave me alone, I need just to tell him the truth. Maybe then, he'll go away.

"He's the demon who saved me the night of the accident. He pulled me from the car. I made a deal with him to save my life, and now I belong to him."

Joshua furrows his brow. "Saved you? Demon? No, Contessa, I think you're confused."

"I'm not confused!" I scream at him.

He holds his hands up in front of him and says, "Alright, calm down. Why don't you get into my car, and we can go back to the hospital? There's a warm fire in the lobby and—"

"No!" I shout. "No fires. He travels through the flames."

His arm slides around my lower back, guiding me toward his car. "Fine. Just get in. We need to get out of the rain."

I hesitate at first and then give in. I'm going to hell either way, I might as well make it worth it. My wet clothes soak into his seats the second I sit down. He drops into the seat beside me and cranks the heat inside the car. "Where to?"

"I don't know." I lean my head against the window beside me and sob.

Joshua sighs. "Well, I don't think you should go home if this demon may be waiting for you." He pulls away from the curb and twists the windshield wipers up to high. They slap back and forth across the window, doing their best to flick off the pounding rain. "I don't think you should be alone, either. Besides…" He glances over at my cast, "…I think I'm going to have to rewrap that." We pull up to a traffic light, and he gazes over at me. "I can take you to my place."

"No. That's not a good idea." I wipe my runny nose with the side of my hand, then wipe my hand on my sopping wet sweats.

"There are tissues in the glovebox." He reaches in front of me and pulls it open.

I snatch a few and blow my nose. "Where are we going?" I ask as we pass the last traffic light in town and breeze by the sign that reads Sassafras Mountain, fifteen miles.

"On the other side of the mountain, my family owns a small cabin. You'll be safe there. It has an electric fireplace, no real flames, food in the cupboards, and no one around for miles." He steers toward the exit ramp and takes a left turn. "I have medical supplies there, too, in case your cast needs to be redone."

I squeeze the wet, mushy cast with my fingers. "I'm sorry."

"Don't be sorry."

For the next fifteen minutes, we say nothing to each other. I can feel the stale air between us and the unspoken thoughts emanating from him. I know he has more questions, but his eyes and mind are trying to stay focused on the road so we don't hit any deer.

When we reach the top of the mountain, we coast down the other side for several minutes before turning onto a wide gravel-coated road that leads to a muddy path. The car splashes through puddles, bouncing me around in the car. It rocks side to side, snapping my neck before finally coming to a halt outside a quaint cabin.

Solar lights illuminate the landscape running the length of the low front porch. We pull around the side, where there's a side door with two steps leading inside. I grip my pants on my lap, squeezing the fabric with one hand, whitening my knuckles. Joshua turns off the car, rests his hand on mine, and says, "Don't be afraid. You're safe here."

"I'm not safe anywhere," I say matter-of-factly before climbing out into the rain. I stand by the side door, waiting impatiently while he fumbles with his keys.

After trying three different keys, the lock turns, and he pushes the door open. He gestures for me to go first, but I shake my head, not keen on entering a dark, unfamiliar space. His hand slides inside and moves up and down the wall until finally a light flickers on, illuminating the space. I peer around the small but efficient kitchen, an apartment-sized electric-coil-top stove set off to one side. Beside it, rests a chest freezer that vibrates noisily.

"Deer meat," Joshua says, removing his coat and hanging it on a hook by the door. "The fridge is there, although there are probably only condiments and bottles of water inside. But in the cupboard…" he grabs the knob of an upper cabinet and swings it open. "…we have canned beans, raviolis, Ramen noodles and such. You know, easy stuff."

A shiver runs down my spine, and I tremor violently. Joshua rubs my chilled arms and says, "Let's get you some dry clothes. I'm sure my mom has something here for you to wear from the last time we came."

Mom? Great. Hopefully, they aren't pleated pants and a wool sweater.

He leaves me standing in the space between the living room and the kitchen, then takes the stairs to the second floor. A puddle grows around me as I wait for him to return. When he comes back down, he's wearing a pair of red flannel pajama pants and a clean white T-shirt that reads, 'Baby Bear' in brown lettering with a teddy bear on the front.

"Don't laugh." I try to hide my smile as he passes me the same outfit. "These are from our family Christmas photos, but it's all I have."

I shake it out and frown. "Mama Bear?" My eyes lock on his. "Does this mean I'm your mama?"

"Only if you want to be."

Heat rises in my face, and I know I'm blushing, which makes me feel awkward and vulnerable. I look around the room for somewhere to change.

"Over there is the half bath." He points to a door beside the electric fireplace. "Want any help?' He slides his hands into his pockets, the tension stretching the gap at the front of his pants, exposing flesh and hair. He's not wearing any underwear. If he pushes his hand any further into his pockets, the button keeping the front flap of the pants together may burst, releasing his cock.

There's a twitch between my legs, and I quickly turn away from him. "No, thanks. I can do it." I quickly shut the door behind me and cover my mouth with my hand.

Hold it together, Tessa.

I slide my pants down and kick them away from me, before pulling up the flannel ones one-handed. They are slightly large but should work. After fighting for my life to get the wet T-shirt clinging to my skin off, I realize I may have an even harder time putting on the fresh shirt. I lay it across the vanity, feed my bad arm through it first, and then my head and the other arm. The t-shirt rolls over my wet skin, bunching it up around my upper body. I dig into the fabric, trying to get it to unravel and pull down, but it's stuck.

"Umm, Joshua. I think I need some help."

The door rattles, and I grip the handle, holding it closed. "Wait. Close your eyes."

"What? Contessa, how am I supposed to help you with my eyes closed?"

"Just do it," I say, raising my voice.

"Okay, they are closed."

I open the door a crack and peer through the gap. Joshua's eyes spring open.

"No, peeking," I yell.

A broad smile stretches across his face. "Okay, fine."

He holds the smile, his eyes pinched closed as I slide into the space in front of him. "Reach out with your right hand."

He does as he's told, and I take his hand, guiding it along my waist to where the material of the t-shirt is tightly crumpled against my skin. "Feel it? It's all bunched up."

His other hand slides up my opposite side, and his smile fades away. "Yes, I can feel you."

A tremor rises in my abdomen, and I take a step back. He grabs my waist, holding me there, grips the sides of the shirt on both sides, and pulls it down. "Can I open my eyes now?"

"Yes," I murmur, his hands still holding the bottom hem of my shirt.

Our eyes lock, and the heat rises between us. I can feel his longing for me and me for him. I want to dive into his eyes and swim for eternity. Fuck, Tessa, break away. Don't let him be so close. His head angles just so, and he leans toward me, his eyes drifting from mine to my lips and back again.

"I can't." I push him away, and he staggers back several feet. "I'm sorry. It's too dangerous."

"No, I'm sorry. I crossed a line I shouldn't have. You're my patient." He gestures to the couch. "Have a seat." He clears his throat. "I'll go grab the supplies I need to take care of your arm."

"Aren't you crossing the line, just by having me here?" I say to his back as he walks away.

He stops walking, putting his head down before nodding. "Yes."

That's it. That's all he says before disappearing into the next room. I'm jeopardizing his life and career just by being in the same room as him. When he comes back into the room, I say, "After you've rewrapped the cast, I think you should take me home. I don't want you to get into any trouble, having me here."

"Contessa." He sits on the coffee table in front of me, setting a saw and supplies beside him. "My job as a doctor is also to protect you. Now, is being here crossing a line? Yes, but I'm doing it to keep you from getting hurt."

"I can't sleep with you," I blurt, closing my eyes and pressing my lips together, immediately regretting my presumptive statement.

When I open my eyes, Joshua shakes his head. He takes my arm, blows out a relieved breath and says, "Well, I wasn't planning on sleeping."

The tingle returns, and my legs inadvertently clamp together. God, I want this man so bad, I can taste it.

"My plan was to watch you sleep. I'll stay awake so you can get some sleep—keep an eye on you. You look like you could use a good night's rest."

Oh, now I feel dumb. He wasn't going to be awake because he was fucking my brains out; he plans on babysitting me while I slumber. I don't know if I can sleep when someone is watching me.

"It's fine," I say, swiping my face with my hand. "I can just go home after this. You don't need to watch me." When I rest my hand on my knee, it trembles, the thought of going home sending a fresh wave of fear through me.

Joshua places a heavy hand on mine. "You're staying here, at least for tonight." He picks up a remote from beside him, holds it over his shoulder and presses a button. The electric fireplace kicks on. "You know, you're the reason I wanted to be a doctor. That night, the night of your accident, sparked something inside me. I became driven, determined almost. It was like I was meant to find you."

"Really?" I raise my eyebrows. "Well, I'm glad at least one thing good came out of this whole mess."

Heat filters around him and into my face as the fireplace blower kicks on. "Ready?"

I gaze down at the cutting tool that hovers between us. "Ready," I say with a nod.

Chapter Thirty-Six
Helpless

After removing my sopping wet cast, cleaning my arm and replacing the cast with a new one, Joshua leads me upstairs. The loft has a massive bed, probably king-size, and it's covered with a heavy, fluffy blanket.

I run my fingertips along the furry fabric. "What is this?"

"It's faux rabbit fur." He pulls the coverlet back and pats the mattress. "Come on. Let's get you to bed."

The sheets are warm and soft like brushed cotton when I sit down and rub my palm across them. Joshua holds the blankets up, waiting for me to tuck my legs under, before covering me up to my waist. "How's that feel?"

I curl my good arm fingers over the blanket's edge, tuck it under my chin and snuggle into the warmth. "Perfect."

He smiles at me before turning toward a chair in the corner. The armchair staggers across the floor, making me cringe, before he drops it at my bedside.

"What does it mean?" I ask, pointing to the tattoo running down his arm.

His arm twists toward me. "Redemption through forgiveness means saving someone by bringing the person back from a state of sin through forgiveness."

"Meaning?"

"Meaning…" he leans forward and rests his elbows on his knees. "…you confess everything—all your sins. Take responsibility for your actions and change, not just because you may be forgiven, but because your sins will continue to eat away at your soul until nothing is left." His hand warms the side of my face, and I close my eyes. "I can forgive you for everything you may have done, Contessa, but you may never find your inner peace unless you change."

"I don't think I could ever be forgiven for everything I've done." I open my eyes, and a tear slides down my face, soaking into the feather pillow beneath my head. "It's too late for me."

He wipes the next tear that falls from my eyes with his finger. "This demon, or whatever it is that you're afraid of, is preying on you, using deception and lies disguised as truth to justify its actions. It's controlling you by keeping you focused on life's physicality. You need to focus on saving your soul—your spirit. Steer clear of his temptations, his promises, because I can guarantee you, they are only half-truths."

"But I owe him my life?" I whimper. "He saved me."

"Contessa, why do you keep saying that?"

I roll over, turning my back on him. "I don't want to talk about this anymore. It's not going to make a difference. No one can stop him. Not even God."

He sighs heavily behind me, and the chair creaks. Footsteps grow fainter and then descend the stairs. I'm alone in this, forced to face the music when the next full moon comes or when the next flame ignites nearby. I can feel it coming—my death. Hope is slipping further away by the second. All is lost.

His footsteps grow closer as he ascends the steps, reentering the loft space. He carries the chair around to the other side of the bed, so he's facing me once more. When he sinks into the floral cushion of the chair, I see he's holding a book on his lap.

"I'm going to stay here, right by your side, reading aloud, until you fall asleep." The spine cracks, and he begins to read.

It's the bible. He's reading verses from the bible.

The longer his smooth voice drones on with words I've never understood, the heavier my eyes feel. They flicker closed, and I force them back open, trying hard to stay conscious.

"Be sober-minded: be watchful. Your adversary, the devil, prowls around like a roaring lion, seeking someone to devour...1 Peter 5:8-9"

Darkness consumes me, and I dream of a place where the landscape is covered in wildflowers, and the sun beams feel warm on my face. Butterflies flutter around me, and bees bob in and out of tulips, collecting nectar and pollen.

The crisp air fills my lungs, and I stretch them wide open, heaving in its freshness with a broad smile. I pluck a rose and bring it to my nose, sniffing its fragrance.

A thorn pricks my finger, and I drop the red flower, watching the droplet of blood fall in slow motion before striking the ground, turning the grass by my feet black.

I step away as a plague of darkness spreads around me, and the sun disappears behind an angry cloud. Thunder claps loudly in the sky, rumbling the ground beneath my bare feet. A bolt of lightning travels from the onyx sky down to the earth, striking a wayward tree on a hill in the distance, setting it on fire. I run toward it, hoping that this destruction doesn't extend into the valley below.

When I reach the burning tree, its flames lash out at me, keeping me from coming any closer, from seeing what lies beyond the fire.

A hissing sound draws my eyes down to the space by my feet. A black cobra slithers around my legs before wrapping around them tightly. I lose balance and fall to the ground, crawling backward and sliding my bottom through blackened ash that stirs up in a cloud around me.

The serpent slithers closer, its scaly body coils in and out of my legs before gliding across my chest. Flames rise in its eyes, and its mouth opens wide, revealing overly long, hooked fangs. It hisses in a low, gritty tone. "Mine."

"No!" I scream, and with my mouth wide open, the serpent strikes, only it doesn't bite me. It's inside my mouth, forcing its head further and further inside my throat. I feel it slithering its way down my esophagus, writhing back and forth, trying to fit its whole body inside me. I grab its center and pull it hard, but it won't budge.

I can't breathe.

"Contessa!" Joshua shouts from somewhere far away.

My nails dig into the scales of the serpent as I wake to find Josuha standing over me, his eyes wild and in a panic. But my nails aren't trying to pull a scaly creature from my airway, it's Mastyx tongue.

Tears flood my face, and Joshua swings wildly at the space above me. He can't see Mastyx, but he knows something is there, something is killing me in the darkness.

My eyes flit to the windowpane, the sky lighting up with another round of thunder and lightning. Just outside the window, a small fire flickers across the ground, ignited by sky-to-ground lightning, giving Mastyx a way in—a way to find me.

Mastyx's face, engulfed in flames, holds no human form. He's a beast, a predator, and I am his prey. His tail wraps around my chest, squeezing it tight like a constrictor, forcing what little air I have left from my lungs.

"She's mine." His voice booms.

Joshua stands back, shaking his head, his eyes locked on mine. He heard Mastyx. He can't see him, but he heard his voice just now. Urine soaks the sheets beneath me, and my arms fall away from Mastyx's tongue. I can't beat him. I'm not strong enough.

Words flood from Joshua's mouth as he reads passages from the bible, trying anything to set me free.

A loud, ominous, diabolical laugh fills the room, Mastyx amused by his attempts. Mastyx's claws clamp down on the bible, tearing its pages and ripping it out of Joshua's hand. He launches it at the window, shattering it with a devilish grin.

The book tumbles across the ground, landing in the small fire, making the flames rise higher. "Our contract is binding."

My body leaves the bed, levitating just above it. Joshua dives on top of me, trying to keep me from hitting the ceiling. He wraps his hands around my face, my eyes wide with horror. "I don't know what to do. Tell me what I can do."

My body convulses—the lack of oxygen affecting my brain. Mastyx yanks my body to the side, knocking Joshua off me, then rips my pants off and tears my shirt from my body, throwing them at Joshua before forcing me face down on the mattress, completely naked.

His cock enters me, completely on fire. My silent screams go unheard, but as the room begins to darken before me, Joshua's tear-filled eyes widen, seeing everything that's happening—the flesh of my pussy widening and smoldering as Mastyx rams his giant flaming cock in and out of me, the burning handprints pressing into my skin, the scent of my scorched flesh.

He's witnessing my assault, my inevitable death.

My eyes drift closed for the last time, and my body melts into the mattress, weighing heavier by the second as I give up hope, give up fighting, and let him have me.

The pounding in my head and the rush in my ears grow distant. I fade into the darkness that is death, my soul floating away from my body, the last solemn words of Joshua's filtering into my head before death consumes me.

"God forgive me."

Chapter Thirty-Seven
Another
Life

My eyes flicker open, and dark branches from blackened trees hang over me. Where the sun should be is a deep-red circle from which something is continuously falling.

I curl my fingers into the hot, damp earth beside me, and something crawls across my hand. My eyes dart to the left, and a black serpent with crimson eyes lashes its tongue in my direction before slithering away, disappearing beneath an oozing leafless bush.

"Where am I?" I say to the emptiness around me.

No one answers. I'm alone. I sit up slowly and rub my eyes, trying to focus on the sky and what's falling from it.

That's when I see it. The closer the items falling through the hole in the sky get to the ground, the more they take shape.

A body slams into the ground beside me, its face twisted in a permanent state of horror. I back away from it, and the ground vibrates behind me. When I turn around, a woman, her body fully intact, reaches for me. "Please don't kill me."

My eyes scan the area around me, wondering who she's speaking to. She reaches her hand out to me, and when I reach back, I realize my hands don't look the same. My nails are long, black and pointed. The blood coursing through my veins is like crude oil, leaving lines similar to the branches hanging around me. I glance down at my feet and gawk at the long, onyx talons that took the place of my toenails.

Something touches my leg, and I spin around to see what it is. A tail wags at me, and I snatch it quickly, squeezing it tight. My eyes widen and rage floods through me as I realize it's mine.

He killed me. Fucking Mastyx killed me, and I'm in hell.

The woman on the ground staggers to a slow stand and wanders away. A few seconds later, another body drops in her place. I toss my tail behind me and storm away. If I stay stationary, a body may drop on me like a house. This isn't fucking Oz, that's for sure.

I follow the same path the woman takes, keeping my distance. The black pebbles on the ground massage my feet, and the scorching heat feels nice on my skin.

My skin.

I twist my arms out in front of me. Outwardly, they look the same, with the exception of my blood being black. I touch my face. Nothing feels different.

We walk for what feels like forever, bats flying from one tree to the next over our heads until finally, in the distance, the reflection of water catches my eye.

The woman runs toward it and slams into an invisible wall, bouncing back into the forest like a boomerang. She leaps to her feet, brushes off the black sludge coating her hands and tries again, yielding the same result. She's not allowed to leave. Banished to the Black Forest, where she will wander lost for eternity, her futile attempts will be endless.

How do I know that?

I don't know how I know, but I do. I walk directly to the wall and step right through it. The massive lake, rimmed with fire, bubbles like boiling tar, popping and bursting intermittently.

Above it, a man stands on a high, pointed cliff, crying. His body launches forward, and his arms and legs flail as he screams on the way down to the water. He hits it hard and fire envelopes his body.

I'm not afraid, though. It's like I don't…care. My breathing doesn't quicken, and my heart no longer pounds with fear. It all seems…normal, like I've always lived here in this land of sin.

I lean over the water's edge and gaze at my reflection. My hair and eyes are the same, except for a small set of pointed horns protruding from the top of my head. I run my fingers over them before tapping their sharp, pointed tips. My skin is ashen with shadows darkening the space above my eyes like a heavy powder, and my lips are a bright cherry red, sultry and seductive. In that moment, I realize I'm naked. Clothes and modesty are pointless in hell, I guess.

Another body drops into the water and disappears into its depths. I extend my finger to one of the ripples created by a third body dropping and touch the surface of the lake. To my surprise, it feels cool to the touch, and suddenly I have the overwhelming urge to swim. I raise my claws to the sky and leap into the lake of fire.

When my eyes adjust to the darkness in its depths, bones appear before me, covering the bottom of the lake

I return to the surface, lie on my back and float as another person is pushed to their death by a horned man-like creature, their souls filling the basin with chilled water.

"Little Sinner?"

I sit up and tread water.

Mastyx stands on the shore, his brow furrowed in confusion. "Get out of the lake." He extends his hand to me. "It's not safe."

Not safe for him.

Again, how do I know I'm allowed? How do I know it wouldn't drag me to the bottom, my bones joining the rest?

I swim in the opposite direction. Who does he think he is? He fucking killed me and now expects me to take his hand and walk by his side? I exit the water, the sheen of souls draining off my skin like an oil slick. I walk toward a massive empty throne. Its seat comes up to my hips, and the entire thing is made from stacked human skulls charred by fire. On either side of it are arched doorways, leading somewhere unknown.

A spine-tingling sensation encapsulates me from behind and oversized claws rest harshly on my shoulders and heat up, forcing me to the ground. I kneel before the throne as the devil steps over me and takes his seat.

I shudder for the first time since my arrival, his power radiating outward around me like a swirling tornado of fire. A long fingernail hooks under my chin, lifting it. I keep my eyes closed, afraid to look, afraid of what I may think, say, or do.

"Open your eyes, Conteeeeeeesssssssaaaa." His voice filters into my head like a hundred hissing snakes.

I force them open and find nothing but black smoke that floats away from the throne and disappears inside one of the archways. I rise and walk slowly toward it. Flames launch from torches inside the entrance, lighting my way.

The smoke drifts side to side, dancing its way down the long corridor before disappearing inside a room. When I step inside, multiple chandeliers light up with hundreds, if not thousands, of candles, illuminating a gigantic library. Rows and rows of books fill the shelves. In the center of the room, a single stool sits.

"Sssssit," the devil orders.

I move my tail to the side, sit on the stool and gaze around the room. The smoky figure floats down a long row of books and vanishes. Water trickles down the cave-like charcoal walls, and unfamiliar symbols decorate the floors. Smoke fills the room, blinding me, and when it dissipates, a scroll sits on a table that wasn't there before. Beside it is a book rimmed with what appears to be gold, held closed by twine.

"Reeeeeeaaad."

The room falls silent and empty. The devil has given me my first task. I wonder if there will be a quiz.

I tug the twine holding the book together and open it slowly. In ancient lettering, there is one name.

Mastyx.

Holy shit, this is Mastyx history, his story. I flip through the pages, caring little about the beginning and more interested in the period from when we met to the present. When I find the page, that's when the handwritten words change.

Contessa.

It's about us, everything about Mastyx and me. From the time he pulled me from the car to the moment he sav—.

Wait a minute. What the fuck? It's all right here in his own words, that fucking bastard. He never fucking saved me. Joshua did. Mastyx pulled me from the car, but he admits that by leaving me, he may have risked losing me for good and voiding the contract. But when I survived, thanks to the doctor finding me at a young age and the paramedics bringing me back, the contract remained intact. He was there the whole time, watching them save me through the flames.

Mastyx lied to me, telling me a twisted tale, his version of the truth, and my mind, blinded by tragedy, remembered everything all wrong. Tucked between the two pages that follow is a flowchart. It shows Mastyx's soul collection changing substantially after we met, the hierarchy shifting in his favor over the years.

He's been using me this whole time, collecting souls of sinners before their time, his status in hell growing exponentially.

And I helped him get there. With every drive of my blade into my victim's hearts, I sent them to an early grave and him to his new position.

The right hand of the devil.

He answers to no one but him now. I slam the book shut and grip the scroll in my hand. The wax seal, a half-rose and half-skull, holds it tightly closed. I tear it off and unroll it.

It's our contract. I read it, and now I understand everything I couldn't before. My eyes narrow at a symbol, like an asterisk, beside the stipulations of our contract. The same symbol appears in a very tiny paragraph at the bottom of the page—the footnote, the terms and conditions. I bring the paper close to my face and read.

A devious smile curves on my lips, and my mood shifts from hopeless to elated.

Chapter Thirty-Eight
Mine

Mastyx thinks he's won. But as I sit here, devouring this ancient book, running the tip of my finger along its golden trim, I realize that I'm more powerful. It's not typical. Usually, we are considered equals in strength, with varying degrees of power and abilities.

I stop reading briefly and take in the room around me. Symbols that once were illegible to me, suddenly become words and images that weren't there before now decorate the walls. It's as though the longer I sit here, the more I adjust and absorb the knowledge and power of this place. I feel…at home.

Comfortable.

My eyes drift back to the tome's pages, where I continue reading what seems like familiar text, despite reading it for the first time.

Where Mastyx messed up is that I've been seducing and killing men in the human world for years before he killed me. That seduction, combined with my sacrifices for him, not only binds us together, making us essentially one entity split in two, but also gives me access to his strengths and his only weakness.

Me.

He can still read my mind if I let him, but now that I'm here, in this world of fire, there are no otherworldly thoughts. Since I've entered this space, I haven't thought about my past, the present, or my future. It's as though time no longer exists or matters.

Everyone thinks when you go to hell, you're tormented mind, body and spirit for eternity. But the truth is, unless you serve a purpose in this realm, you're cast into the lake of fire or banished into the Black Forest, where lost souls wander. Because Mastyx chose me years ago and we have a contract signed in blood, I can walk in the forest and find my way out. I can dip my toes or my whole body into the flaming waters of Fire Lake without being incinerated. This is my hellscape as much as it is his and every other incubus and succubus pairing.

Some others merge completely, choosing to live as one, traveling as a single demon to the earthly plane, where they take their human lovers as a couple.

Not me.

I decide.

I'm the only human lover Mastyx has ever had. What I didn't know before, but I do now, is that when he decided to pull me from my burning car, it was conditional not only for me, but for him as well. The devil gave him a choice. He always gives his creatures the option to choose the lesser of the two evils.

Mastyx could have let me burn, and I could have been brought into the depths of this inferno to face my fate—the devil's assignment, if there was one for me. If the devil let me stay, I could be Mastyx's lover, and he could still take on other lovers if he chooses.

But…if the devil decides I don't have a purpose, a place, I would be sent to my second death in the lake of fire or banished to the Black Forest, lost for eternity.

I shake my head as I thoroughly scan the contract I signed with him years ago, my bloody fingerprint still fresh, the metallic scent wafting into my nostrils making my mouth water.

Tsk, tsk, someone didn't read the fine print, but I did.

By giving me a chance to live, Mastyx committed himself to me and only me, but the door doesn't swing both ways. I can do what I want, and I intend to.

I rest the heavy tome back on the table, closing our contract between the pages like a bookmark.

Knowledge is power, some people say. And now, after reading over everything— the rules, the contract, the abilities I likely possess, I now know that Mastyx no longer has control over me or what I do. I stand from my stool, and it vanishes as I walk out of the room and make my way back to the wasteland, which I now call home.

When I emerge from the tunnel, Mastyx stands beside the devil's empty throne, his eyes fixed on mine. He's in full beast mode, his hooves shifting toward me as I strut in his direction. The odd thing is, I'm not afraid. What once repulsed me about him, I find strangely attractive now. It's as if this place changed my perspective on what's important.

Power.

Here he is, the right hand of the devil, making him a very alluring specimen indeed. But there is one more powerful.

I rest my hand on his hairy chest and shove him hard, moving him from my path. He throws his hands against his chest, his eyes wide with shock at my bold actions. I slide my ass up and onto the devil's throne and run my fingers along its arms.

"What are you doing?" Mastyx's eyes darken. "You can't sit there; no one can."

Yes, I can, I think to myself, letting him read my mind—words from the ancient book filtering from my head into his.

I see all. I know all. I own all.

The devil's rules play on repeat, over and over again. The last line of his list of rules may be my favorite yet. I push the memory of the words into Mastyx's head, letting him read them.

The chosen may sit on my throne and call to me, letting their desire be known.

I run my fingers down the length of my tail, its smooth, hot surface sending a wave of pleasure through me as I thrust it inside my pussy and slide it in and out, moaning.

Mastyx's eyes fill with fire, and his cock bursts into flames. The desire he feels for me here multiplied tenfold. He takes a step toward me, and the massive onyx hand of the devil strikes him in the chest, knocking him back several feet. The Prince of Darkness, his skin entirely black like high gloss paint and muscles that rise and fall with heaving breaths, approaches me, his swinging cock hardening to stone. I let my tail drop from inside me and swing it up toward his face. He catches it in his mouth, sucking the tip of it like a cock.

A low throaty moan escapes his lips as I stand, curl my tail around his lower row of teeth and pull him closer to me. I dig my long, sharp black nails into his arms, drawing onyx blood and push him down on his throne. He grips my hips as I straddle him and lower myself down onto his lap before peering over my shoulder.

Mastyx frowns at us from his hands and knees, forced to bow and watch as I ride his boss on the throne of death. I rock my body harder and faster, the devil's grip on me growing tighter, making me feel pain for the first time. I cry out in pleasure, and he lifts me from his lap, forcing me to the ground in front of Mastyx and climbs onto my spine. His claws tangle into my hair before yanking my head back, keeping my eyes level with Mastyx. I smile at him, my tongue sliding across my lips as I pant and groan before shouting, "Harder!"

My body launches forward, my forehead cracking into Mastyx as the devil slams into me. He closes his eyes, not wanting to see the pain his boss is causing me and how much I'm enjoying it.

"Ooooopen your eeeeyes," the devil hisses.

Mastyx forces them open, the fire in them burning with jealousy-fueled rage. The devil's cum fills my insides like hot magma, and I screech. He grabs me by the throat from behind, holds me against his chest and murmurs, "You're mine now, more than his." His eyes flit to Mastyx, whose jaw clenches and fists tighten. "I take what I want, when I want. Do not forget your place."

I reach over my head and stroke the sharp jawline of the devil as his cock slides from inside me, a trail of cooling lava spilling on the ground. Mastyx nods to him, surrendering to his boss's will.

The devil climbs from my back and turns me to face him. "He is still your incubus, your mate, but you…" His sharp nail curls a lock of hair around my ear. "…can sit on my throne and I will take you anytime I please."

And with his final wishes known, he dematerializes between us and vanishes into a cloud of smoke.

I stand slowly and run my hands over my breasts, circling my nipples, teasing Mastyx. "Do you regret saving me?"

His tail wraps around my waist, pulling me against his chest. Claws glide up my legs before wrapping around my body and clenching my fiery ass. "Never."

I smile devilishly at him before removing his hands from my body. "You will."

My feet slide over shiny lava rocks, their smooth texture like sheets of silk, grazing across my soles before I sink into a deep bed of black sand up to my ankles, a dusty smoke rising around me, enveloping my lower body.

A round portal opens beside me, flames licking into our world and the next. Mastyx races toward me, his arms stretching out beyond their normal length, trying to stop me from passing through.

My newfound freedom sends a flood of desire straight to my pussy. I've been forced to stay with Mastyx for years, and now, I can fuck whomever I want, whenever I want, in the human world, and there's nothing he can do to stop me.

I step into Joshua's living room on the night of the first full moon. He's asleep on the sectional, wearing nothing but his boxers, a bottle of whisky resting on the coffee table beside him. The remembrance card from my funeral dangles between his fingers.

Mastyx enters the room, the portal closing behind him, and grabs my arms, his sharp talons tearing into my flesh. "No. Anyone but him."

My fingers glide down his sternum before walking down to his cock where I yank it hard, making him clench his pointed teeth. "I decide. Remember?"

He releases me, and my torn skin seals itself, stopping the flow of inky blood. I chuckle softly. "Silly Little Mastyx, you know you can't hurt me."

I back away from him, turn toward the doctor and run my fingers through his soft hair, my blackened veins bulging as onyx blood races through them. "I can't wait to taste you," I whisper.

Joshua stirs but does not wake.

The portal opens in the fireplace, and I whip my head in Mastyx's direction. His hoofed foot disappears inside the opening. I lash my tail out and grab him around the throat, tossing him back into the room. He slams into the hardwood floor, sliding across it before hitting the wall, leaving a scorch mark and a hole. "Stay," I order. "You're going to watch."

I turn my attention back to my human lover. His eyes flutter beneath his lids before partially opening. "Contessa?" His eyes widen. "No, you're dead." He sits up, and I shove him back against the couch cushions. His eyes drift to my hands for the first time, and the realization that I'm no longer who I once was settles into the deep frown line on his forehead. "No. This can't be." He squeezes his eyes closed, his lips moving rapidly, murmuring what sounds like a passage from scripture, before opening them again.

Don't be afraid, I say inside his head, using my new telepathic powers.

His lips part, and I cover them with my clawed finger, straddle his abdomen, and run the tip of my tail down his thigh. "Hush, now." My sharp talons glide along the elastic of his boxers before ripping them off and tossing them toward Mastyx. "I don't want to hurt you, Joshua. So, you lie there like a good boy and enjoy the ride."

My tongue extends from my mouth and slides between his lips, kissing him deeply. He gags, his arms flailing as he fights to breathe. I pull my tongue from his throat and lick my way down to his cock where I flick my tongue over the tip, tasting his precum.

"Mmm." My heightened senses send waves of pleasure surging through my body. I long for him more than anyone in my entire life. "I knew you would taste good."

"Tessa, please, don't." Fear washes over the good doctor's features, making him look older.

I cup his frowning face in my hands and plant a soft kiss on his tender lips. "Don't worry, I'll be gentle if you're a good boy." I lift my ass, move my tail out of the way and lower my flaming hot pussy lips around his cock.

His upper body launches upward, and he cries out, the fire inside me stinging his cock like hundreds of bees. A blood-curdling scream fills the room, and he tries to push me off him, my flaming hot skin scorching his, but I grab his head and bury his tear-filled face in between my breasts.

My eyes dart to Mastyx, rage encapsulating his entire being, his body in full beast form. He digs the floor with his hooves, leaving gouges in the wood and smoke filters from his furious nostrils.

He charges us, but before he can reach me, I snatch him up with my tail and hold him at bay. He dangles inches from the ceiling, his hairy limbs thrashing about trying to get free. I launch my head back and howl as an indescribable surge of passion courses through me.

I moan and wrap my arms around Joshua, rocking into him, harder, faster, hungry for release.

The feeling, unlike anything I've ever felt in the world of the living, can only be described as an unapologetic and violent orgasm that won't stop bursting from my body. As I bounce up and down on Joshua's cock, his screams sing through my ears like a high-pitched soprano at an opera. It's an intoxicating sound, one that I never want to end. But it can't be all about me. I'm not like Mastyx. If I'm to return to the good doctor, I need him to understand that it's for his benefit, not just mine.

I slide back, letting his cock slip out of me and take the entire length of him into my mouth, sucking it harder than any human ever could. The doctor's toes curl, and his body flies back on the couch, his hips arching up to meet me. "Oh, God, Contessa."

I peer up at Mastyx, his livid eyes glaring down at me, and groan, pushing the doctor's cock deeper into my throat, his fingers curling into my scalp.

Puffs of radiant heat encapsulate us in waves, Mastyx's seething fury ready to escape his mouth like a flame from a dragon. My mouth fills with the doctor's salty cum, and I smile, swallowing it down like the drink of life.

Mastyx roars, vibrating the entire room. His legs kick in the air like a toddler throwing a tantrum. I release Joshua's blistered cock from between my lips, and it slaps against his stomach, softening. His heavy panting subsides, and his eyes fight to stay open. I stand, bend at the waist and kiss his sweating forehead. He opens his mouth to speak, but only gargles escape before his eyes roll back into his head, fainting within seconds.

I lower Mastyx to eye level. "Taste my rage." I ram my cum-coated tongue into his mouth and yank it quickly back out. "You killed me, and my punishment for your sin is an eternity of not only watching me fuck the man you hate but tasting his cum on my lips." My lips press hard against his, inhaling his fury like an invigorating essential oil, dimming the fire in Mastyx's eyes. I release him, letting him fall harshly to the floor. He puts his head down, and I yank it back, forcing him to look at me. My eyes heat up with his flame, a devious smile curling on my lips. "Now, you are mine."

I call open the portal and point to the opening. "Go."

He stands and walks toward the gateway, heavy footsteps echoing through the room as he shakes his head in astonishment. His eyes drift to mine. There are no more flames, no more rage, just disbelief. He can't beat me. He can't stop me. The only thing he can do now is accept the fact that I'm going to keep not only my human lover, his enemy, despite him, but fuck his boss, the devil, in front of him any time I wish.

I rest my hand on the side of his face, smacking it gently. "We are no longer in your hell, my love." I pull the fire curtain back and shove him inside with a strike from the heel of my palm. "You're in mine."

The End

If you loved this story, please leave a kind review on Amazon and Goodreads.

Thank you.

Blow
You Should've Kept Driving (book 1)
You Should've Stayed Home (book 2)
You Should've Stayed Dead (book 3)
Libitina
The Prickling
No One Leaves
The Unnerving
Sidero (book 1)
The Carpenter's Chameleon (book 2)

Anthologies and other books in which this author is included.

Horror for the Holidays
Thrills and Chills
Pretty Little Slashers (including the above story titled Blow)
Halloween Horror Show
Thousand Word Thrills
Bloody Tidings